SHATTER POINT

JEFF ALTABEF

To Sarah
Congrats on joining a great family
Jeff Altabef

SHATTER POINT

FIRST EDITION

ISBN: 1622533127
ISBN-13: 9781622533121

Editor: Megan Harris
Senior Editor: Lane Diamond
Cover & interior layout & design by Mallory Rock

Printed in the U.S.A.

www.EvolvedPub.com
Evolved Publishing LLC
Cartersville, Georgia

Other Books by Jeff Altabef

Fourteenth Colony

What Others Are Saying About Jeff Altabef's Books:

Fourteenth Colony:

"The synopsis gives a reliable example of author Jeff Altabef's genuine talent as an articulate and engaging story teller. The "Fourteenth Colony" is an original entertainment from beginning to end and documents its author as a contemporary novelist of considerable merit and imagination. Highly recommended for summer reading lists and community library collections."

- Midwest Book Review

Fourteenth Colony:

"Jeff Altabef's clean writing style shines in Fourteenth Colony. His descriptions are thorough and fresh without overloading the reader.... His ideas of the future are believable, and they function as an extreme version of the path some believe America is headed down. At the conclusion of the book, instead of events and characters being drawn in black and white, as one might expect, they turn gray in an enjoyable turn of events.

- Foreword Clarion

Fourteenth Colony:

"In this gripping dystopia story, we see just what happens when power and wealth are concentrated among a few. Fourteenth Colony is a clever tale of intrigue, in a future where the poor get poorer and the rich control access to health and education, but the plucky may still survive.

"Jeff Altabef has surprises in store as his carefully-crafted characters discover the mysteries of the Fourteenth Colony. You'll find yourself rooting for these working-class kids held back by an unjust society, and for this bright new story-telling talent to come out with his anticipated sequel. Kudos for a fast-paced well written work that is full of heart and a sense of justice in regards to young people. Fourteenth Colony is a thought-provoking, fast-paced thriller that you should treat yourself to today!"

- Kevin Ryan, Bestselling Co-Author of "Almost Home"

For Karen, Emily, and Erynn, who are the sparks that make my heart beat, and to my pops for his contribution to this book and his tireless work as the "Editor and Chief" of my life.

CHAPTER 1

I'm a killer. No better than a common murderer, and worse, really. More like a serial killer who can't help himself as he takes life after life, unable to stop even if he wished he could.

Darian frowned at the corpse on the stainless steel autopsy table. "Damn it, Zeus, I thought you were going to make it." His frown deepened until long lines etched into his face. Remorse wasn't good enough. It was useless. Pointless, really. Remorse would not bring Zeus or any of the others back.

He glanced at the video projections of Zeus's brain development. His original brain on the left screen appeared normally formed and perfectly functional. The one on the right showed Zeus's brain after he had injected him. Misshapen and grotesque, it was so overdeveloped it strained against the skull.

Darian shook his head. "Not again. I can't lose another batch of test subjects."

"We're making progress, Doctor Beck. This time, the brain enlargement slowed at the end. With some adjustments, next time it might stop before...." George attempted to smile, but only the tips of his lips responded. Twice Darian's age, he was so optimistic he could see the silver lining in a hurricane, but this lethal turn of events left even him speechless.

"We're missing something critical. We need to stop the brain development *before* it overwhelms the subject." Darian peered through the glass wall that separated the autopsy room from the rest of the laboratory. The remaining five subjects sat perfectly straight and stared mournfully at the glass as if Darian and Zeus and the table with death hovering above it drew their gaze.

An icy chill tickled its way up his spine. The others had no idea Zeus had died. They were often separated. To them, the glass wall was a simple mirror. They had no idea—could have no idea—a laboratory sat beyond the glass, yet he suspected they knew the truth: that Zeus was dead and he the killer.

Darian nodded toward the remaining subjects. "It's odd that they haven't eaten their breakfast. It's already past noon. They must be hungry."

Color drained from George's face. "It's unnatural for them to stare at the mirror like that."

Darian pressed a button on a keypad and the one-way glass window turned gray, blocking the other subjects from view. Led Zeppelin started playing. "It's just our imagination. Hand me the circular saw. Let's hope we can learn enough from Zeus to save his friends."

George handed him the shiny autopsy tool, but before he switched it on, the lab door swung open and Brenda Callaghan darted into the room. The normally composed, rather attractive young researcher appeared ashen, her jaw clenched tight.

"What's wrong, Brenda?"

"I came as soon as I heard. I'm sorry about Zeus, but there's something else you should know."

Darian stared patiently and waited for her to continue. She clutched a thin hospital issued tablet in her hands. His chest tightened.

"Wickersham authorized EBF-202 to be administered to a new patient. He doesn't know that Zeus died, but the injection is scheduled for later today." She handed Darian the tablet.

Darian narrowed his eyes until they were nothing more than slits. "This is a young patient. How can he do this? This is *my* trial! We're not ready! We'll end up killing him." The tablet cracked under his tightening grip. "I'm going to…." The violent images flashing through his mind came too fast and were too graphic to put into words. He hurled the tablet across the room and raced from the lab.

Darian hurried toward the elevator, his white lab coat flapping open, revealing a vintage Grateful Dead t-shirt, worn blue jeans, and flip-flops. His usually affable face twisted into an angry grimace as he repeatedly jabbed the call button. He cursed under his breath and shifted his weight back and forth. When the bell rang, the door *swished* open, and he darted inside the empty elevator.

"Please hold the doors!" a voice called.

He instinctively thrust out his hand as they began to shut. A young female lab assistant strolled into the elevator. Her long, pin-straight blonde hair was pulled back in a ponytail and swayed as she walked. Her golden brown tan contrasted with her white lab coat, and her jade eyes that flirted behind long eyelashes. She smelled like jasmine and vanilla. *She must be new,* he thought. Perfume was discouraged in the labs, and no one stayed tan after working the long hours the research facility required.

"Thanks for holding it for me." She smiled.

"No problem." Darian tapped the button for the top floor, raised his eyebrows, and glanced at the lab assistant.

"That's good for me," she said.

When the elevator stopped on the main floor to let in three additional passengers, Darian stepped back, and she slid closer to him. The fragrance of her perfume grew stronger. A current zipped through his body as he breathed the scented air deep into his lungs.

"My name is Vanessa." She held out her hand.

Darian squeezed and let go, but her hand lingered for a second longer than it needed to. Electricity flowed between them.

"I'm Darian Beck." He had been so angry and preoccupied that he almost forgot to notice that she was a knockout. Almost, but his eyes wandered to her thin neck and started to wash down the rest of her body when he admonished himself and pulled away.

The elevator stopped at the fourth floor and let out everyone except Darian and Vanessa. He used the space to furtively study her reflection off the elevator doors. Her eyes were wide, lips full and red. A small beauty mark dotted her right cheek, which made her perfectly symmetrical face beyond beautiful—unique.

Vanessa stayed close to his side. A seductive smile snuck across her lips. "I've heard your name mentioned before, Doctor."

He grinned despite his surly mood. "Only good things, I hope."

"Mostly." She winked good-naturedly at him.

When the doors opened, he raced from the elevator, eager to be on his way, temporarily forgetting about the new lab assistant with the sweet smile and perfume.

The top floor hardly resembled the rest of the research hospital. Gone were the gray tile floors, fluorescent lights, plain hallways, and metal doors. Dark cherry paneling, antique ink drawings, and white wooden doors replaced them.

He stomped toward the corner office. With each step he grew more agitated, as if his anger rolled down a steep hill, gathering intensity as it went. He stared hard at the nameplate on the corner office door—*Samuel Wickersham, PHD - Head of Research*—and shoved it open.

The receptionist screeched in surprise at his sudden entrance. She regained her composure and grinned at him. "I'm sorry, Doctor Beck, but we don't have an appointment for you."

"Not to worry, Clair. He'll want to see me." He quickened his pace toward Wickersham's door, turned the doorknob, and plunged into the corner office.

Wickersham's cavernous office was larger than Darian's entire studio apartment. Floor-to-ceiling windows covered both exterior walls and offered stunning views of New York City. He huffed to Wickersham's massive desk. Four inch risers lifted his desk and chair. In reality, Wickersham was short, well below average, but from Darian's vantage point, he seemed imposing.

Wickersham immediately raised his left hand with his palm facing Darian, without looking up, as if he'd been expecting him. Wickersham's vast oval desk contained only a flat screen computer monitor, a new holographic video display that was turned off, an old-fashioned intercom box, and a photograph of a smiling Wickersham with his left arm draped over the Vice President's shoulders. He told everyone that they were childhood friends. No one believed him.

Wickersham's eyes never lifted from his keyboard.

Darian seethed as he watched the snail-like progress of his fingers drag across the keyboard. He balled his hands into tight fists. Wickersham shifted in his seat, but his perfectly tailored, crisp navy suit moved seamlessly with him. He paused for a second and gently stroked his dyed blond hair, but not one hair moved. He used so much hair gel, Darian thought it would take a tsunami to move any out of place.

When Wickersham finished typing, he looked up from the keyboard. Darian couldn't read his emotions; Wickersham had injected a river of Botox into his face. It was like dealing with a mannequin.

"Doctor Beck, I didn't know that we had a meeting scheduled. I imagine you have something important to tell me. Perhaps you have a breakthrough to report? Please, take a seat." Wickersham gestured toward one of the two leather wingback chairs facing the desk, but Darian remained standing.

"We can't try EBF-202 on a new patient. It's not ready."

"I disagree. The drug has shown remarkable potential." Wickersham crossed his manicured hands on the desk in front of him. He sat absolutely straight, tried his best to smile, and sighed slightly when the effort failed.

"The first version of the drug ended up killing all the test subjects." Darian leaned on the desk, wondering if he could hurtle it and reach Wickersham's throat in one leap.

"That was the first version. The second version hasn't produced any fatalities. I visited all six of our research subjects last night. They all looked healthy."

"Zeus died this morning!" Darian glared at him, hoping Zeus's death would cause him to reconsider, or at least bother him, but if it did, the head of research showed no signs of it.

"We only started this trial two months ago. Their brains are still developing. The pace has slowed considerably, but it hasn't stopped yet. If the development continues, they will all die over the next month. Plus, their behavior has altered. It's just not safe! We don't understand all the ramifications of the drug. We can't use EBF-202 on humans. I didn't go into research to kill people! It's bad enough the dogs have died."

Wickersham leaned back in his chair and folded his arms across his chest. "How did you know I planned on using a human test subject?"

Darian's face grew hot.

"I see. Callaghan must have told you. My mistake."

"That's not important. EBF-202 regenerates brain tissue, but we can't control the effects. It will likely kill anyone you inject with it! We need more time with the animal control subjects." His anger crested like a wave headed to shore, and crashed as it mingled with sand and surf and the knowledge that he was helpless.

"This drug will revolutionize how we view the brain. The treatment will not only end Alzheimer's and senility, but can increase cognitive powers. The applications are endless, and so are the profits. You're young still. You must understand the bigger picture. With your share of the money, most of your educational costs will be paid off." Wickersham's moss-colored eyes gleamed brightly.

Darian's spirit sank. That look in Wickersham's eyes meant that he sniffed money, and when he thought he might get paid, nothing changed his mind. "Did the patient's guardian sign the consent forms?"

Wickersham tried to smirk, but he gave up under the strain well before Darian could have recognized the reaction. "You've seen the young man's chart. He's not going to recover from his head wound if we do nothing. At least we'll be giving him a chance to benefit all humankind. Besides, he's the perfect test subject—young and strong with a severe head trauma."

"He still has a fighting chance to come out of the coma using traditional treatments. His guardian should be told about the choices and the risks."

Wickersham stood, his head clearing the high back of his chair by an inch. "This is 2041, Doctor Beck. The law was changed two years ago. Without premium insurance, I can make this decision, and he doesn't have the proper coverage."

Darian's nails dug into the palms of his hands. "But the Sheppard Group is paying all his bills. They have the required riders in their insurance."

Wickersham slithered toward the side of his desk. "Yes, but the tennis instructor is not covered by that insurance. They're paying for his costs out of pocket." Wickersham waved his arms in the air as if he were conducting a symphony. "This is for the best, Darian. Don't worry about the ethics. You should stick to what you're good at: neurobiology and making friends among the female staff members."

"Just give me another two months with the dogs. We'll be in a better place."

Wickersham stood beside him, his head just inches above Darian's shoulder despite the man's ridiculous platform shoes. "You'll be fully involved in his case study. Just imagine how much we'll learn! Think of all the people he'll be helping."

The intercom buzzed. Wickersham might have been the only person alive who still used one of those things. "Your daughter is here for your meeting, Doctor Wickersham."

"Great. I've just finished with Doctor Beck. Good day, Doctor."

"His name is Jack."

"Whose name?"

"The tennis instructor. Your *case study.*" He had a fleeting fantasy about smashing his fists into Wickersham's surgically altered nose, but spun and stormed toward the door instead. He reached for the doorknob, but the door swung open and he collided with Wickersham's daughter. Their eyes met.

"Vanessa?"

CHAPTER 2

Thump-thump-thump-thump.

Cooper brushed his fingertips across the smooth, soft flesh of her chest and chuckled. "Your heart is racing like a small, scared rabbit."

He offered his brightest smile, and willed his sapphire eyes to twinkle. He used one of his direct irresistible looks, one that never failed to melt a woman's heart.

"It's you, baby. You make me... cr-crazy." Her lips quivered, and her eyes brimmed with tears. Young and lovely, her naked form stretched out on the freshly cut emerald grass, which bent against the weight of her thin body. Her chestnut eyes were wide with excitement, her hair pulled back in pigtails and tied with pink ribbons. A smattering of freckles playfully dotted her nose and cheeks. She had worked as a waitress before they met, before he took her away from that life to give her a better one.

"Have you enjoyed spending time with me?" He stroked the cream-colored skin on her upper arm. Goose bumps sprouted in response.

"Of course, baby. You're an angel."

The answer pleased him. He tipped back a crystal wine glass, taking a sip of the 2021 Lafite Rothschild Bordeaux. He let the liquid linger in his mouth before swallowing. "Some people say superb wine is determined solely by the conditions in which the grapes are grown. They argue that if the soil content is just right, and you have ideal amounts of rain and sun, great wine is sure to follow."

He took another sip from his glass. "I disagree. Without extraordinary vines, truly superior wine cannot flourish. The same is true with humans. Only those with the proper genetic code can truly be exceptional."

She stared back with a blank expression on her face.

Cooper shrugged. "It is a trick of fate." He opened a wicker picnic basket and removed a piece of aged, sharp cheddar cheese and sliced off two paper-thin pieces. He fed one to her, fingertips sweeping against her pink lips.

He nodded toward the sky. "It is a near perfect day, and you are almost perfect."

"I can try to be perfect. I'll do anything you want."

He smiled and stroked her cheek with the back of his hand. "I know you would try, but there are things you can't be—certain... deficiencies you cannot overcome." His smile vanished and his demeanor turned cold and hard like blue ice.

A singular tear rolled down the girl's cheek. When she pulled her hand away from him, a jolt shot through her and she whimpered.

"Struggling won't help you. The restraints are electrified. If you struggle against them you will only feel pain—a tremendous amount of pain. And we wouldn't want that, would we?" The words dripped out of his mouth like sickly sweet syrup.

"No, don't hurt me. Please don't." She glanced toward an athletic-looking young man standing behind her tormentor, the only other person in the field. She pleaded at him with her eyes.

The attendant smiled coolly back at her, casual in a plain white t-shirt and blue pants, eyes lit with an unnatural gleam. He was trim and well muscled, but a softness to his features indicated that he lived a life of privilege.

"You can call out to Terry if you'd like. You can beg him to help you, but I don't think your pleas will do you any good."

She tried to kick, but the restraint held and jolted her with another blast of electricity. She screeched. Tears rolled down her face freely now.

"Terry, bring me the case."

Terry placed a plain wooden case on the grass next to the girl and opened it. He removed a red velvet cloth and draped it next to her. On top of the cloth he placed a dozen stainless steel surgical instruments.

Cooper's blue eyes reflected off the stainless steel, creating dozens of sapphire orbs.

The girl turned away.

"Don't be afraid. I'll explain each one of these tools to you and what I plan on doing with them."

She turned her head to face him again. "But why? I did everything I could to please you. I'll do anything you want."

Cooper beamed an angelic smile at her again. "You can't give me the one thing I need."

"Just name it. I'll do it. I can do it!" She gasped between sobs.

"You can never be *Maggie*." He grabbed the scalpel, knuckles white with rage.

"No! Please don't!"

CHAPTER 3

Darian stood stiffly in the open doorway clutching a tablet against his chest. His throat had tightened so much he had a hard time swallowing.

Jack lay on his hospital bed with a cup of red Jell-O in his hand. His mother sat on a chair beside him while his younger brother stood nearby observing him carefully. The relief in the room was palpable. Jack had people who loved him, people who deserved more than this charade.

Jack's mom glanced Darian's way and locked eyes with him. She left her son's bedside, and approached him warily.

He thought about retreating, but that would be cowardly. He was responsible for Jack now. Turning and running was not an option.

A bright smile lightened her face as she got close. She appeared decades younger than she had earlier in the day, before Jack's eyes had fluttered to life.

"Doctor Beck? I'm Jack's mother, Maggie. Thank you so much for helping my son. I was so worried." Relief rippled through her voice like a breeze through a wheat field.

Darian stammered and glanced toward his feet as he spoke. "He recovered... on his own. He's a strong young man." The truth was useless now.

Maggie shot Darian a piercing look. "I have a feeling there's more to it than that." Without warning, she closed the gap between the two and threw her arms around the researcher's shoulders.

He stood woodenly, the tablet's hard edge jabbing into his side.

After a few awkward moments, she stepped back. Tears welled in the corners of her eyes and a slight pink hue flushed her face. "I'd better go inside."

He nodded and watched her return to her son's bedside.

He felt like a thief. Wickersham had injected Jack with EBF-202 two hours after Darian had confronted him. *Two hours.* More than enough time for him to have warned Maggie. He could have marched straight to Jack's room and given her all the information she needed, but instead, he had studied Jack's file, paced his office, and convinced himself that Jack's best chance to recover was the experimental treatment.

Two days had passed, and he knew he had lied to himself. He wanted to find out if the drug would work. That desire doomed him, and now he judged himself guilty. His only chance at redemption was controlling the drug. He had to find an inhibitor to save Jack's life.

Samuel Wickersham's Clive Christian knockoff cologne drifted into the hallway like a pregnant rain cloud, as he materialized behind Darian as silently as a shadow. He slapped Darian on the back. "Congratulations, Doctor. You've saved the tennis instructor's life."

Darian glared at his boss while random violent thoughts flashed through his mind.

"You don't look well, Doctor Beck." Wickersham's throaty voice hung like a wisp in the air. "Have you had problems sleeping? Those dark circles under your eyes don't inspire confidence. You're not in the lab now. You have a patient to take care of."

The bastard was right. Darian hadn't slept more than a couple of hours since Jack had been injected, but he didn't feel tired. More than enough anger raged through him to power his body—some directed at Wickersham, but most reserved for himself.

He scanned the hallway, found an empty room across the hall, and motioned for Wickersham to follow. When the director hesitated, Darian grabbed his arm, pulled him into the room, and closed the door behind them.

"I lost Lucy this morning," Darian growled.

Wickersham stumbled backward. "Lucy? Should I know what you're talking about?" His face was flaccid, but his eyes brightened with alarm and fear. He plunged his hand deep into his front pocket.

"Lucy is one of our canine test subjects, and Desi has turned violent. He's never been violent before. The treatment has changed his personality completely." Darian's jaw ached as he clenched it shut.

He had taken Lucy's death hard. Death was the enemy. It needed to be defeated. Beaten down. Crushed. Even George seemed depressed when he had to separate Desi from the other test subjects.

"That's a shame, Doctor. I hope you learn enough from her death to help our new friend." Wickersham crossed his arms against his chest.

Darian ran his hand through his shaggy blond hair in frustration. "I need Jack to stay with us so I can monitor his condition until I think it's safe for him to leave."

"That will be impossible, Doctor. As you know, the tennis instructor's family knows nothing about our *unconventional* treatment. We can't keep him here without arousing their suspicions."

"I thought you weren't worried about the legality of the treatment or the family's reaction."

"I'm not worried about the law or their little family." He snickered. "They are a bunch of nobodies. I am concerned about the Sheppard Group. They're part owners of the hospital, and I haven't figured out their connection to the tennis instructor. Apparently, Charles Sheppard doesn't play tennis."

The law was ambiguous. Without the proper insurance riders, Wickersham could use experimental methods on a patient *if* the patient was otherwise deemed terminal. Normally, the hospital wouldn't be worried about being dragged to court; most patients couldn't afford the expensive attorneys. With Charles Sheppard involved, however, the equation changed.

Darian could see the thin layer of concealer Wickersham used under his eyes. *I'm not the only one having trouble sleeping.*

Wickersham continued in a softer voice just above a whisper. "If they learn of our treatment, I will deny everything. As far as the records show, you acted without my knowledge. The consequences would be severe. You would be taken off the project, lose your license, and maybe serve jail time." He reached for the doorknob with his left hand, as though clutching something with his right.

Darian's face reddened as he spotted what appeared to be a taser in his boss's right hand. He took a half step toward his boss. "I'm not worried about myself. I need to protect the patient."

"Then I suggest you persuade him to help you in an academic study involving head traumas. Have him come in as often as he will agree. The younger brother is something of a science progeny. His scores on the preliminary assessment test rival yours. Perhaps he can be useful to you. Otherwise, I'll make sure that we acquire the autopsy. Good day, Doctor." Wickersham opened the door, spun, and left the room without looking back.

Darian pounded his fist into the wall, scraping his knuckles, but the pain felt good. He deserved pain—even welcomed it.

He opened the tablet and studied a series of brain scans using the latest neuro-imaging technology. The first group was a baseline series of Jack's brain before EBF-202. The next series had been taken after he woke from the coma this morning. Already, the drug worked its magic. The damaged area was largely repaired, but a well-trained eye could detect the beginnings of more subtle differences.

What will those changes do to him?

Zeus and Lucy had died, Desi turned violent, and the other dogs acted more somber than before they were treated, as if they understood more than they could possibly know.

A cold chill crept down his back. *What have I done?*

CHAPTER 4

Jack swerved his red Indian Chief motorcycle into a spot between a gray Mercedes and a silver BMW SUV. He pulled off his helmet, and his short curly brown hair fell in tight, untamed circles around his face. He checked his appearance in the side mirror and traced the thin white scar by his temple with his finger—the only visible reminder of a dangerous episode four months earlier, when a psychotic businessman had kidnapped him. He would have died if his younger brother, Tom, hadn't risked everything to save him—a debt he could never repay.

He placed the helmet on the seat and instinctively reached for the pannier to retrieve the heavy chain he used to secure the bike, but stopped mid-step. *Who would steal an old motorcycle in a hospital parking lot full of luxury autos?* Besides, his bike was still dented and scratched from when he ditched it four months earlier. Tom had repaired the engine for him, increasing horsepower and gas mileage, but had no interest in the cosmetic stuff. Jack hoped to save enough money to fix the bike, but tennis instructors didn't earn much.

An hour late for his appointment, he ambled toward the hospital as if wading along a sandy beach. He didn't want to keep the doctor waiting, but he hated hospitals and doctors, so his legs would only go so fast.

He would have dropped out of the study by now if his mom and brother hadn't made such a fuss about it. They were adamant, so he'd relented. It was the least he could do after what he put them through a few months ago, and if it meant that his mom would sleep better, he really had no choice.

Sweat rolled down the side of his face as the heat rose off the pavement in thick waves. New York suffered through what seemed like an endless heat wave. Scorching temperatures had soared past 110 degrees for two weeks straight, as if Mother Nature flipped humanity the bird for treating her so shabbily.

He trudged toward the massive glass and steel facility, t-shirt soaked and blue jeans already stuck to his long legs. He passed the armed guards and swiped his citizen's identification card at the reader. The glass doors swung open with a smooth *swoosh,* and he smiled as a cool breeze engulfed him.

He took an immediate right and sauntered down the long hallway away from the three patient wings. Heading to the basement and the research laboratories below ground, he pressed the call button for the elevator at the end of the hallway.

When he arrived in the basement, Brenda welcomed him with a broad smile and a soft touch on the arm. "Hi, Jack, you're a little late today."

"One of my clients had a heart attack during his lesson. He collapsed right along the baseline. I had to give him CPR until the ambulance came." He widened his eyes and grinned, trying his best impression of a humble, life-saving hero.

"And the time before that you raced into a burning building. Then there was the time a child was drowning at the pool at the club." She turned from him and strode down the hallway. "Let's not forget the traffic accident where you had to pry open the door right before the car exploded. You live quite the heroic life."

She smiled mischievously at him as she brushed back her short, black hair. She had a fair complexion, bright hazel eyes, and a wide smile that transformed her pretty oval face into something extraordinary.

"I'm sorry, Brenda, the traffic was crazy."

"I'm sure, Jack. Next time, let us send you a car. Doctor Beck isn't happy with you driving the bike while you're having those headaches." She led him to the examining rooms.

"You know I only come to see you."

"You're sweet, but I don't think I'm your type." She chuckled. "Besides, you live too dangerous a life with all of those fires and traffic accidents you're saving people from. I would never sleep at night from the worry."

The hallway stretched out in solid white, as if a splash of color might disrupt the experiments. Research labs dotted both sides of the corridor, with Doctor Beck's workspace larger than most.

Jack hesitated at the doorway. "Run away with me! We can make a break for it." The serious tone in his voice surprised him as he gently grabbed Brenda's arm. For a moment, her smile melted away like snow on a hot day, and the wave of melancholy that replaced it shocked him like an electrical jolt. He recoiled as if the wave of emotion caused him pain.

Her smile instantly returned. "Maybe next time, Jack. Come on, Doctor Beck is waiting for you." She shoved him out of the snow-white hallway and into a world of color.

Vibrant posters hung on the walls, many of them depicting lush Italian and English country sides. The largest showed Da Vinci's drawing of a naked male human body—multiple arms and legs stretched out wide and enclosed in a grand circle.

Darian sat behind a large metal desk with three flat-screen monitors and two keyboards perched on top, but he examined a color illustration of the brain in an old textbook. He stood and grinned as Jack leaned over the desk before him, closing the book on the desk as he shook Jack's hand. "Good to see you." He wore a wrinkled U2 t-shirt and jeans.

Jack noticed dark circles under his eyes and stress lines on his forehead that hadn't been there when he first met the doctor four months earlier.

"Sorry I'm late, Doc."

Brenda followed him into the office. "Jack stopped to save a poor helpless child from a burning building."

"That was last time. This time I had to give CPR to one of my clients who had a heart attack."

Darian smiled. "Don't worry about being late. You're the only patient we're seeing today. Tell me, how have you been feeling?"

Jack shrugged. "I feel good, Doc. How about you? You need to escape and do some biking."

"Why do you say that?"

Jack pointed to his desk. "You've had the same six pictures on display since I started seeing you."

"That's very perceptive of you, Jack. I haven't biked outside in four months. The head trauma study is keeping me busy, but I still have

Bessie." He pointed to a well-used stationary bike in the corner of the lab, with worn pedals and a slightly tattered seat. "But enough about me. I see you still have sensitivity to light." He gestured toward Jack's sunglasses.

Jack shrugged. "It's not that bad."

Darian frowned. "Obviously it's bothering you a good deal. You've got to be honest with me to help with the study. Tell me about your hearing issues. I can see the ear plugs, so don't deny it."

"Okay, you've got me." Jack smiled sheepishly. "Lately everything sounds louder, more intense, as if the volume on the world has been turned up. I figure that's a good thing."

Darian pointed to a couch on one end of the room. Jack sat on one end while Darian and Brenda settled onto chairs next to him. "And the headaches?"

"They're about the same. I get a quick flash of pain that goes away in a second or two. I can cope with them." The headaches were becoming more frequent and intense, but he didn't want to tell Darian. He didn't want to come for more tests, and he didn't want his family to know. Tom would want him admitted, and he had the sneaking suspicion that if he were admitted to the hospital he would never be released. He could deal with the headaches on his own.

"How about we go through a series of ten math problems before we head to the imaging center?"

"You know, math is not my thing. You should be asking Tom the questions. He's got the brains in the family. They're just numbers to me."

Darian lowered the clipboard. "How's your brother doing? I understand ICS gave him an education contract."

"The Sheppard Group bought out the contract. Tom's going to be a star!"

"That sounds great. Have you met Charles Sheppard? What do you think of him?" Darian locked his eyes on him.

"Tom's met him a couple of times, says he's a straight shooter, someone who seems to care about ordinary people. Why do you ask?"

"The Sheppard Group is a part owner in this facility. I was just wondering. I've never met him." Darian raised the clipboard. "Give me the first number that comes to your mind. Remember, it doesn't matter if it's correct. I just want the first number that pops into your mind."

Jack nodded and Darian began. "3,657 multiplied by 876...." The questions became progressively more difficult. Darian checked off the responses as Jack correctly answered each one.

After the last question, Jack said, "I told you I'm not good at math. Did I come close to any of them?"

"It's not important whether you got them right or wrong. I just need your first impression."

Darian smiled and patted him on the knee, but Jack noticed that his shoulders sagged and worry crept into his eyes like a shadow from a candle. He assumed he had answered them all wrong.

A searing pain burned through his head—another headache. It lasted only a few seconds, but he got the unmistakable image of a barking golden lab. "Do you have a dog, Doc?"

He looked up from his notes. "No."

Darian glanced at the small refrigerator tucked away in the corner of his lab. He kept one syringe of EBF-202 hidden in the back. When they'd first treated Jack, he considered injecting himself as well. If he increased his own intelligence, maybe he could discover the key to reigning in the drug. Maybe he could save Jack. Maybe he could be useful.

Maybe, maybe, maybe....

Treating himself would have been too reckless. He had no idea how the drug would affect him, and he remained Jack's best chance at survival. If Jack died though, he would have no choice but to inject himself, because Wickersham would find another patient to test EBF-202 on.

He couldn't go through this again. He couldn't fail again. He couldn't be responsible for someone else dying. If EBF-202 increased his chances of finding a cure, he would take that bet with his life. This was his responsibility, his mess to cleanup.

He turned on music from his phone and The Who's "Tommy" flooded the workspace. Sometimes rock inspired him—the driving beat, the chords, the emotions behind the music—but this time, the music fell flat as he studied the new images of Jack's brain.

It had changed so substantially that if he didn't know any better, he would have sworn that it was a different brain altogether. The new video showed a denser brain with more developed creases and wrinkles in all four lobes, increased brain branching and complex linking between brain cells, and substantially more activity during even the simplest questioning.

Frustrated, he paced the lab. He had spent the past four months trying to develop an inhibitor for EBF-202, hoping to stop it before Jack's brain developed so much it killed him. If he couldn't stop the drug somehow, it would prove fatal to anyone injected with it, rendering it worse than useless.

The growth rate of Jack's brain had slowed, but it still progressed steadily. Unsure how much longer Jack had, Darian feared time was running out. Only one canine test subject still lived—Lassie, the golden lab. Her body had unexpectedly rejected the drug three months ago. She now lived as the key, but Darian couldn't unlock the mystery. He groaned, jumped on the stationary bike, and began pedaling. He'd been studying the dog's blood for three months now, and nothing stood out as unique or unusual.

As sweat trickled down his face, he looked back at the refrigerator that held the extra dose of EBF-202. Lassie's blood contained the secret. Could he find the key before time ran out for both of them?

CHAPTER 5

Vanessa studied Darian from the doorway as he pedaled hard on the stationary bike, sweat soaking his shirt. He remained a mystery—an exciting, brilliant, funny, slightly dangerous mystery.

Usually, he attracted fun like screens attract dust. At least, he was like that when they had first started dating. On their second date, they ended up at the boathouse in Central Pepsi Park, where they borrowed masks from departing revelers, joined a costume party, and stayed until the sun came up. On their fourth date, they stumbled upon an underground rock bar and spent the night.

The list continued, but had trailed off dramatically the last few months. He worried about Jack, but she wanted the fun Darian back.

She silently swerved around a chair, slid behind him, and whispered an inch from his ear, "Hello, Doctor Beck."

He jumped and almost bolted off the bike. "How did you sneak in?"

She chuckled. "I borrowed a master card key from my father." She dangled her lab coat in her hand. The first three buttons of her white shirt were unbuttoned and her dark blue shorts ended mid-thigh, the top snap undone. She swayed her hips and played with the open collar of her shirt. The room filled with the sweet scent of her perfume. She knew how that fragrance drove him wild.

"You could have killed me." He shut off the music and slowed his pace on the bike. "I might be forced to report you to your father. Breaking into a lab is serious business." He rolled his eyes and scowled in an exaggerated show of indignation.

"That would be awkward, Doctor Beck. I'd hate to tell Daddy how you've taken advantage of his little girl." She batted her eyes and pursed her lips.

He smiled. "I'd be happy to talk to your father and tell him all about us. We'll have to do it sometime soon anyway."

"Not now. He might kill you, and it would be a shame if you died. I have more important things planned for you," she said, her voice husky.

He stopped pedaling.

She nibbled his ear and blew hot air against his neck. "It's already past midnight. I think you should take me home." She shot him her best pouting face, full red lips moist and inviting.

"I thought you had left for the day." He raked a hand through his shaggy hair. "I'd love to go with you, but I've got more work to finish tonight before I trudge home."

"You work too hard. You need to have more fun." She crossed her arms and frowned at him as if she were the parent and he a mischievous boy. "What happened to the guy who stayed out all night?"

Darian grinned. "I don't know what you're talking about."

"Let's see," teased Vanessa. "I've heard the stories—the illegal gambling houses, mansions filled with movie stars, yachts with the rich and famous. Even an unexpected trip to the Cayman Islands."

"All exaggerations. I'm really a homebody. I never go out."

"What about the time you ended up in the Knicks' locker room at Madison Square Garden with two cheerleaders?"

"Well, that one is true, but in my defense, I have no memory of how I ended up there." He smiled sheepishly.

"Come on, Doctor Beck, how about we go for a stroll?" She stroked the handlebars on his stationary bike seductively.

Darian groaned.

She could tell that he fought with himself. She imagined the war waging in his mind, but his face narrowed. She had lost this time.

"I can't tonight. I have a date with the couch." He jumped from the bike.

"I'm beginning to become jealous of Bessie." Vanessa waved her hand at the empty office. "George has gone for the day. He's probably home with his wife and two kids."

"George is a morning guy. He'll be in by the time the sun comes up." He shrugged.

"I bet he starts every day knowing he's going to find a breakthrough." Everyone in the research facility was familiar with George's sunny disposition.

"Yes, it's very annoying." He frowned and pointed to the video screens on his desk. "The answer is here somewhere. I just need to find it."

"Why are you studying two different brains? The one on the left seems normal while the one on the right is clearly extraordinary."

"That's the problem. Both scans come from Jack. The left one is when we first treated him with EBF-202, and the right is from earlier today. He answered all the advanced math questions correctly during today's exam. When I extrapolate that sampling to an IQ, it zooms off the charts."

"But that's what's supposed to happen, right? Your drug should improve intelligence?"

"Yes, but Jack's brain is developing so extensively, it's causing pressure against the skull that I can't stop. Plus his hearing and sensitivity to light have increased. That's unexpected, and if those changes could happen, who knows what else is happening to him."

He twisted his face angrily as he raked his hand through his hair. "This is all my fault. I'd change places with him if I could."

"But you can't, and this isn't all your fault. We've been through this dozens of times. You can only do your best for him. Is there anything I can do to help?"

"I've got to figure this out." Darian started walking her toward the door. "This is my responsibility, although you could tell me what you're working on. Your team has taken over the entire southern end of the facility. Security is as tight as Fort Knox."

"You sound jealous, Doctor Beck. You know *Project Qing* is highly confidential." She smiled seductively and lifted her hand to her open mouth. "Whoops, I wasn't supposed to tell you the name. I might let something else slip if you come home with me."

Darian shook his head.

"It was worth one last shot, but I have something planned for you Friday night. It's going to be special. You'll have no excuses." She turned and strolled out of the lab, letting her hand linger on the doorframe for a moment before she left.

"Project Qing," Darian muttered to himself. "That name sounds oddly familiar. Where have I heard it before?"

Cooper twirled a fine Swiss fountain pen in his hand with one crisp piece of cotton stationary stretched out before him. He glanced at the latest surveillance photographs of Maggie on his computer screen and smiled. She would be his. After all these years, she would finally be his.

He had started to write her a letter, but he paused, his imagination whirling with details of a meeting he would soon have with her. It was a lifetime since he had spoken with her last. *She will be so pleased to see me, to finally realize the happiness only I can grant her.*

He'd last seen her in person at her wedding, where he watched her from the back pew and left before the service ended. She looked happy at the altar, but he knew she was miserable inside. How could she be anything else—settling for a loser when she could have had him?

It was all so idiotic, so stupid of her to waste those years, but he would give her one more chance at happiness.

Snap! He pulled himself from the daydream and glanced down at the paper. It had a jagged rip down the center, and he'd snapped the pen cleanly in half.

CHAPTER 6

Maggie squinted against the sun's bright glare as she hustled from the office building where she worked to the park across the street.

Her best friend, Susan, complained as she huffed from just behind her. "I hate August. It's just not human out here." A familiar refrain—she also hated parts of April, all of May, June, July, and most of September.

"Come on, let's grab our bench!" Maggie scooted through the security gate and into the small park toward her favorite spot. Entry to the park was limited to employees of corporate sponsors, one of which was the law firm where they worked.

Maggie reached the bench first.

Susan ran more than a few steps behind. Her pretty, heart-shaped face had already turned beet red from the heat and the quick jaunt. "Why don't we eat lunch inside during the summer?" She settled onto the bench and sighed heavily.

Only four other people braved the afternoon heat, scattered in pairs on far-flung benches.

"You can eat inside anytime you like. I need to see the sun for a few minutes each day. Otherwise I become claustrophobic." Maggie opened her lunch bag containing the usual—a sandwich, an apple, and a bottle of Canadian water. Their favorite bench offered a partial view of

Madison Avenue on one side and a small reflecting pool on the other. Susan liked to people-watch on the Avenue, while Maggie usually spent her time looking at the water. None of the other benches worked as well for the pair.

"I hear you've pulled Mr. Grabby Hands tonight for overtime," Maggie said.

Susan groaned and shrugged. "What can I do? We really need the money."

"Jane and I are both working tonight, so we'll have to implement operation *Chastity Belt*," Maggie explained. "It's never safe to be alone with Mr. Grabby Hands. If he needs to speak to you in his office, call one of us. We'll alternate and make up an excuse to be with you. And don't be fooled by an unexpected trip to the copy center on the fifth floor. He grabbed Darlene in there between a couple of three dimensional laser printers the other night."

Susan frowned. "I've been told that it might be a late one." She had brought a small container of leftover pasta for lunch, and sipped from a can of cheap domestic beer, which was less expensive than Canadian water and safer to drink than tap water.

"You know our motto." Maggie smiled. "We leave no girl behind. We'll share a transport home. I've brought my sketchpad just in case we're super late and I finish early." Maggie had organized a dozen women at the firm into a vigilante group of sorts for their mutual protection against partners like Hawkins, a.k.a. Mr. Grabby Hands, but operation *Chastity Belt* was not foolproof. The winter holiday party was her greatest challenge—three years running and she'd had no casualties.

"Thanks." Relief flooded Susan's face as her worry lines smoothed. "Are you taking tomorrow off?"

"Yes. I call it my Solitary Day. Every year, I take one day off in August to be alone." Maggie faced the reflecting pool, lips turned down and eyes sad as she contemplated the true purpose of Solitary Day. She would say nothing about that to Susan. She would never burden her with it.

"We've got to find you a guy. It's been over eight years since Paul passed on."

Susan thought all her problems could be solved with the right guy, but Maggie had already had the right guy, and now he was gone. No one could replace Paul. Why bother trying?

"I'm too busy with work and my boys to take time for romance." She stared into the reflecting pool. The water reminded her of a lake from her childhood, at a resort where she had once lived with her parents. A lifetime had passed since then, but her days there still haunted her. The hair on the back of her neck stood on end, and her skin became clammy.

Susan tugged her arm. "Looks like there's a VIP on the avenue. Look at all the security guys."

A phalanx of eight beefy-looking men dressed in dark suits, with assault rifles slung over their shoulders, briskly marched down the avenue past where they sat.

"I wonder who's so important?" Susan whispered.

In the center of the group walked four civilians.

Maggie saw a flash of royal blue and shuddered—her mind momentarily thrown back in time. Some memories grew more vivid than the present.

CHAPTER 7

Thirty Years Ago —

Maggie stumbled out of her bedroom dressed in pink cotton pajamas, her steps tentative, as if unsure the ground was solid underneath her feet. She usually woke refreshed in those days, but she'd had a hard time sleeping. She dreamed about her friend, Cooper, and each dream left her more shaken and soaked in sweat than the one before. His volcanic temper had worsened as the summer progressed, and he'd started to scare her.

She plopped down on her chair at the kitchen table. The frayed wicker seat protested even the slight weight of her small body.

"Good morning, sleepyhead," her mom said, smiling. Young and beautiful, she twirled in a tight three hundred and sixty degree spin. Her plain blue maid's uniform ballooned out slightly from her knees as she completed the pirouette. "How do I look? There's not much I can do wearing this."

"You look pretty, and I love the pink ribbon."

She always found a way to wear something pink to break up the ugly blue sameness of her uniform.

Mom smiled as she poured Cheerios into a small bowl from the single serving box she had "borrowed" from the resort. "Eat quickly. I want you dressed and out the door before I leave."

Maggie launched into her cereal, spilling milk over the top of the bowl. After the first few bites, she noticed a new rip in the bright green linoleum floor. At least, she believed it had originally been bright green. Most of the floor was now dark and dingy, but when her father had moved the mini-refrigerator last week, they uncovered a small bright green patch with tiny yellow flowers. She had never noticed the flowers before. Even now she had to hunch down on her hands and knees and look closely to find any.

"Come on, I thought you were eating your breakfast. I can't be late this morning." Mom hovered over her, frowning with only the edges of her lips.

Maggie's face warmed. "Sorry, Mom, I didn't mean to." She twisted her chair so the offensive, attention-grabbing linoleum rip was no longer in clear sight, and gobbled down three quick spoonfuls of cereal, forgetting to breathe between bites. By the time the last jumble of breakfast entered her mouth, she had no air left in her lungs and coughed up half-eaten circles of toasted oats across the table.

Mom chuckled. "I think that's enough breakfast. Get changed and I'll clean up the table."

Maggie skipped into her room and got dressed after some agonizing moments over her small wardrobe.

"Grab your book and let's go."

"Do I need the book? I thought I would do some drawing. The lake is *so* pretty."

"You drew all day yesterday and you have to finish that book before summer vacation ends."

"Pleeeease!"

"Bring both, but you had better make progress on that book, or no more drawing."

She grabbed her book off the table and her small backpack off the floor, which already contained her sketching materials.

"Find your father at lunch time. He's going to let you feed the horses."

Maggie eyed her mother suspiciously. "Feed the horses or clean up the stables?"

"You're old enough to do both!"

She marched to her favorite place, a small clearing opposite the boathouse. Hidden from the hiking trail, it had become her secret spot. A tall evergreen bush that she couldn't see over guarded her private sanctuary. Eyeing the bush carefully, she bent back a few branches and pushed through to the other side. Yesterday, the angry bush had snapped back at her, scratching her leg. Today, it tossed morning dew on top of her head. She began to think it didn't like her very much. On the other side, a circular fifteen-foot clearing with thick green grass and one towering weeping willow edged the lakeshore, hiding the clearing from the lake.

Only two other people knew about her secret spot. Well, that wasn't quite right... one person and a cat, but she thought of the cat as another person. At the beginning of the summer, she'd been hiking along the trail when she heard meowing. The cat sounded hungry and scared, so without hesitation, she pushed her way through the evergreen bush and found the clearing. A scrawny, feral cat sat in the middle of the grass opening, looking sad and lonely. She sort of adopted it.

Each day, she brought food to the clearing. She had stuffed a small container in her backpack last night. "I have some milk for you, Mr. Cat."

At the sound of her voice, the cat appeared from behind the willow tree. It looked healthy and gracefully stalked toward her, stopping to rub its head against her leg.

She stroked his thick, soft black and white fur. "The milk is a little warm, but I think you'll like it just fine."

Cooper also knew about the clearing. She had met him at the beginning of the summer. He was a guest at the resort and a few years older than she was. One day, she skipped her way to the lake and he popped out from behind an oak tree, startling her. She considered making a run for it, but he'd smiled broadly and introduced himself. His voice had a friendly, soothing quality, and he had the deepest blue eyes she'd ever seen. For a moment, the broad smile and the sapphire eyes froze her, but she eventually thawed and found her voice. It seemed weird, but he always popped out of someplace: along the lake, or by the rose garden, or in the maze. She hadn't told her parents about him because fraternizing with guests was off limits, and they would be angry if they found out.

She sat in the grass, opened her backpack, found her sketchpad and colored pencils, and neatly placed them in front of her.

The hair on the back of her neck stood on end. "Cooper, are you watching me?" she shouted.

He dropped out of a nearby oak tree and landed with a quiet thud, and the cat bolted from the clearing.

"Cooper, you scared away Mr. Cat."

His eyes narrowed and followed the cat's path out of the clearing. "Sometimes I think you like that cat more than me."

She tried to ignore him, but he dropped down in front of her and blocked her view of the lake.

A wide grin beamed on his face. "Draw me, Maggs!"

"I'm not good at people yet. I thought I would draw a frog." She pointed to a fat one that sat comfortably on a lily pad.

He darted toward the amphibian and scooped it up in one hand. "Now you have no choice. You can draw me holding the frog." He made a funny face and crossed his eyes, making her laugh. He could be fun when he wanted.

"Okay, just this one time, but don't get mad if you don't like how it turns out." She shot him a knowing look, wary of the latent volcano.

"I'll love it." He posed while he held the frog in one hand close to his face.

She went to work, starting with his face, trying to capture his smile and eyes just right.

"We're leaving the resort tomorrow. I wish you could come with us."

"What?"

"You've got to come with us. I'm sure my parents won't mind. We have plenty of rooms at my house."

"What about my parents?"

"They can stay here." His smile vanished. His jaw tightened and his eyes pinched together.

"Don't be silly. I can't leave my parents and come with you. What would I do about Mr. Cat?"

Cooper simmered and pink tint flushed his face. A scowl spoiled his good looks.

She finished the drawing, but squinted at it and frowned.

He jumped toward her. "Let me see."

She turned the page and stuffed the pad into her backpack. "You can't see it. It's not any good."

"That's not fair!" His grip tightened around the frog.

"Tough!"

His nostrils flared as he flung the frog hard against the trunk of the willow tree. After a sickening thud it fell lifeless to the ground.

She screeched and tears rained down her cheeks.

He stormed out of the clearing without looking back.

The next day, Maggie faced the evergreen bush, uncertain what to do. She stared hard into the green tangled branches, looking for some sign of Cooper. She inspected the ground for footprints. Sneakers had scuffed the ground at the base of the bush, but she couldn't be sure whether they were old or to whom they belonged.

The pink backpack tugged heavily on her shoulders. She particularly felt the weight of the small can of tuna that she had "borrowed" for Mr. Cat. He would be waiting. If it were not for him, she would have turned and gone someplace else, probably to the stables where her dad worked.

She steeled her nerves, took a deep breath, and shoved her way through the bush. She pushed a little harder than usual and stumbled into the clearing, lucky to catch her balance. As she glanced around the open space, her heart hammered and her stomach ached. Nothing appeared out of the ordinary, but something was wrong. The clearing was too quiet.

She spun in a circle. "Cooper, are you here?" She had intended to shout, but her voice sounded soft, barely above a whisper. She looked carefully in the old oak tree to see if he hid among the branches, but couldn't see much against the bright morning sun.

An uneasy relief washed over her as she walked to the middle of the clearing. "I've got breakfast, Mr. Cat. Come and eat it."

She dropped her backpack and inched toward the edge of the lake. Something white and black swayed in the wind against the weeping willow tree. She snuck up on it, unreasonably worried that it was dangerous, slowly placing one foot in front of the other. Time seemed to stretch on. She strained her eyes until she realized it was just a piece of paper pinned to the tree.

It can't hurt me. Still, she crept forward, eyes darting around suspiciously. A rustling sound behind her startled her, and she spun to see a squirrel looking for nuts. She unpinned the note with shaking hands, careful not to rip the fancy linen paper that felt coarse and heavy against her fingers. It contained the Lake Country Resort watermark.

Turning her back to the lake, she read the note, each letter perfectly formed in neat block letters.

> Dear Maggs,
> You should have shown me the picture. I know you like me best! See you next summer.
> Your Special Friend,
> Cooper

The breeze picked up and a small thumping sound came from the willow.

Then she saw it, and dropped the note.

The collar she had made for Mr. Cat swung in the breeze, thumping against the branches of the tree. He was nowhere in sight.

She called out, but he didn't appear.

"Maggie, are you okay?" Susan, still seated on the bench next to her, shook her shoulders. Concern had sprung on her face like weeds in a garden.

Maggie woke from her daze. "I'm fine. I'm just a little under the weather, that's all."

"You were trembling and all the color drained from your face."

"It's nothing. Let's go back." She rose from the bench and shook the memory from her mind. That had only been the beginning of her nightmare.

The rest was worse. Much worse.

CHAPTER 8

"You're going to be late for the bus!"

Maggie pushed Tom toward the front door. At the beginning of summer, he began an internship for the Sheppard Group, where he specialized in robotics. When summer break ended in two weeks, he would start his senior year in high school and the internship would transform into a part-time paid position.

"I'll make it on time. I like the mornings better when you're already at work." He shuffled his feet while she playfully pushed his tall, athletic frame.

"You know the date. This is my Solitary Day."

"Okay, Mom." Tom laughed. "No need to push. I'm working the benefit with Jack tonight. We'll be back late." He turned, kissed her on the cheek and leapt out the front door, his long, curly brown hair falling to his shoulders. The bus had just turned up their block as he bounded down the front stoop.

Maggie watched her son board the bus. *He's seventeen and I still feel anxious until he's safely on his way.* She wondered if the worry that accompanied motherhood would ever go away as she turned and locked the door behind her.

She wore her favorite shirt—a plain pink cotton blouse with buttons down the front. Paul had bought it for her. The soft cotton felt like a hug from an old friend. Of course it was pink. She always wore pink on Solitary Day. The color reminded her of her mother and lifted her spirits, which was not easy to do on Solitary Day.

She somberly walked the length of the small apartment, her footsteps heavy. She moved woodenly, feeling older than her age, her nerves frazzled. Noises in the apartment were louder than they should be. A creak on the staircase sounded like a stampede. She sighed. It would be a long day. Solitary Day always was.

She crossed into her tidy bedroom and, breathing deeply, inched her way to the closet. The door opened with a squeak. She frowned at her small wardrobe, just a dozen dresses and some casual clothes hung on plastic hangers. She heaved them all to the far right of the closet. The floor angled upward at a thirty-degree angle toward the left side. She bent low, and her hand trembled. She searched the coarse wood for a small indentation in the wood with her fingers, found the small nook, clasped it and pulled upward. The wooden latch caught and the top of the false floor sprung open with a metallic popping sound.

The acid in her stomach churned as she sat on the floor and stared at the now open hiding spot, her breath shallow. She wanted to close it and run. She didn't even care where she would go—anywhere would be good so long as it was far away—but she couldn't. She had a responsibility.

She reached into the opening, pulled out a small metal container, rose robotically, and brought the metal box to her unmade bed.

The container wasn't heavy, but it felt like an anvil. Tears welled in her eyes as she flipped open the lid and pulled out the file. It was her Cooper File and it was Solitary Day, and that meant that she had to reread the letters and study the pictures. If she closed her eyes, she heard the screams from the girls in the photographs.

She called it Solitary Day, but she was never really alone. The girls in the pictures kept her company, and the letters terrified her, filling her with overwhelming fear. Cooper watched her, her boys, her friends, everyone she cared about. If she acted on the letters, he would take his revenge, and there would be nothing she could do to protect them.

What evidence do I have? Nothing connected the letters and pictures to him. No one would believe me.

He was rich and powerful.

She was nobody.

It was all too monstrous to believe. The letters came on Solitary Day each year, and her sense of helplessness grew each year as well. She feared that one day nothing would be left of her but a pile of helplessness.

The afternoon light streamed through the kitchen windows. She had long ago put down her e-reader and started drawing. She never quite finished the books she started for her book club. She wanted to quit the group, except that every time she made up her mind to quit, her mother's voice chastised her in her head, and she felt guilty.

She sat at the kitchen table with her sketchpad open to a mostly finished drawing of her son Jack. While he had lain unconscious in a hospital bed, she promised to draw him when he was better, *if* he got better. He had asked her numerous times in the past to draw him, but she had always declined. She was still reluctant to draw faces after all these years, but she had to keep this particular promise.

Almost finished, she studied the drawing for a long moment. *It's not half bad, but I need to add more fun to the eyes.*

A computerized voice interrupted her thoughts. "You've got mail." The recording repeated the message three times through a small speaker in the hallway.

Her heart leaped forward and she doubled over in pain as cramps squeezed her stomach. She knew the letter would come, but each year, the pain got worse. Tears cascaded down her face. With each passing year, she felt more culpable, more responsible for the latest victims. She hated herself on Solitary Day and most days thereafter.

Her head slumped to the kitchen table. She covered it with her arms, shielding herself from Cooper and the shame of inaction. She had no idea how long she stayed sitting that way.

Eventually, the sun shifted and its hot rays beat against the back of her neck. A fly buzzed by her ear and snapped her back to the world. She shooed it away, rose, and wiped her face on a cloth towel. Maybe this year would be different. *I am a strong woman. I'm not responsible for him.*

She didn't really believe it.

Maggie trudged to the front door, noticing details in the hallway that she usually ignored—a chipped tile outside Tom's door; a dark dirt stain on the wall next to Jack's door looked, as if someone had leaned against the wall before grabbing the doorknob; a small stain on the ceiling where one of her boys had killed a flying bug and hadn't cleaned up the mess.

She reached the front door, opened it, blinked her eyes against the bright summer sun, and eyed her mailbox as if she could determine what was hidden within the dark metal box by staring hard at it. When her x-ray vision failed, she reached across the doorway and opened it. The thin white envelope felt familiar to her touch, a fine cotton linen—the same as the other letters. The familiar neat handwriting jumped out, and as always, there was no return address.

Dazed, she went back inside, leaving the front door slightly ajar.

Something odd about the envelope caught her attention. It was thinner than past letters. She opened it and unfolded the single sheet of paper held within.

Dear Maggs,

I've given up trying to replace you. There will be no other women.

Your Special Friend,

Cooper

The handwriting was exactly the same as it had been thirty years earlier, the signature with the same flourish, as if frozen in time.

Cooper stared at Maggie through the glass windowpanes of the back door. He breathed heavily and butterflies fluttered in his stomach. He had last seen her in person over twenty years ago. She was older now, but the person he knew thirty years ago was still there. Freckles dotted her cheeks like stars, and she kept her hair pulled back in a ponytail with a pink ribbon. She wore a pink shirt and beige pants, but if he squinted just a little, he could visualize her in pigtails and pink shorts, just like the ones she wore that first summer he met her.

She let the paper flutter to the ground. Fresh tears moistened her face.

The letter deeply moved her, he thought. *She must be upset with herself.*

She probably misunderstood the letter's meaning. She probably assumed that he wouldn't contact her anymore or that she had lost her chance to be with him.

She must have been afraid she wasn't good enough for him—a perfectly reasonable fear. Any outsider would have reached the same conclusion, but she had qualities that defied description and logic.

Today, everything would change.

The letter fluttered to the ground as if in slow motion. Her thoughts whirled in circles, creating a small tornado in her mind. Relief washed over her. There were no new pictures, no new victims to mourn or screams to imagine.

Is it possible that I'm freed from this hell?

The words kept spinning around in her mind, gathering speed. She would never be free. *'There will be no other women.'* What did that mean?

A noise at the front door startled her, and she suppressed a scream. She spun and found a mountain-sized man in the doorway who filled the entire space. A black t-shirt stretched tightly across his broad chest and an automatic pistol hung holstered at his hip. The words "Private Security" were written in white on his baseball cap. His dark skin blended in with his black clothes, short black beard, and dead eyes.

With a scream still frozen in her throat, she spun toward the back door, hoping to make a run for it.

Two more men had entered through the kitchen door. Another granite-sized security man who looked eerily similar to the man at the front door blocked her retreat out back. Her eyes focused on the second man, and ice-cold fingers wrapped their way around her heart and squeezed.

He stood a good deal taller than her, tanned with straight, short, coffee-colored hair feathered to the side. He looked comfortable in a silk buttoned-down pink shirt, crisp gray slacks, and highly polished black shoes.

She froze before his electric blue eyes and broad smile. It could have been a hundred years since she'd last seen him, but she would always recognize those eyes and that smile.

Cooper casually strolled into the kitchen and examined her pad. "I like your sketch. You've got so much talent. I recognized it when we first met."

She regained her composure. She had dreaded this day her whole life, but she'd always known she would have to confront him again. Now that he stood before her, an odd sense of relief washed through her. Perhaps her nightmare would finally end.

Her face twisted into a scowl. "Put that down!" She marched toward him and snatched the sketchpad from his outstretched hand.

He seemed amused as his fingertips ripped the edges of the paper. "I've come to take you away from all this." He laughed as he waved his arms around the kitchen. "I'm sure you won't miss it."

"Leave me alone! Stop bothering me. Just go!"

"I don't think you understand. You don't have to worry that you're not good enough for me. To me, you're the same girl I met thirty years ago. Nothing else matters. No substitutes will do. I must have you." His perfectly tanned face turned up in a wide smile. "I've wasted enough time as it is."

"No, I don't want to go!" Tears returned to her face as she crept her way to the kitchen counter, inching away from him. The small kitchen shrunk further as the two giant-sized security men edged toward her.

A butcher block with a set of knives sat on the white plastic countertop. Jack had given her the set as a gift last Christmas.

Cooper stood his ground, but his left eye twitched and his smile turned tight and forced. "We can come back later and retrieve anything you're attached to, but we must go now. I have an extremely busy day planned. I'm sure you understand."

She snatched the eight-inch carving knife from the butcher block with her right hand, while still clutching the sketchpad close to her chest in her left. She was scared, but she wasn't a little girl any longer.

"You're just in shock. Put down the knife, Maggs." Cooper raised his hands in the air with his palms outward. The cuffs on his sleeves dropped down towards his elbows and revealed a platinum wristwatch on his left wrist. One of the security guards slid silently and gracefully behind her.

"We can talk about this. I'm going to give you everything you deserve." His silky smooth tone showed no worry or concern.

She slashed the knife toward him in a long, violent arch. The knife missed by two feet, but the swipe gave one of the security guards the time he needed to grab her arm and twist her wrist. The knife clanged against the tile floor.

As the guard held her still, Cooper stepped forward and snatched the sketchpad. "I look forward to you drawing me."

She staggered backward against the security man's broad chest. "Never! You're a monster!"

The smile disappeared from Cooper's face. Quick as a snake, he slapped her hard across the cheek with an open palm. The guard let her go and she sprawled backward, twisting to her knees.

"You'll do as I say." Cooper spit out the words, the volcano still active after all these years.

Pain seared her cheek and she spit blood. "You can't make me."

Cooper laughed and examined the drawing of Jack for a long moment. "You have nice looking boys, Maggs." He ripped the drawing from the sketchpad, crumpled it into a ball, and dropped it to the ground.

Nausea washed through her body.

"There is no limit to the things I can make you do." He sneered, his handsome face twisting with malice.

CHAPTER 9

Darian floated about his small studio apartment like driftwood along a shoreline, aimlessly bumping into his bed and wandering past his tiny living space toward an alcove kitchen. His bare feet left faint footprints behind on the tightly woven carpet.

He had been watching Vanessa sleep. The darkness covered her naked body, but not completely, so he glimpsed the outline of her lovely curves from different angles. He had found her sleeping in the nude, a bottle of champagne chilling alongside a small spread of chilled caviar and artisan crackers, and a handwritten note to wake her. He had no idea how she'd entered his apartment. She certainly didn't have a key, but he complied with her wishes to the best of his ability.

He smiled despite his champagne-induced headache. She was no ordinary lab assistant. She was special and nothing like her father. Even though he warned himself that they could never have a future, he still found himself falling for her.

The Great Romantic Fool. She will never truly understand me.

Her world embodied privilege and luxury compared to the place where he'd started—a dark place full of despair.

He turned from her, leaned against the wall of his apartment and peered through rain-streaked windows. Purple and white spotlights lit the stone arch at the entrance to Washington Square Park. Sometimes, when weary, his mind roamed back to his childhood. He usually tried to keep that door shut, but exhaustion and his subconscious desire to punish himself for his role in Jack's plight overcame his defenses. The door to the past creaked open... painfully.

Born in the Upper Manhattan Ghetto, he had never known his father. His mother probably didn't know who he was, either. Whenever Darian asked about him, his mother smiled, shrugged her thin shoulders, and told him that his father must have been an angel. He didn't believe in immaculate conceptions, nor did he see any sign of divinity at work, so he ruled out angels or God. At times, he created his own version of his father, alternating between hero and villain, knowing neither probably fit, and that he would never discover the truth.

His mother was addicted to a slew of drugs. It didn't seem to matter which ones—really anything that transported her from everyday reality to somewhere else, *anywhere* else. The Upper Manhattan Ghetto became the first Free Commercial Zone where recreational drugs could be sold legally, as long as they were taken in the Zone. Major drug companies made a fortune, developing cheap addicting pharmaceuticals like the Sugar Shot, the Orgasm, the Chilly Dipper, the Almighty Aspirin, the Devil's Downer, and the Afterlife.

His mom took them all.

His earliest childhood memories revolved around drugs: his mother's need to acquire them, to use them, and a few failed attempts to free herself from those shackles. Each time she'd tried to quit, his hopes soared, only to crash hard when she failed. He never blamed her. She'd tried hard, but some chains were too strong to break.

Most of those early days blurred together, but one day stood out among the misery-filled days. He was nine and the rain fell in torrents while his mom suffered through a particularly bad patch. They lived on the streets, in a cardboard box beneath an overpass, with the rats and other vermin. The weather had been cold and wet, and the concrete felt rough and dirty against his bare feet.

His mother had been passed out for over a day. All he ate during that time were a few stale pieces of bread he nicked from a bakery. He glanced across the street even though he didn't want to. He thought someone might have died not more than twenty feet away; the person hadn't moved in two days. He should check, go through the man's pockets for anything useful, but death hovered too close. He didn't want to tempt the Reaper with his mom in such a precarious position.

A police van pulled up and four officers piled out to do a routine sweep. They tried to rouse his mother, but she lacked the energy or the will to respond. A female officer with a kind face who smelled of lilacs spoke softly to him, and he willingly followed her into the van. Even at the tender age of nine, he knew he was better off in the orphanage, and his mom was better off in jail for vagrancy than under that overpass with death lurking so close across the street.

At least the orphanage kept him fed and the rain off his head.

His mom visited at first. She tried to come every week, but long stretches passed when she didn't show up. Those were the scariest times; he always imagined the worst, until that day when the Warden called for him. He had just turned eleven.

The bald Warden always wore a poorly fitting gray suit and tie. He spoke with a booming voice and an unfortunate habit of spitting while he spoke. Officially, they called him the "Headmaster" because the orphanage had its own school, but that was a joke. The kids called him Warden because they knew better. The orphans weren't free to leave, and where would they go if they could?

Darian's memory of the Warden's office remained mostly fuzzy. He recalled a spacious room with many windows and a thick carpet, but he vividly remembered the large oak desk, which came up to his chest. A thin piece of wood pulled out to give the person sitting opposite the desk something to write against.

As Darian entered the office, the Warden placed a bowl of vanilla ice cream on that thin piece of wood. Darian stared at the ice cream, frozen like a statue. Two small scoops stared back at him.

The Warden beckoned for him to sit. "Come closer. The ice cream is for you." He smiled, but no genuine affection lit his face.

Darian walked with stiff arms and legs and sat on the small metal stool next to the frozen dessert.

"There's a spoon next to the bowl. Please eat the ice cream before it melts." The Warden smiled and nodded at the bowl as if it were the most precious thing in the world.

Darian glared at it as though it were poison. The other kids had a saying: "Two scoops of vanilla means death's come to get ya."

The ice cream meant.... His throat closed up. He refused to eat it, to even look at it.

The smile disappeared from the Warden's face. "I'm sorry to tell you this, son, but your mom won't be visiting any longer. She passed away."

He stared at the Warden for a long moment. His mother was broken, but he'd hoped that one day he'd fix her. Anger flushed to his face, and he turned his little hands into fists. "Can I see her?"

He didn't know what else to say or ask, but he wanted to see her one last time. Why, he couldn't explain. Thinking back, he now realized he desired closure, certainty, but at eleven, he couldn't put his need into words even if he had tried.

The Warden shook his head. "That would be impossible. She's already been... disposed of." Those were his words—*disposed of.*

He pounded his fist into his leg, stood, knocked the bowl of ice cream onto the floor, turned his back on the Warden, and left the office. A nurse waited for him outside, but he ignored her and stalked back to his dormitory.

Tears never came.

Over the next few years, he spent most of his time fighting with the other kids, arguing with his teachers, and spending long hours in the orphanage factory weaving bags, processing food for food distribution centers, or assembling basic furniture.

On his thirteenth birthday, when English class ended, the teacher stood tall and thin and smiled with crooked yellow teeth. "Stay seated, Darian." The teacher often held him after class for some type of punishment. They enjoyed a mutual distaste for each other.

The other kids gladly scampered from class. One muttered, "I wonder what he did this time?" just loud enough for Darian to hear.

He sat stiffly in his chair. His ribs ached, a cut above his left eye hurt, and the scraped knuckles on his right hand burned. The day before, he had fought with three other children. He gave better than he got, but they still got some licks in.

The English teacher approached with a pamphlet and a sharp number two pencil. He leaned low and slammed the pamphlet on the metal desk. "Take this test. You have an hour, but we both know it's pointless. Just fill in the bubbles and be on your way."

He smiled slyly at the teacher. He didn't like taking tests, but the teacher's tone and attitude angered him. He grabbed the pencil and bore down on the exam, determined to take the full hour and answer all the questions correctly just to spite his teacher.

That was exactly what he did: used the full hour and got every question correct.

The next day, the principal summoned him and required him to retake the assessment test, explaining that there must have been some mistake with the prior one. Darian finished in half an hour with the same result.

From then on, his life in the orphanage changed. He still fought with the other kids regularly and argued with the teachers, but now the teachers realized he was often right, and they stopped underestimating him. No longer required to work in the factory, his teachers encouraged him to spend time reading and on his studies.

By the time he turned sixteen, his scores on the Preliminary Assessment Test soared through the roof, securing him an educational contract that paid back his debt to the orphanage. Education beyond tenth grade required an educational contract or some other guaranteed means to pay for further schooling. Either a student was rich or they secured a contract. They could also attend vocational school, but it still cost too much for many of the kids.

He remembered the day he left the state-run facility. He had hardly any possessions: a small knapsack with a few articles of clothing, an e-reader one of his teachers had given him, an old photograph of his mother, and his first pair of sneakers. The shiny white footwear felt tight against his feet, so he yanked them off when he entered the car that brought him to the prep school that would serve as his new home.

Through an accelerated and winding path, he'd earned a doctorate in neurobiology and started work for the New York Teaching and Research Hospital. He focused his research on brain function, selling the concept behind EBF-202 as a way to prevent Alzheimer's and senility, but secretly hoping that it would unlock the key to drug addiction. He remembered what addiction had done to his mom and other addicts in the ghetto, and he hated the disease. He wanted to kill it, to end it, not just for any particular drug, but for *all* drugs.

The brain held the key to that puzzle, and EBF-202 was the first step.

Darian turned from the window, flopped down on his one comfortable chair, donned his virtual entertainment visor, and turned on the television. The picture instantly projected on the visor in perfect three dimensions.

He switched to a rock music station and groaned. They were replaying the concert Bono had performed for his eighty-first birthday. The epic went on for three hours, fifty-two minutes, and twenty seconds. The aging rocker could only recall parts of three songs, which caused a mash-up of epic proportions. Darian had watched the entire concert last month, unable to shut off the station, as if he were watching a massive pile-up on the freeway.

He switched off the concert and scrolled through the endless list of choices, unsure what most of them were. Usually too busy with work, biking, or catching up with the latest scientific journals, he rarely watched anything on TV but the rock station. Still, he needed a break from the world of neurobiology, the brain, Lassie, and Jack, so he settled on a twenty-four-hour news station.

The station replayed a press conference from the new Ghetto Czar. Actually, his official title was Secretary in Charge of Domestic Priorities, but the news show ran a caption underneath his picture identifying him as the Ghetto Czar, the more common street term. Darian turned up the volume. The man appeared comfortable in front of the cameras, his good-looking face unlined and his short white hair in place. He looked physically fit for someone in his sixties, and sounded silky smooth and sincere.

"I am pleased to announce that we are making the new brain cancer vaccine available to every citizen without charge. By distributing this vaccine we'll end this plague that has affected so many of our citizens.

"The government has contracted to produce the vaccine in enough quantity for every citizen. Along with private doctors, police will distribute the vaccine through detention centers. The plan is to distribute the vaccine alphabetically by last name. Over a period of three months, we'll roll out the distribution to every region. Please consult your local police office to obtain details about distribution in your area. I'm happy to take any questions."

A tremendous breakthrough, the new vaccine should help millions of people and eradicate the disease within a generation. Darian smiled. It was important that the government make it available to everyone.

The new Ghetto Czar had certainly made a good first impression. Darian read the caption on the bottom of the screen: "Charles Sheppard - New Ghetto Czar - Announces Free Distribution of Brain Cancer Vaccine."

Darian shut off the television. Charles Sheppard looked like someone who cared. *Was it real or a good acting job*?

CHAPTER 10

Jack pulled the motorcycle onto the curb and locked it to a lamppost with a thick steel chain. "You're never going to win at craps if you only play the odds, Tom. Craps just doesn't work that way."

Tom shook his head. "Jack, the entire game is odds and math. There's no such thing as streaks. The numbers will always even out in the end."

Jack grinned as he clasped the lock around the heavy chains. "What were the odds that I'd be the big winner and you the big loser?"

"Not very high."

"Intuition and streaks are part of the game. Not everything can be boiled down to numbers and math."

Both brothers plodded to their apartment. It was two-thirty in the morning.

Jack chuckled. "Did you lose everything you made from working the benefit?"

"I've had better nights," Tom mumbled.

Jack surreptitiously grabbed a few bills from his winnings, slapped Tom hard on the back, and secretly slipped the bills into his brother's back pocket.

Tom turned angrily from the sharp slap, but Jack's wide smile disarmed him.

"You aren't going to start with that karate stuff, are you, Tom?"

"How many times have I told you I study jujitsu? I've only been practicing since age five."

Jack staggered a step under the grip of a fierce headache.

"Are you all right?"

The pain came and went quickly. "I'm fine. Just a little tired after taking all your money." He winked. "So how come you're fighting with Mary? I really like her."

Tom stopped cold. "How do you know that I'm arguing with Mary? Did she say something?"

"No, brother, she didn't say anything. I think you mentioned it." Jack shrugged. "Besides, you're hopeless with women."

"She's awesome, but she drives me crazy. She can be so stubborn." Tom had met Mary four months earlier when Jack had been kidnapped. At first Tom thought she hated him, but she helped him save Jack and the relationship flourished. They had a lot in common, and it didn't hurt she was the prettiest woman he had ever met. "I just feel lost sometimes, like I've got no idea what I'm doing and what she's thinking."

"She's special, Tom. You're never going to figure her out with math and numbers. Just go with your heart."

"That's easy for you to say. You've always had lots of girlfriends. It's a little harder for me." Mary was Tom's first real girlfriend if he didn't count Carol Douglas in eighth grade, and he certainly didn't count her. She only made out with him once to make her boyfriend jealous.

He swiped his card key at the common entranceway to their apartment building. The lock flashed green and the door opened. The porch creaked loudly as they stepped through the entrance to the building and turned from the staircase that led up to the other apartments. "Let's be quiet. Mom should be asleep, and she always looks so worn out after her Solitary Day."

A jolt of electricity shot through Tom. "Jack, the front door's open," he whispered. "Mom never leaves the door unlocked." He carefully treaded into the apartment.

"Maybe she just forgot to lock it. It happens to everyone."

They crept down the hallway toward the kitchen. The doors to the three bedrooms were closed.

Tom's skin felt clammy as he instantly calculated probabilities and equations in his head. Something didn't add up. "The light in the kitchen is on." They were vigilant about shutting off lights and reducing energy costs.

What's the probability that Mom forgot to lock the door and *shut off the kitchen lights*?

He led the way to the kitchen. The back door was shut, but not locked, and Mom's e-reader lay on the table.

Jack picked up a crumpled piece of drawing paper from the floor.

Tom swept his eyes across the room. The kitchen chairs were out of place—one pushed too far under the table—and three small red drops had splattered on the floor by the stove. He squatted to look closer at the liquid.

Jack smoothed out the creased paper. His eyes widened. "It's the drawing Mom was sketching of me. Why would she crumple it?"

Tom touched the sticky red fluid on the floor. "Jack, this is blood." His heart pounded hard in his chest. He followed Jack to their mother's bedroom door, where they both paused and stared at the doorknob as if it were red hot.

Jack reached for the handle but hesitated. A light sheen of sweat coated his face as he twisted the doorknob and pushed the door open into the dark room.

At first, Tom saw the sheets bunched together on his mom's bed and thought she slept safely. Then his eyes adjusted to the darkness and he realized she wasn't there.

Jack flipped the lights on and they stared into their mother's empty, unmade bed.

"What's going on?" Tom asked.

Jack grabbed his cell phone and dialed his mother's number. The ring tone blared in the kitchen.

Tom went to fetch the phone, and returned ashen-faced. "This is bad, Jack. Something's happened to Mom. She hasn't called anyone since yesterday. She has two missed calls—one from Aunt Jackie and one from her friend Susan."

"Give me the phone and I'll dial Rachel. Maybe she knows what happened to her. Look around and see if you find anything else that looks weird."

Tom handed the phone to Jack and left the bedroom in search of clues.

Jack's hands trembled as he hit the speed dial number 14. "Rachel, it's Jack. Have you heard from Maggie? She's missing."

Rachel was the leader of a secretive underground political movement called the Fourteenth Colony. America had become a nation divided between the fabulously wealthy and everyone else. The Fourteenth Colony dedicated itself to restoring balance and fairness to American society through nonviolent means. Rachel and Maggie were old friends, and Jack had been a member of the group for a few years. Tom had joined four months ago when he saved Jack with the covert group's help.

"I haven't heard anything, Jack. It's been slow tonight. What can I do to help?"

"Let me talk it over with Tom. There have to be some clues around here. I'll call when we figure something out."

"Okay, Jack. I'm going to ask some discrete questions. I'll let you know if I hear anything."

Tom joined Jack in Maggie's bedroom. "There's nothing else out of place. There's no sign of an accident. I have a really bad feeling about this."

"Let's look around some more."

They began a detailed search of Maggie's bedroom with Jack looking through her dresser and Tom pulling out a plastic bin from under her bed.

Tom opened the box and carefully sorted through the contents. "It feels weird going through Mom's stuff." When he finished with the bin, he pushed it back under the bed.

Jack still worked his way through the dresser, so he turned his attention to the closet. The door creaked as he opened it. "That's odd. All of mom's clothes are pushed over to the right."

Tom scanned the closet. "Check this out. The floor's angled upward at the corner for no reason. There's a false floor. Mom must have hidden something underneath."

"Why would Mom need a hiding spot?'

Tom used the flashlight mode on his phone to sweep the light over the floor. The rays lingered over the wood. "You see how the dust has been swept away? Mom recently opened this thing. There should be a latch or some lever on the box to spring it." He brushed the outside of the box with his fingertips and found a small nook. He reached in and pulled, and the wooden trap door popped open with a clunk.

He leaned over and peered inside. "That's weird. It's empty."

CHAPTER 11

Cooper sat next to his mother, Ethel, at a round table toward the front of the main ballroom. His fashionable Italian-made tuxedo fit him flawlessly, yet he hated it. It had become a second skin, squeezing him and suffocating the breath from his body. He so wanted to rip it off.

He fidgeted with his shirt's silver and onyx studs, and upon catching himself doing so, he took a deep breath and placed his hands flat on the table. He had discipline.

Over two hundred people crowded the main room like cattle in a giant pen. He had gone to far too many of these formal events. All the men wore tuxedos. Most of the women were a decade younger than their companions and wore formal gowns with enough diamonds and gold to fill the best jewelry stores on Rodeo Drive. Ethel would not be outdone. Her brilliant diamond necklace and matching earrings sparkled even in the dim light, and were easily the most expensive pieces of jewelry at the event.

Ethel was one of three children born to Frank "The Bulldog" Simmens. Cooper's grandfather had made a fortune in real estate. He was a tall, beefy man with large thick fingers and strong hands and self-described as a "hard man." Cooper would never admit it to anyone now, but Frank terrorized him. Physically imposing, he liked to cause pain, usually by pinching or stomping or pulling.

Physical pain wasn't the worst type of pain Frank doled out. He used to say nasty things to Cooper when they were alone—"you're a rather dumb boy," or "you're a weak little thing," or "stop crying so much, you baby." Cooper wasn't the only one Frank aimed his derogatory comments at. Everyone else in the family got their share of poison—everyone except Ethel. He spared only her.

At first, Cooper thought he spared her because of her gender, but then he realized that Grandmother endured the worst treatment. Eventually, he decided either Ethel scared him or he respected her more than anyone else in the family. Either way, she was safe from the poison dripping from Frank's tongue.

One month after Cooper's tenth birthday, Frank fell victim to a serious stroke. He could no longer walk or talk, but his eyes, those deep blue eyes, burned. Luckily, Frank died not long after the stroke. Cooper remembered the funeral, less a memorial for The Bulldog than a crowning ceremony for Ethel. Everyone kissed her ring, including both her brothers, Uncle Jay and Frank Jr. She had been running the company during Frank's illness anyway, and no one was dumb enough to cross her.

Cooper bounced his leg under the table as he fidgeted with his napkin. His mother forced him to attend the event because she had been named *The Philanthropist of the Year.* He had no idea why she'd won the award. A holographic video explained everything, but he paid no attention to it. A lovely raven-haired woman sitting a few tables away had distracted him. Her short black dress revealed a shapely thigh as she played seductively with a strand of pearls that hung around her alabaster neck. Her full, wet, candy-apple lips teased him as she seductively licked a teaspoon while staring at him.

His heart jumped. When she had his attention, she strolled toward the restrooms, glancing back over her shoulder with a pouty expression on her face, inviting Cooper to join her. He fought hard against that impulse, but he didn't want to be here in the first place. He glanced at his mother, annoyed.

Who cares about philanthropy? Would it really hurt anyone if I left now for a little fun?

He could control himself if he went. He wouldn't spoil his tuxedo with blood.

His hands trembled, and just when he decided to join the young woman, an official announced Ethel as the recipient of the award. The entire table stood and clapped enthusiastically as she strode purposefully toward the stage to accept the honor and make her speech.

The black haired seductress's spell had been broken. The troops held the front line. He wouldn't budge while Ethel gave her speech. He silently congratulated himself on his extraordinary willpower.

After Ethel returned to the table, Cooper left. He thought about finding the young woman, but too many people strolled about for him to fully enjoy himself, so he fled to the back rooms. Both were similarly appointed with lush carpeting, dark wood paneled walls, long mahogany bars, and numerous sitting areas with leather chairs grouped around small, dark cocktail tables.

All the action took place in the back rooms, which guests needed an extra layer of clearance to enter. Big, muscled security guards checked identifications with portable card readers. The important people always gravitated to the back as the night progressed.

He leaned casually against a rich mahogany bar. Two dozen people, mostly men, milled about in the dark room. The band in the main ballroom began to play a Nat King Cole song.

He held a vodka martini in the fingertips of his left hand and wore a placid smile on his face, as if it were an accessory. Three acquaintances stood uncomfortably close and discussed a future real estate deal in hushed tones just loud enough for those around them to hear every detail.

Cooper smiled.

A short gray-haired woman not more than five feet away strained to eavesdrop on their conversation, her spine tilted backward in an uncomfortable angle, and her lips pinched tight in concentration. She obviously wanted to listen to what *he* had to say.

Does she really believe that I would discuss anything important with these people?

He regarded the man closest to him, Wade Angus, with a measure of distaste. Wade's wide shoulders were uncomfortably close to his arm, almost brushing against him. Almost, but thankfully still a few inches apart. A slight red rash sprouted where the man's bull neck bristled against the collar of his tuxedo shirt.

Wade's family had made their money in commodities. Cooper thought he was only slightly smarter than the wooden bar he leaned against, and that was generous. Wade's grandfather was clever, but as far as Cooper could tell, Wade and his father failed to inherit that gene.

Nothing can be done for those who did not inherit the raw material necessary to be exemplary. Unfortunately, so few people are extraordinary. So few count or mean anything. The rest are mere cattle to be used and discarded.

Cooper stood out, superior from birth, and his superiority had nothing to do with his upbringing. He owed his success to superior genes and his extraordinary willpower and discipline.

The three men discussed the financial merits of their transaction. They anticipated making three times their money with a thirty percent annualized return. Of course, he could invest with them if he wanted.

"We build the apartment buildings on gigantic pontoons supported by helium buoys. We'll call them boats. Then we won't have to pay real estate taxes. The views...."

Cooper's mind drifted away from Wade's blathering and toward Maggie. Now that he had her, he needed to see her, to do things to her. He wanted to leave, but his mother would be angry if he left so early, and he didn't want to make Ethel angry. No one wanted to make her angry.

He noticed a lull in the conversation around him as three expectant faces waited for him to cast judgment on their potential business deal. An image floated to his mind of Wade sinking into the river on one of his pontoon apartment buildings wearing nothing but a captain's hat. "Can you swim, Wade?"

Wade screwed his face into a question mark. "No."

Cooper chuckled. "The transaction sounds ill-conceived to me."

Wade's face turned pink and the color drained from the other men's faces.

The eavesdropping woman snorted in laughter.

Cooper clasped the beefy man on the shoulder, excused himself, and left them standing by themselves to share a heavy dose of disappointment.

He sauntered away from the riverboat real estate team and scanned the room, looking for a diversion. He found one in the person of Samuel Wickersham. Under most circumstances, Wickersham would not have gained clearance to a room like this one, but Cooper had made sure the *list* had included him. He caught Wickersham's eye and nodded toward the corner of the room, where he met the doctor.

"Samuel, it looks like you've lost some weight. You must share your diet and exercise regime with me." Cooper smiled.

Wickersham wasn't dieting or exercising. A surgeon's scalpel and a small vacuum had sucked away unwanted fat. Still, Cooper offered the praise in case anyone else listened in to their conversation.

Wickersham patted his stomach. "I'd send it to you, but you haven't gained a pound in twenty years."

Cooper nodded. He had never felt in better shape. He enjoyed exercise, most particularly rock climbing and cliff diving and his time with the Maggies, which always made his blood race.

They stood far away from the bar, well out of hearing range of others, but Cooper spoke softly anyway. "So how is Project Qing going?"

Wickersham inched closer, and his right sleeve brushed against Cooper's arm. He scowled, and Wickersham retreated to his previous position. "It's going remarkably well. We're close to implementation. I'll be ready for the presentation in a few days."

Cooper smiled blandly. He didn't want anyone to think this conversation interested him too much. "And EBF-202? How's that going?" He leaned closer.

"It's very exciting. We're on the brink of a major breakthrough."

"Excellent. I want a presentation on that also. Nothing long and boring, Samuel. Limit the eggheads."

Cooper straightened and beamed a full smile as Ethel swaggered toward him. She had inherited The Bulldog's gait—short, purposeful, and aggressive. "Mother, you look wonderful. Congratulations on the award again. Very well deserved."

She joined the two men and shot him a piercing look with her bright hazel eyes. She knew him better than anyone else.

He detected a note of disappointment in her gaze.

"Thank you, son. I've been looking for you. Is everything well?"

"Everything is superb, Mother. You remember Samuel Wickersham?" Cooper nudged him on the shoulder, pushing the doctor away from him. "Unfortunately, he was just leaving."

Ethel gave Wickersham a sideways, cursory glance.

Not sure what to do, Wickersham awkwardly bowed his head as if Ethel were recently coronated queen, and stumbled his way toward the bar. He knocked into a table and caused two champagne flutes to fall and shatter on the floor next to him.

"You should upgrade the people you spend time with." Ethel pinched her face together as if she had just eaten a bad piece of fruit.

"Samuel's a useful person. He serves a purpose. Where's father?"

Ethel frowned. "He's in the main ballroom. He found some Hollywood types. You know him—he can't help but talk about the next project. I'm sure he'll find you before the night is over."

"He loves his work." Cooper's father kept a small movie production company, which he had owned before he met Ethel.

Ethel huffed and wrapped her arm around Cooper's. "Did you listen to my speech?"

"Of course, Mother. Quite a wonderful speech. Very well received."

"You didn't hear a word of it. You should pay more attention to the downtrodden. We have a responsibility." Ethel smiled for the benefit of any onlookers, but her eyes told a different story.

Cooper cringed. She was angry with him, which was unusual. Disappointment was common—anger not so.

"Haven't you heard? The President appointed a new Ghetto Czar. He's supposed to fix everything."

Ethel locked her eyes tight on him, like a bulldog on a bone. "Charles Sheppard is a formidable man. You should keep an eye on him. Use him well, but be careful. He has important allies."

"I know all about him." Cooper chuckled. "We'll be fast friends in no time."

"Don't underestimate him! I hear some of the ghettos are becoming increasingly violent. They've started coordinating amongst themselves. This is a dangerous time."

Cooper detected a slight note of fear in his mother's voice, which surprised him. "Don't worry, Mother, I have something in the works that will solve all our problems. Leave it to me."

Ethel nodded toward the security station as Uncle Jay strolled into the room with a young-looking blonde attached to his arm. He wore a bright Simmens Racing Team pin stuck to the lapel of his tuxedo, next to his red and white checked bowtie. Uncle Jay used to race cars when younger and was reasonably good but never won any major races. He always spent too much time chasing blondes. Now he headed the company's racing division, which cost Ethel twenty million a year, but at least he left her alone to run the company.

"I guess Aunt Jane couldn't make it to the benefit," he said.

"What an embarrassment! Thank goodness Father isn't alive to see him make such a fool of himself." She shook her head and huffed. "That's his new driver. I hear she gets lost going around an oval track."

Ethel squeezed Cooper's arm tighter. "I've noticed that your lovely wife isn't here tonight, either. I hope everything is fine."

"She's just under the weather with the pregnancy. They say the first is the hardest. She sends her regrets. She would've loved to have shared in your success," Cooper lied.

Lori had no interest in coming to the award ceremony. A good deal younger than him, she came from a prominent Texas oil family, and could not have been more different from Maggie, which was a good thing. The more a woman looked and seemed to be like Maggie, the more Cooper ended up hating her, and those instances never ended well. They had been married for seven years, and Lori was two months pregnant. His publicist and Ethel had come up with the idea. They thought a new baby would soften his image.

Ethel disentangled her arm from his. "I had better talk to Jay before he makes a bigger fool of himself than he has already. Be careful, son. There are sharks out there circling. Don't let your *passions* overwhelm you."

She glided toward Uncle Jay, making her way through the crowd as effortlessly as any great white might swim through a coral reef.

Suddenly, the people in the room morphed into sharks. He shook his head to clear his vision, but the image remained. Everyone stared at him except Ethel.

Cooper broke out in a cold sweat, closed his eyes, and rubbed his face. When he opened them again, all the sharks had returned to their human form.

The benefit ran late, but he had to see Maggie before morning.

He ignored the physically fit young male attendant who sat next to the bed as she slept. He approached her with short steps, gently placing his hands on the fine Egyptian cotton sheets, which felt soft and cool to the touch.

Sedated, her chest moved up and down rhythmically, peacefully. Over time, she would overcome her fears and insecurities and voluntarily stay as his guest. He would spoil her with luxuries she could only dream about.

He gently whisked back a few strands of hair from her cheek and away from the new red bruise on her face, and his finger brushed against her swollen lower lip. The bruises would subside in a few days and be forgotten. Perhaps they would laugh at the incident, like old married couples do when recalling an argument that lost its steam many years ago.

He peeled back the sheet to her waist. She wore a soft white cotton robe. Her lily-white skin sparkled beneath the plush fabric. She had the same coloring as she had thirty years earlier. In fact, she looked exactly as he might have guessed she would when he was just a boy.

He resisted the urge to untie her robe. He knew from experience that if he delayed his enjoyment, it would be all the more pleasurable. He maintained his discipline.

CHAPTER 12

Tom paced the small kitchen, clutching his tablet in one hand and waving his other about as if he were perpetually shooing away a pesky housefly. Intense concentration darkened his demeanor. Two looping strides brought him from one side of the room to the other. His mind worked supercomputer fast, sorting everything he knew about his mom into categories and subcategories, applying probabilities to each possibility. With each round of calculations, his heart sank deeper as he realized he didn't know much about her life.

Who are her friends? What does she like to do outside of work? Who would want to harm her? Who, who, who?

He glanced at Jack, who sat on the kitchen floor with his back to one wall as he bounced a tennis ball against the floor and off the refrigerator, catching the ball in one hand.

Kathunk, kathunk, kathunk.

The morning sunlight filtered into the kitchen and the smell of stale coffee permeated the air.

"Do you think we should call the police?" Tom asked.

"No, Mom's only been missing for a few hours, and they won't care about us because we don't live in one of the good neighborhoods. They'll fill out a form, and it will be a waste of time." Jack shrugged. "We're going to have to figure this out on our own. How's the list coming?"

Kathunk, kathunk.

Tom glanced at the computer screen as he spoke. "I've typed a few categories: work, friends, book club, Fourteenth Colony. Each category has a list of possibilities and an action plan we can implement to check them out. If Rachel doesn't know anything, then I think we should start with the people Mom works with. Maybe a client of the law firm, or one of her coworkers with a grudge might have taken her."

Kathunk, kathunk.

He rifled a hand through his curly brown hair, doing his best to ignore the constant thumping, but the noise started to grate against his frazzled nerves.

Jack shook his head. "I don't know, Tom. This doesn't feel like a law firm type of thing. Something else is going on. It's got to be tied to mom's Solitary Day. I've never understood what she did on Solitary Day. And for a day off, why did Mom always look so terrible by that night? I've always thought that was weird."

An awkward silence filled the kitchen as Tom thought about Solitary Day. *It definitely wasn't a holiday.*

Kathunk.

Why didn't I ask her more questions about it?

Kathunk, kathunk, kathunk.

"You should call Mary. She's going to be pissed if she finds out about Mom from Rachel without hearing from you first."

Tom sighed. "I know, Jack, but she's gotten really close to Mom over the past few months. Her own mother died when she was young. I don't know what to tell her. We need a plan or some clues first." He hunched lower as he leaned against the kitchen counter.

Kathunk.

He couldn't talk to Mary like this. He needed something positive to tell her, some insight that proved he wasn't useless—some breakthrough or plan or really *anything* besides, "Guess what? My mom's been taken." If he just crunched the numbers hard enough, a pattern would have to develop. Then he could face Mary.

Kathunk.

He continued to sort the choices by probabilities and into lists, but he lacked enough data for any useful conclusions and cursed to himself. He was just wasting time, hoping that inspiration would strike.

Kathunk, kathunk.

He snatched the tennis ball and chucked it down the hallway.

"Hey!"

Three sharp raps on the front door froze Jack's protests in his throat.

Startled, Tom almost dropped the tablet.

"Expecting anyone, Tom?"

He shook his head.

Jack grabbed his sunglasses from the kitchen table. By the time they reached the front door, they saw a small round fist banging on the door again with three crisp knocks.

"Open up. It's Aunt Jackie! I'm too old to be standing here all day!"

Jack groaned and slowly opened the door.

Aunt Jackie wore a gloomy frown on her wrinkled face as she briskly marched into the apartment and brushed past him, her shiny white sneakers squeaking against the tile floor. She used to be just over five feet tall, but she had given back a few inches over the years.

"Hello, Thomas." She smiled thinly at Tom and nodded stiffly at Jack.

Jack stepped over and shut the door, looking even more miserable than he had a moment earlier.

Aunt Jackie carried an oversized canvas purse slung over her shoulder, which she always brought with her. "Take my coat, Jack." She placed her bag on the floor near the door and handed her brown quilted coat to him.

Jack begrudgingly took it, held it far away from his body as if it were contaminated with lice, and tossed it on a chair with the flick of his wrist.

She trudged toward Maggie's room. "You've heard no word from your mother?"

Before the brothers could respond, she threw open the door. The room felt even emptier than it had last night.

"I called her yesterday and she didn't answer."

"We came home late last night and she wasn't here," Tom said. "We've called her friends and no one knows where she is."

Aunt Jackie stood quietly for a few seconds as she scanned the room. Finding nothing useful, she sat stiffly on the edge of the bed, her feet barely touching the floor. She glared at Jack. "How come you didn't call me?" The question was more of an accusation than a query.

Aunt Jackie was really Maggie's aunt and Jack and Tom's great aunt. Together, they were the only living relations Maggie had left in the world.

All three clustered around her bed, worried about her safety.

"We didn't want to disturb you. We know how important rest is to someone your age." The end of Jack's lips twitched in a tentative smile.

"*Right*. I'm not pushing up any daisies yet, sonny boy." Her gaze focused on the closet. "Have you found the hiding spot yet?"

The boys shared a look. "We found it last night, but it was empty," Tom said.

"Of course *you* did." She grinned at him, but worry lines carved deep canyons into her already wrinkled face. She ran her hand through her short gray hair. She wore three golden hoop earrings in her left ear and one in her right. A half visible horse-shaped tattoo snuck above where the collar of her shirt brushed against her neck. She kept herself in good physical condition for a woman in her seventies, and still had clear, penetrating blue eyes. "I was worried that something like this might happen."

"Something like what? What's going on, Aunt Jackie?" Jack asked impatiently. "We need to know. We've got to find her!"

She wearily rose off the bed. Moving a little slower than she did when she first entered the apartment, she took short, uncertain steps, as if unsure where to go next. Dark circles smudged under her eyes.

"I need some coffee. Bring me my bag, Jack." She squeezed Tom's shoulder as she shuffled past him to the kitchen.

Jack muttered under his breath as he went to fetch her bag.

She could see the worry on the boys' faces. They were smart kids, especially Tom. They knew their mom was in trouble.

A small trace of steam twirled above the half empty pot of coffee on the kitchen counter. "Thomas, be a dear and pour me a cup, will you? You know how I like it, black as the devil."

She settled into a chair with the back door behind her and watched him pour the coffee. *Only seventeen and he's already a man. Everyone grows up so fast these days.* "When are you going to cut your hair, Thomas? It's down to your shoulders."

He handed her a mug of coffee, black with no sugar, and smiled. "You didn't come here to offer me grooming tips."

Jack trudged back into the room with her bag in his hand.

"Just drop the bag over here." He complied, and she took a long sip from her mug. The coffee was awful, too weak for her taste. Her face contorted sourly when she drank it, but she kept silent.

They sat at the table and stared at her, hoping she had all the answers. Jack leaned forward on his elbows.

The boy is always so impatient.

"Why are you wearing those sunglasses? Is it some new thing? Take them off. They look stupid."

"The light has been bothering my eyes lately. Now tell us what you know about Mom!"

She took another long sip from the cup. *What am I going to tell them?*

She felt foolish. After all her years and experience, how could she not know what to do? But she was conflicted on so many levels. She spotted a ball on the kitchen table. "Are you still teaching racquetball, Jack?" She tried to buy a little time while she decided on the right path.

"It's not racquetball, Aunt Jackie! It's tennis, and don't change the subject!"

He is always so easily baited.

"They play with a racquet. How am I supposed to know the difference?" Her comment met with icy stares from her nephews. She sighed. "What do you boys know?" She danced her eyes between the two young men.

"We know that Mom went missing last night," Tom said. "We found some blood on the floor and the doors were unlocked, so we think she must have been kidnapped from the apartment. No one seems to know what happened. She had a hiding spot in her closet that we never knew about, and whatever she had hidden was stolen last night with her."

"All this happened on Solitary Day," Jack added, "so we know it has to do with that. You know something, or you wouldn't have dragged your wrinkled self out here at this time of the morning."

They don't know much. I still have a choice to make.

She spoke softly, almost as if her nephews were not in the room. "I love your mother very much. She and you two boys are the only family I've got. I knew she was special when she was a baby. I bought her first sketchpad and drawing pencils. She was always drawing something, and had enough talent to pursue it, but your grandparents weren't in a position to give her that chance. I wish I could've, but there were many lean years. The circus didn't pay well, even when I was the star."

For a brief period, she had been a star, famous for wearing seductive outfits while performing eye-popping gymnastics on horseback. She proudly displayed her portfolio of pictures during every holiday. At age five, Jack snuck away with the scrapbook and decorated the pictures with his mom's drawing pencils. Their relationship hadn't been the same since.

"Maggie always lit up the room with her smile. She still does. She's been a daughter to me. You know that I never had any children. I've taken a different road than the conventional route, but Maggie's always been in my life, and I'm better for it."

She paused and exchanged looks with both of her great nephews. "I've made certain promises to her, boys. If you already knew, then maybe I could help, but she made me promise not to involve you. She's worried about your safety, and I can't blame her. I can't break those promises now. They have me wrapped up tight." She removed her hands from her cup and placed them flat on the table.

"We're going after her. We need to find her. You can't stop us." Tom's voice shook while his right hand balled into a fist. "We'll be in more danger if we don't understand what's going on."

Jack grabbed Jackie's right hand with both of his, and a shock zapped through her. She tried to pull back, but he held tight, so she brought down her left hand in a forceful chop. He released his grip. She felt short of breath. Sharper and more intense than an ordinary shock, she had never experienced anything like that before.

Jack groaned and brought his hands to his head, as if worried that it might shatter and he needed to hold it all together.

"Jack, are you all right?" Tom asked.

Jack took off his sunglasses and rubbed his face. "I'm fine. I have a headache, and Aunt Jackie isn't making it any better."

She massaged her hand and regarded Jack suspiciously. "I should be going."

"You're not going anywhere," Jack growled. "Not until you show us what's in the bag."

CHAPTER 13

"Don't take that tone with me, young man! You're not so big that I can't take a belt to you!"

Tom observed as Aunt Jackie stared at Jack, a razor edge in her eyes as she clutched her bag close to her chest. He sneered back at her, eyes equally dangerous.

Maggie always played peacekeeper between them, but in her absence, Tom jumped in between the two. "Come on, Aunt Jackie. You've never touched us in your life, and we're too old for you to start now. We need to find Mom, and we're not going to stop until we figure out what's going on."

Her face softened. "You shouldn't have looked in my bag, Jack. You've been raised better than that."

"I didn't look in that giant sack you carry around."

"How'd you know what I brought with me, then?"

"I just guessed. We're wasting time. Tell us what we need to know!" His voice rumbled in a tone Tom had never heard him use before.

Her eyes shifted from Jack to Tom and back again to Jack. Her shoulders drooped as she leaned back in her chair. "Okay, I guess you boys are old enough to make your own decisions. I'm going to need some real coffee. This stuff tastes like rusty water."

She removed a small tin of coffee grounds from her bag and made her way to the coffee pot. As the coffee brewed, she began. "Solitary Day for your mom wasn't a holiday, or some day for her to be alone and meditate or any of that New Age crap. It meant much more to her."

She brought a full cup of coffee back to the table. "It all started when she was young. Your grandparents worked in various resorts when she was little. Your grandmother worked as a maid, and your grandfather liked to work with horses, but more often than not, he worked as a handyman. They traveled around a lot back then. At one of their stops one summer, your mom met a boy named Cooper. She was young—I don't know exactly how young—but not quite a teenager when she met him. Initially, they became friends.

"This boy was a guest at one of these resorts. He began following Maggie around, and by the end of the first summer, he started scaring your mother. She wanted nothing to do with him and told him so, but he wasn't the type to settle for that. The next summer, he came back and things just got worse. Maggie tried to avoid him, but he kept popping up."

"Didn't Mom tell Grandpa?" Tom asked. "He wouldn't stand for that."

"No, she never did. Maggie worried that he would act rashly and lose his job. He had a hot temper. Much like you, Jack."

Jack rolled his eyes.

"Anyway, this boy Cooper wanted Maggie to come home with him and leave her parents behind forever. She refused, of course, and things got even worse. The boy was disturbed. He'd hurt animals like cats or dogs and even horses. He was quite creepy and scary.

"After your mom refused to go with him, something bad happened at that resort. She wouldn't tell me what, but I could tell by the way she told the story that she realized how dangerous he was. Your mom never spoke to him again after that summer, but she thought she saw him out of the corner of her eye every once in a while. He haunted her, becoming her personal bogeyman.

"When she became an adult, she started receiving letters. Every August 25th Cooper would send one—nasty, horrible, letters. As time went on, the letters became more involved, and came with pictures in them—horrifying pictures of girls that were tortured before they died."

"Why would someone send letters like that?" Jack asked.

She shrugged. "It's hard to say. Who knows why he sent them? In his twisted mind, maybe he thought they connected him with your mom. Perhaps they were his sick way of showing his devotion to her. Perhaps he just wanted to hurt Maggie because she rejected him." She sipped her coffee.

"Didn't she ever tell the police or anyone else?" Tom asked.

She shook her head. "Maggie was afraid. Cooper was a powerful person from a powerful family. She was sure that the police would protect him. Besides, she had no proof that he had sent her those letters, and they always contained nasty threats. At first there were threats against her parents, and then your father, and then you boys. He included pictures of you. He always knew where she lived and what she was doing. The letters arrived on the 25th of August like clockwork. She spent that day mourning the girls in those pictures and hoping it would all end."

Aunt Jackie placed her coffee cup back on the kitchen table. "It tore her up. She felt so useless, afraid. Guilty, even. I'm the only person she ever told about Cooper. She worried about you two boys, and said if something were to happen to her, she wanted me to protect you from this monster."

Jack's knuckles turned white as he gripped the tennis ball. "So who is this Cooper?"

"I'm not sure your mom knew. She never told me. She worried I would go after him."

"But you do have the letters in your bag, right?" Rough and angry, Jack's voice sounded as if it had been rubbed raw over a cheese grater.

"I have some of the letters and photographs. There were others that Maggie wouldn't give me. They must've been truly terrible because these are pretty bad."

She hoisted her bag on her lap, pulled out a thin yellow folder and steadily placed it on the table. Shifting her eyes between her nephews, she left her hand on top of the folder. "She didn't want you two involved in this, and spent the past nineteen years protecting you. I'm sure she wouldn't want you going after her."

The brothers looked at each other.

"We'll do whatever it takes to get Mom back," Tom said.

"Whatever it takes," Jack repeated.

CHAPTER 14

Charles Sheppard sat comfortably in the supple leather backseat of the sedan. It hummed as hidden mechanical fingers dug into his back and gave him a shiatsu-style massage, burrowing into tense muscle. His nerves bothered him, and that rarely happened.

He had taken the special plain-looking car for this meeting instead of the typical limo. From the outside, the nondescript car appeared old and battered. The cracked back right brake light didn't work and duct tape secured the trunk. Only upon close inspection would someone notice the bulletproof glass, the steel reinforced carriage, and the purr from an engine much too powerful for anything caged in such a rundown exterior.

The car had just entered the Westchester Ghetto. He scanned the streets and frowned. "How did we let things become so bad?" Every time he entered one of the awful ghettos, the same feeling of loss buffeted him.

He thought about all the lives ruined and futures destroyed, as they made their way through a once vibrant downtown street. Metal bars protected window frames, and plastic bulletproof sheets were installed where glass should have been. The more common vacant stores had broken windows, the shards of glass scattered across the sidewalk and sparkling in the morning sunlight.

He detected movement within some of the dark spaces, and a chill blew through his body.

Once a week, the state sent in powerful street vacuum cleaners to suck away the mess and prevent pestilence. Rat poison distribution trucks followed the street cleaners, spreading toxic pellets across the concrete like fertilizer on plowed fields. Whenever the pestilence problem worsened, the pesticides grew stronger.

The effects on the human population were not well understood. He'd commissioned a study to determine safe levels for the toxins, but most within the government didn't care. The stupid, small-minded men only cared about keeping the vermin away from other areas—*their* areas.

Charles shook his head as the car's efficient air purification system blew a cool, scented breeze against his face—lilacs.

The sun had just risen, and only a few cars navigated the pitted streets. A couple slept under the protection of an awning beside a garbage bag filled with their possessions. A few prostitutes leaned against buildings, hoping for one last trick for the night. Glazed expressions shone dully behind exhausted eyes.

He took a long sip from his vitamin-infused water bottle. A specially designed cylinder tucked into the back door kept it cool.

Steven drove the car, his blue eyes razor-sharp and bright. He expertly weaved around potholes and larger debris in the street as he navigated their way to the meeting place. "We can still turn back, Mr. Sheppard. I don't like this meeting." He spoke plainly, almost mechanical in tone, his military training showing through.

He'd started working for Charles four months earlier and, though average in height and thinly built, was lethal as a cobra. Charles knew other security men with bulging muscles and wide chests, but they all paled in comparison to Steven. Training, decisiveness, and ruthlessness were the necessary ingredients in a good bodyguard, and Steven had all three in abundance. Charles trusted him completely, and had immediately installed him as the head of his private security.

"I realize there's some risk involved, but I need to meet with them in person and in secret. We could both gain from a mutual friendship. They'd be stupid to try something and, from everything I've been told, they're not stupid." Charles had never met the ghetto leaders before. He was sure they weren't stupid, but he wondered whether they would buy what he needed to sell them.

"Yes, Mr. Sheppard. We'll be at the meeting place in a minute." Steven swung the car to the left and drove down a narrow side street.

Once-magnificent Victorian houses dotted both sides of the road. Windows were boarded up and the paint had peeled off wooden shingles. Many of the structures looked unsound, and weed-infested gravel had replaced glass yards.

"I think this car suits you, Steven. It's beaten up on the outside, but has a lot left in the engine."

"It suits me just fine, Mr. Sheppard, but I'd rather take you fishing." As an avid fisherman, Steven made his own equipment.

"Maybe in a month or so when things slow down. I've always wanted to try my hand at fishing." Charles sounded far away. They both knew things wouldn't slow down in a month or two or three.

Steven slowed the car as two men blocked their path. He lowered the glass and showed one of the guards Sheppard's citizen identification card.

The man took a long look at the card and then an even longer look at Sheppard. Eventually, he handed the card back and nodded toward a spot by the curb. "We saved the best parking space for you."

Steven swung the car in front of a pink Victorian house, and turned toward Sheppard. "Remember to stay with me at all times, Mr. Sheppard. I can't protect you if I'm not near you."

Charles smiled and nodded. Steven meant well. He wanted to protect him, would even die trying if he had to, but Charles would do what he wanted, trusting in his instinct and luck. It had gotten him this far.

He gracefully stepped out of the sedan, dressed casually with a light brown sport coat, a plain Egyptian cotton dress shirt, and tan slacks. His antique gold Rolex wristwatch gleamed in the morning sun. He always wore the antique, given to him by his father, to important meetings. It was his lucky watch.

Two hulking armed guards led them through the front door of the old house.

Charles's eyes widened. The inside had been restored to its original condition, with sparkling, polished cherry wood, newly painted textured ceilings, and even a slight air-conditioned breeze.

The larger of the two guards grinned at his reaction. "You'll be meeting Mr. Moses and Mr. Gabriel in the library." He waved them inside a room to the right.

Black bookcases covered all four walls of the large rectangular library. Stamped tin squares decorated the tall ceiling, and a clean oval desk sat on one end of the room with a leather chair behind it. A sitting area had been set up at the opposite end of the room with four wingback leather chairs arranged around a square cocktail table. Centered on the wooden table sat a glass bowl with a pomegranate in it.

The guard shut the door, leaving them alone.

Charles smiled. "I guess we aren't the only ones who use deception."

He eyed the fruit suspiciously. He had been briefly known as the "Miracle of the Pennsylvania Pomegranate" when he survived a train wreck aboard the Pennsylvania Pomegranate as an infant. Both his biological parents died in the crash, and the rich Sheppards had surreptitiously adopted him. He thought that secret well buried, but apparently it rose from the dead like a zombie fruit.

Ignoring the pomegranate and what it meant, he wandered over to the bookcases on the far end of the room. "This is a substantial collection. You don't see many hardcover books anymore." He pulled out *To Kill a Mockingbird*. "Have you read this one, Steven?"

"No, Mr. Sheppard. I can't say that I have. I read mostly historical novels."

"It's a classic. I have a copy just like this one back at my apartment. I'll give it to you." He replaced the book in the bookcase as Moses and Gabriel entered the room.

The two men couldn't have looked more different.

Moses, short and wiry with a pasty white complexion, wore his shockingly bright yellow hair shaggy and long, falling in front of his light blue eyes.

Gabriel, on the other hand, was dark skinned, had short, curly red hair that matched his tight beard, and stood five inches taller than Moses. He also appeared twice as broad, with wide shoulders and rippling muscles.

They both looked young, neither man appearing older than late twenties, and both dressed casually with loose-fitting, long-sleeved shirts, blue jeans, and sneakers.

Charles smiled at them.

The shorter man stepped forward with his hand out, his voice soft but strong. "It's nice to meet you, Mr. Secretary. I'm Moses."

Charles shook it firmly and Moses clasped his second hand on top in a European style greeting. He held onto Charles's hands for an uncomfortably long moment while he stared deeply into his eyes.

The smile stayed fixed on Charles's face as the seconds melted away. He would not look away. Trust was important.

Moses released him.

"Please, call me Charles."

"This is Mr. Gabriel." Moses nodded at Gabriel, who stood a step behind him with his arms crossed over his chest.

Charles stepped forward and proffered his hand, but Gabriel stayed behind, stubbornly refusing to move. Charles nodded at the big man and returned his hand to his side. *He's going to be tough,* Charles thought, but he had confidence in his skills, if not in what he offered.

"I was admiring your library. You have some great works in here."

"Reading opens up windows for the soul to explore, and imagination for the mind to ponder. Without it, we are stuck only with the current, depressing circumstances." Moses waved at the bookcases. "We have a collection of history books and fiction. I prefer fiction, while Gabriel reads history."

"Most people have e-readers these days, but I don't think you can fully appreciate a book without feeling the pages in your hands," Charles commented. "There is something about the feel of paper and the written word that e-readers and audio files cannot provide."

"It's a luxury we're happy to enjoy, Mr. Secretary. All of these books were castoffs from abandoned homes."

Gabriel whispered into Moses's ear.

Moses nodded toward Steven. "I thought this was a private meeting. Your friend can wait in the hallway with Jayden."

Steven's face remained an unreadable rock, but Charles knew he wanted to stay with him. "Yes, of course it's a private discussion. Steven, if you would be so kind as to wait outside. I am sure that I'm perfectly safe with Moses and Gabriel."

Gabriel shut the door when Steven left, leaving Charles unprotected. He wasn't sure they wouldn't harm him, but his instinct said to trust the two men, and in the end, he always sided with his instinct.

CHAPTER 15

Moses gestured at the vacant chairs in the sitting area. "Please, take a seat."

Charles and Moses sat while Gabriel stood behind Moses, his arms still crossed, his face tight, and his eyes hard.

"Thank you for meeting with me," Charles began. "I've heard complimentary things about both of you from our mutual friend. I think we share many of the same goals."

Moses nodded. "We respect the work of the Fourteenth Colony and Rachel in particular. She has spoken highly of your motives, but it would be a mistake to confuse us. We are different from Rachel and her organization. Our people are suffering greatly. Time is running out."

"I understand your situation. I didn't come alone. There are others who agree with me—important people. We must restore balance in this country—to what it can be—with opportunities for everyone willing to work for them. We're making progress, but both our efforts can be facilitated if we learn to trust each other and work together."

As a master salesman, Charles had built a wide-ranging empire. The Sheppard Group invested in cutting edge computer technology, biotechnology, military hardware, and a small but popular swimsuit collection.

Gabriel whispered into Moses's ear.

Moses smiled. "We appreciate the efforts you've made with the brain cancer vaccine. When will the vaccine be made available to us?"

Not everyone in the government wanted to make the cure widely available. Some wanted to use it to reduce the population, dispensing it only to those considered worthy. Charles, as his first act as Secretary of Domestic Priorities, had persuaded the administration to release the vaccine to everyone. The vaccine's release, which would save millions of lives, had been a pre-condition for him to take the job. Not many people knew about that argument, and he was certainly not going to mention it here.

"The vaccine will be widely distributed within the month. We'll disseminate it throughout Westchester, but that's only a start. There are other things we can do immediately. The food distribution effort will be increased. There's too much waste and greed and not enough food for dissemination. I've received clearance to change that right away."

Gabriel spoke, his baritone voice hot and angry. "You think you can buy us with trinkets! You've been starving these people for a decade!"

"You're right." Charles clasped his hands together. "These things are nothing but a sign of my good faith. There's much more work to be done—important things like jobs, education, healthcare, political power—but we start with the basics and go from there. We can make the changes nonviolently if we work together—*if* we work together."

Moses leaned forward, and flecks of gray burned brightly against the blue swirls in his eyes. "I don't doubt your sincerity, but there are those in the administration that view us as animals. We're no longer human beings to them, merely beasts of burden they throw away after using us up."

Charles knew they were right, but he needed to convince them of the possibility of change, something he believed in himself. "My influence with the president is increasing. We are making progress, and the people I represent are influential. They want change. If we coordinate our efforts, then we'll see real progress that will improve millions of lives without bloodshed. If you act independently and widespread violence erupts, then we can't help. My powerful friends will run for cover. Thousands of lives will be wasted, and the results will be much harder to predict."

Gabriel leaned closer to Moses and they exchanged a short private conversation he couldn't hear.

Gabriel straightened and said, "We're no longer concerned about the president, but his heir—Peter Perfect, as your media has dubbed him—seriously worries us."

"He's done some good," Charles said. "He's initiated the Star program, which will benefit exceptional children and give them a start at newly created magnate schools."

"The Star program is just another way to steal the best and brightest from the ghettos," Moses spat angrily. "Do you know what we call him?"

Charles shook his head.

"We call him the *Razor*. If you didn't know any better, a straight blade is aesthetically pleasing. It looks harmless until you find out its true nature—until it cuts you. We understand that he ordered the military sweep in the Detroit and Midwest Ghettos. If he comes into power, things will accelerate. We have good reason to distrust him."

The Originalist political party ruled the country with an iron fist, having swept into power under a platform of lower taxes, reduced government, and increased personal liberty. Once elected, the party abused their power to support the wealthy class that had financed them, and subsequently changed enough voting rules that no one could realistically oppose them. The vice president was the only candidate seeking the nomination, and once the Originalists selected him, he would run for President without opposition.

"The election is months away. I'm just now becoming acquainted with him. We have time before then to work together, so I propose that we build our relationship and see where it takes us. We share the same goals, and with us rowing the boat in the same direction we can achieve them." Charles smiled with fake confidence. "To see the future, we need to remember the past. Our country was once great for everyone. I know we will restore that greatness again."

"Winston Churchill was a favorite of mine also." Gabriel squeezed Moses's shoulder.

Moses stood. "We need to discuss your proposal. We cannot speak for all ghettos, as our influence is limited, but we have friends across the country. We'll be in touch through our mutual friend."

Charles reached out his hand.

Moses clasped it in both of his for a long moment, as he had when they first met. "Thank you for meeting us, Mr. Secretary."

Gabriel turned toward Moses. "So, can we trust him?"

"Yes. He's sincere in what he says. Who is Winston Churchill?"

"You need to read more history. He was England's prime minister during World War II, but Sheppard changed the quote. He actually said, 'The farther backward you can look, the farther forward you are likely to see.'"

Moses shrugged.

Gabriel paced around the library, sweeping his hands across the book spines. "He's an intriguing person. He could help us, with his powerful friends, but this could backfire on us big time."

"Have I ever steered you wrong before?"

"No, Moses. I'm sure your impression is correct that he's sincere, but we can't be beholden to men like Charles Sheppard. Our power comes from our people and their trust in us. We need to be careful. If word leaks out that we're cooperating with powerful rich men...." Gabriel didn't need to finish the statement.

Moses tossed the pomegranate in the air. "You're the smart one. You've always made the decisions, but I have a strong feeling about the Miracle of the Pennsylvania Pomegranate. He's going to prove useful. You should listen to me. I know it."

"I've learned my lesson the hard way, Moses. I still hate myself for what happened to Izzy. I should have listened to you then. I should never have let her leave that day. I was a fool and you lost your sister." Gabriel leaned heavily on the edge of the desk. Some wounds never healed.

Moses touched him on the shoulder. "I don't blame you, and I'm sure Izzy didn't either."

"I still wake up every morning expecting to see her next to me. I hope we are doing the right thing. Izzy would know what to do. She had the vision."

"I'm sure she'd be impressed with what you've accomplished. She wanted only for us to fight for fairness. 'Every day is a new chance to make the hard choice and do what's right.' She told us that all the time."

"I know, but she knew what was right. What should we do about Sheppard? I will never ignore your premonitions again, but what can he do about Vice President Peter Perfect? I don't see how he can achieve enough before the election. Once Mr. Perfect is sworn in as the next president, we'll have to act. Our counterparts across the country are already making plans. Guns are flooding into the country and violence is increasing."

Moses shrugged. "We still have some time."

"Do you know why I love history books?"

"You hate surprises?" Moses grinned.

"Yes and no. History books contain every worthwhile idea and stupid scheme of humankind. Every great society falls for the same reasons: greed, corruption, power concentrated in too few, economic disparity. Humankind is too stupid to realize it, and we repeat the same mistakes over again. I hope it's not too late for us."

CHAPTER 16

Tom stared at the neatly arranged piles of paper—three straight rows, five deep, letters on top, photographs hidden underneath—and clenched his body.

How did Mom keep this secret for so long? I should have known about this. She must have left clues.

"These are only some of the letters?" he asked through gritted teeth.

Aunt Jackie nodded. "Maggie received one letter every year starting twenty years ago. I only have fifteen letters plus the original note and drawing. She wouldn't show me the others." She leaned back in her chair. "She dated each letter. The last one I have was sent five years ago. The pictures become progressively worse and more numerous each year. There are also many of you two, always with a circle drawn over the face like a target at a shooting range."

"We need to start with this first one." Tom lifted the note off the table. "It's not really a letter, just a note to Mom and a drawing of a face. The drawing is too simple to reveal much, but at least we know he has blue eyes. I think it's fair to assume that Mom sketched the face."

"Cooper never mailed the first note. Maggie met this monster at one of the places where her parents worked and he left that note for her. The letters and the photos started coming years later. She never dated that first one."

Aunt Jackie's face was drawn and her body heavy. She looked away from her nephews. "I've spent too much time studying the letters and pictures over the years to study them now. I've done the best I could, but I've never found any useful clues. I've even given each one a name and a personality. They haunt my dreams, as they did Maggie's. I just wish she would've given me more information to work with. I guess she was too scared and had lived too long as a victim."

Jack lifted a picture from behind one of the more recent letters. "Who could do something like this?" His face twisted sourly.

The young woman in the photograph lay naked in a field of grass, her arms positioned above her head as if signaling a touchdown. Her open eyes and mouth emitted an eternal silent scream. Her legs were spread wide and bent outward awkwardly at the knees, her entire torso covered with bruises, and her chest sliced open to reveal a grizzly peek inside. A bluish-purple bruise around her neck was shaped like a man's hands. Bright red lipstick colored her lips, and a pink ribbon held her hair in pigtails. All the girls in the pictures were positioned the same way. All had red lipstick and wore pink ribbons.

Tom moved next to his brother. "This woman suffered." He pointed to the photograph in Jack's hand. "The wounds on her arms look like they had started healing."

Jack slipped the picture back into its original place and turned away from the letters and the photographs of death. "There are twenty-three photos. The women look as if they could be sisters. They all have the same hair, skin color, size, and body type."

"They're all young versions of Mom," Tom said.

Aunt Jackie sighed. "Yes, Tom, every year this monster chose a substitute for Maggie. Each letter talks about his feelings for your mom and how these girls weren't as good as her. How she should realize that she was meant to be his and run away with him. It's horrifying."

Aunt Jackie's eyes blazed sharp and angry and dangerous. Tom had never seen her like that before. Well, maybe that one time when Jack drew on the pictures in her scrapbook.

Tom read all the letters thoroughly and forced himself to study the photos and take in as much detail as possible. At least he could analyze them—each letter written with the same precise handwriting, signed with the same flourish, and penned on the same expensive stock paper with a faint watermark. All the letters except the first one, which was written on different paper.

He kept going back to the first note, lifting it close to his face and examining every inch of it, looking for something new, wondering what he was missing.

"Mom never told anyone else about Cooper? Not even Dad?" Jack asked.

Aunt Jackie slouched, her voice tired. "No. She was too afraid Cooper would take you away from her. Each letter makes it clear that he had her under surveillance, and the pictures proved it. Do you remember your father's temper?"

Jack nodded.

"She was certain he would do something rash and this devil would take you all away from her. After Paul died, she worried even more. The thought of losing one of you was too much for her to risk." She took another sip of coffee—her third cup, each stronger than the last.

Tom shook his head. "She must know who this pervert is. Surely she gave you some hints, right?"

She shrugged. "I tried hundreds of time, but she wouldn't tell me. I could tell he was someone important and powerful, but she gave me nothing."

"I don't see how we're going to find him from these." Jack waved at the letters. "They're old, so there won't be any fingerprints, and there are no clues. Nothing indicates who wrote them or where he lived when he did." He glanced at his brother for hope. Desperation filled his eyes.

Tom noticed a tiny smudge on the first note that he had missed before, and lifted it toward the light. "Not so fast! There's some type of design on the bottom of the first note."

He dropped the note on the table, grabbed two clear glasses from the kitchen cabinet, filled one with water, and returned with a cagey smile on his face.

"What are you doing?" Jack looked at him as if he had two heads and one spun in circles.

"You'll see." He dripped three drops of water into the bottom of the empty glass and brought it over the smudge. "The water, glass, and light act as a magnifying glass. Check this out, Jack. At the bottom of the page is a logo of some kind. It looks like a building with letters inside."

Aunt Jackie took a turn peering through the homemade magnifying glass, squinting at the image. "Where exactly is the logo?"

Tom shifted the note so she could see it.

"Oh, I've got it now. Son of a bitch, there is something there. I can't believe I've missed it for all these years. I thought it was just a smudge." She put down the glass and started gathering up the notes and photographs from the floor.

Jack and Tom glared at her.

"What're you doing?" Jack asked.

She slipped the papers back into the original folder. "We're going to need help to figure this out. Let's go find Rachel."

Tom's mouth dropped open.

Jack arched his eyebrows. "You know about the Fourteenth Colony?"

"Of course I do. Just because I'm old doesn't mean that I don't know what's going on. We go way back. I introduced her to your mother."

Tom stretched out his hand. "Just give us the file and we'll handle this. We'll go see her."

She snapped back the file and jammed it into her bag. "You'll never take it from me. I'm driving." She hoisted the bag over her shoulder and marched toward the front door, leaving her two nephews in her wake.

The brothers shared a look, and Jack moaned. "I can't believe this."

"Come on, we don't have all day! Jack can sit in the back!"

Tom grinned. He had found a clue, and one clue meant there would be more.

CHAPTER 17

Terry sat in the chair next to the bed and fidgeted, letting a half-sigh, half-scowl slip out under his breath. He watched Maggie sleep under the effects of a heavy sedative and shook his head. He would never have selected this Maggie. She was too old.

He was in charge of selecting Maggies for Cooper. The Peterson twins handled the surveillance work and the actual snatching, but he made the selection. He liked that role—deciding life and death. He didn't believe in God or any common notion of a deity, but each time he selected the next Maggie, he felt all-powerful—as he assumed God would feel, if He existed.

He hadn't selected this Maggie. He'd been robbed of a prized privilege, and now he was stuck with her.

She was the original Maggie, and that made her special to Cooper. Still, she was all wrong—too old, too thin, her hair too short, her skin color two shades too white. He was something of an expert on Maggies, and this one would never have passed his high standards.

He sighed. A small, caramel-colored mole marred Maggie's neck. Most people might have described it as adding texture and beauty to her throat. He hated it. None of his Maggies would have borne such a blemish.

He reached over, pressed his hands against her throat, and squeezed; not particularly hard at first, but he increased the pressure without thinking about it. When her face turned red and her body squirmed, he released her, relieved he hadn't left a mark behind. He would have had a heck of a time explaining that to Cooper. That wasn't his role.

Cooper killed every Maggie by strangulation. Yes, he would cut them before he strangled them. He liked causing pain. Sometimes he let Terry do some of the destruction, but in the end, Cooper always strangled them. He inched his face close to theirs and choked the life out of them, often while weeping with joy.

Terry wanted his turn. He wanted to weep with joy.

What if I've been looking at this problem the wrong way? What if there's no inhibitor for the drug in Lassie's system, but something else is causing her brain to stay in equilibrium?

Darian doodled in his journal, "Look to the brain."

When George strolled into the lab, he pushed the journal to the side. "Have you loaded the latest data into the computer so we can run the simulation?"

"Everything's inputted. We should have the answer in a few hours."

Darian glanced at the note he had written. Yes, he needed to change tracks. He needed to look to the brain. The answer had to be locked in the brain.

He grabbed an old textbook and flipped open to the pages on brain diseases.

The answer is in here, but does Jack have enough time left for me to find it?

CHAPTER 18

Tom and Jack followed Aunt Jackie into the bright, sweltering August sunlight.

Jack groaned and pointed to the old, beaten down silver Ford parked across the street. "I guess we're taking the Silver Bullet." He'd given the car that nickname as a joke seven years ago. It wasn't fast then.

Aunt Jackie took short, energetic strides. Her bag hung low off her shoulder and threatened to scrape across the pavement.

Tom hated to cram into Aunt Jackie's car, but they didn't have one of their own, so they took her car whenever they needed to travel together. Despite its four doors, he always felt squeezed whenever he had to climb into the back seat. His head hit the roof and his knees bumped against the front seat.

This time he sat in the front while Jack stretched out in the back by himself.

He usually got along well with Jack, but being brothers, fighting was coded in their DNA. Lock them in a cramped space and they'd start to argue—as predictable as water running down hill. Usually, they began to push each other. Jack would squeeze his leg in a "horse bite," and Tom would retaliate with a foot stomp. Maggie would yell at them from the front seat within a few minutes.

Jack pointed to a few dents in the front right bumper. "Having problems with trees jumping out at you again, Aunt Jackie?"

"That's my blind spot."

"Your blind spot is the front right bumper?" Jack asked, incredulous. "Maybe I should drive."

"You'd have to pry the keys from my dead hand. I still don't understand why Maggie got you that bicycle."

"Doesn't the car have a sensor that automatically stops it before it hits something?" Tom asked. Every car had a sensor for safety. The Silver Bullet was old, but not *that* old.

"Yes, it used to, but the damn thing kept going off, so I disabled it. Every ten feet the car jerked to a stop. I can't drive like that. I started driving long before those stupid sensors were invented."

"That sensor communicates with the other vehicles on the road, Aunt Jackie," Tom explained. "Without that sensor, they won't automatically stop before they crash into you. Their auto-drive feature won't work."

"Sucks for them." She pressed the door latch on her remote key, and the locks on all four doors responded.

Tom hesitated when he opened the door. The interior was in worse shape than the exterior, with duct tape covering rips in the seats in a dozen places. Still, Aunt Jackie couldn't fit on Jack's bike, even if the idea brought a smile to Tom's face.

Aunt Jackie settled behind the wheel on an orange cushion that squawked under her weight.

Jack snickered from the backseat as Tom calculated the angles and realized the cushion wasn't for her comfort. It raised her body just high enough for her to see over the dashboard. She couldn't see the right front edge of the car because she still sat too low. She needed another four inches, but her toes barely reached the pedals at this height, which explained the blind spot and the dents. He shook his head and reached for the seatbelt.

Aunt Jackie pressed the start button and nothing happened. Jack moaned from the back as she tried again. Still nothing. "I drove over here okay. I don't know what's wrong with the thing. It has enough gas. Sometimes it's a little finicky."

She tapped the start button in rapid fire as if it were a video game controller and she gunned down aliens. Each time, she jammed the button harder. She stopped after a half dozen times and pounded the steering wheel with her small fists.

Tom held up his left hand. "The car has an electrical problem. Let me take a look at the circuit board." He pushed back the front seat as far as it would go, shifted under the dash, and looked for the circuit board. "Do you have a mirror or something I could use to catch a better look under here?"

She rummaged through her bag and handed him a small, round mirror.

After a short search, he found the circuit board, unscrewed it with his fingers, and popped the plastic board off. He squinted at the reflection. The panel contained a series of computer chips lined up in two rows. Tom noticed the problem immediately.

"One of the chips is blown." He pulled a blackened chip off the board and lifted the charred bit of metal so Aunt Jackie and Jack both saw it. "It must control the ignition. You wouldn't have any replacement chips around here anywhere, would you, Aunt Jackie?"

She shook her head.

Of course not.

"How about a small screwdriver?" he asked without much hope for success.

"Sure, I use one of those for my reading glasses." She dug around in her bag and pulled out a small expandable screwdriver.

"That should work." Tom smiled. "Jack, I'm going to need a small strip of wire. Nothing longer than six inches."

"I'll find it." Jack bounded out of the car and jogged back toward the apartment.

Tom went to work on the panel. He unscrewed the board and let it hang down, exposing a series of blue and red wires from behind the panel. He studied them carefully. He knew the basics about car design. His school didn't offer classes in automotive mechanics, but he became interested in the topic when he fixed Jack's bike, so he read up on it. Cars worked just like every other machine—maybe more complicated than most, but his mind reveled in the complicated. At least the mechanical problem gave him a short refuge from obsessing over his mom.

The battery still held a charge, because the doors unlocked when Aunt Jackie used the remote control key. Usually, the wire that connected the battery to the rest of the car was thicker than the ones that connected the chips to the rest of the board. He ran his fingertips against the wires and assessed their gauge. On the third pass, he figured he had the right one.

Jack returned and Tom took the wire from him. "This should do just fine. I'm going to bypass the chip and connect this portal directly to the battery. The wire might burn out when the car starts, but it should work for at least one start." He ducked back under the dashboard. "When I connect the wire, press the start button, Aunt Jackie."

He used the mirror and some nifty handwork to attach the wire, bypass the defective chip, and hook the battery directly into the portal. "Almost done, Aunt Jackie."

"Okay, Thomas."

"Wait—"

Aunt Jackie pressed the start button.

The battery's electric current surged through Tom's fingers. He squealed and jerked his body up, clunking his head hard against the dashboard.

The car started.

He rubbed his scalp as he sat up, his hand still numb. "Aunt Jackie, I said to start the car when I told you it was okay."

"Sorry, Thomas, I thought you said it was okay." She shrugged, shifted the car into drive, and without looking in her rearview mirror, swung away from the curb and cut off a red coupe in the process. At the blaring of the driver's horn, she flipped him the bird.

Country music flooded the small interior.

"You've got to shut off that noise!" Jack shouted from the backseat.

"That's not noise, that's Waylon Jennings. It would do you good to listen to some real music."

Jack clutched both hands over his ears. "I stand corrected."

Tom worked the radio controls without success. "The stereo must be connected to that chip. I can't shut it off."

Aunt Jackie pulled a bulky mobile phone from her bag. "Be a dear, Thomas, and press speed dial 14."

He looked warily at the device, three times the size of any phone he'd ever used. "I've never seen anything like this before. Where'd you find it?"

"It's a low frequency phone, Thomas—hard to trace. Just press the S button and then the one and four for me."

He eyed her suspiciously. The phone wasn't simply old. It was valuable. He dialed the number and handed her the phone.

She drove slowly, working the steering wheel with one hand and the phone with the other. "I've got to come in, Rachel. It's an emergency. It has to do with Maggie. I have the boys with me also. I'll use the usual entrance. We'll be there in ten minutes." She stuffed the phone back into her bag and ignored the surprised look Tom gave her.

He turned to face Jack. "Where'd you get that wire?"

Jack ignored the question and stared out the window, his hands still covering his ears.

"No, seriously, Jack, I need to know so I can calculate whether the wire might last through another start."

Jack grinned. "I used one from your stereo. It's the only place I could think to look."

Tom slumped back into his seat. "Great."

He gazed at Aunt Jackie, who appeared different, more alive than usual, and somehow dangerous. He suddenly felt that he didn't really know much about his family.

Who is she, and what's her connection to the Fourteenth Colony?

CHAPTER 19

Samuel Wickersham leaned back in his leather chair, head hung low, a gloomy mood clouding his day. Having just worked up a sweat playing *Helicopter Madness* for the last two hours, he failed to advance to the championship round. Even worse, his scores had started to slip.

He looked somberly at Emmanuelle, the main character of the game—an attractive, if not impossibly built, bikini-clad female helicopter pilot. Her character's official name was Jane, but he'd renamed her Emmanuelle and spent enough time playing the game to begin having salacious thoughts about her. He switched the game off his new holographic computer monitor.

As head of research, he should have been reviewing the weekly progress reports from the ten different research teams who worked in the labs. Each team leader filmed a short video update on his or her project with supporting documentation, and he watched the videos. He didn't focus on what the team leaders said, really, but studied their body language. He believed his strength was in "reading" people, and rarely opened the documents. What would be the point?

In truth, the weekly progress reports depressed him, and the science behind the projects baffled him. He did his best to keep up, reading the latest articles in academic journals, attending a few of the conferences. He understood enough to ask superficial questions when he met the research teams in person. Still, he focused on the big picture. He had to wade through the shallow end of the pool because the details would drown him.

He drummed his fingers against the desk. He'd heard the talk around the facility—some called him a political hack and joked about his "credentials." No one liked him, and they were right. He had no business being head of research.

Still, he hated the researchers. *God, how I hate them!* He envied their ability and despised their aloofness. The two emotions wrapped around themselves like a double helix until they became inseparable. He wanted to hurt them, but he needed them. Their work would lift him up, so long as he took credit for it.

And he would take credit for it. If only he possessed abilities of his own to see the world differently than others, to figure out truths no one had previously known. Darian's work intrigued him because he imagined it could open those windows for him. Yes, the project could help cure Alzheimer's and senility, but even Wickersham saw other applications. Perhaps he could take the drug himself. Maybe it would change him, make him smarter, make him special. He so wanted to be special.

His family had made a fortune in construction, but his father and two older brothers ran the family business and had excluded him.

His mother had encouraged him to further his education. "Let the rest of the family handle the business," she said. "You should do something else, something important."

Mom had no idea what he should study, and he quickly realized *what* he studied wasn't the point so long as his studies were far removed from the family business. His parents had never physically abused him, but they beat him over the head with low expectations, which might not have been as bad, but certainly left a mark.

Upon his mother's urging, he earned a doctorate in nonverbal communications with a concentration on lower-developed animals from a second rate institution that wanted a new administration building and a new office for the dean. Cooper got him appointed at the hospital. It wasn't the first job Cooper had used his influence to obtain for Samuel, but it was the best so far.

As director of two secret research projects that had far-reaching implications, he almost felt important. He so wanted to win a Nobel Prize, and had already memorized his acceptance speech. He would take credit for the project and finally show his father that he had value—that he mattered. He just hoped his father would live long enough to see it. If the old man croaked the day after his acceptance speech, he would be happy. Elated, really.

He removed the miniature taser from his pocket. Usually, the tiny weapon lifted his mood, but his melancholy persisted. He would rather carry a gun, but he feared shooting himself again. Unfortunately, his record with the taser was only marginally better, including a regrettable incident during a lap dance at a bachelor party two years earlier. Still, he shuddered to think what would have happened if he'd had a gun in his pocket.

The intercom buzzed and he jumped, fumbling the taser on the desk. He pressed the button and his secretary's voice sprang from the box. "Doctor Beck is here to see you, Doctor Wickersham."

He grinned. His assistant always called him *Doctor Wickersham*. He liked how that sounded. "Have him wait five minutes and then let him in."

He unlocked the bottom right drawer of his desk, opened a leather case, took out a small glass vial, and poured the contents of the vial into a glass of water. He needed a little pick-up before confronting Doctor Beck. The drug was the latest mood enhancement narcotic on the underground market. It worked instantly. As he gulped down the glass of water, his spirits rose. Water dribbled off his chin, but he didn't care.

CHAPTER 20

Darian smiled at Clair as he strolled into the waiting area outside Wickersham's office. "I'm here to see the *Doctor*." He dragged out the last part of the word as if it were magically transformed into a dirty dishtowel he had discarded.

Clair frowned, but her eyes twinkled. "You shouldn't tease him, Darian. You know how sensitive he is about his credentials."

He winked mischievously. "I would never doubt his *credentials*."

While she worked the intercom, he scanned the pictures that littered the top of her desk. Most of them showed her family, but a few displayed members of her church. Although not religious himself, he remembered the mandatory sermons at the orphanage. The priest had passionately preached that God was an unfettered capitalist—the original Adam Smith. All other economic systems were the work of Satan himself.

He had his doubts, and sure didn't understand where orphanages, or working children, or addicted mothers fit in to God's plan, so he turned to science. He was smart enough to know that science didn't answer all the questions, but he wasn't ready to give God serious consideration.

"You'll have to wait a few minutes before he sees you," Clair said, interrupting his musings.

He clasped both hands behind his back and pulled, stretching his body. Coiled so tightly, he thought his muscles might explode any second. The results from the latest computer simulation on Jack's condition would be finished any minute, and his stomach soured in anticipation of bad news. "Do you have any idea when his *busy schedule* will allow him to see me?"

"He's in a bit of a mood today, so I'd take it easy with him," she whispered.

He resisted telling her what he really thought about Wickersham's moods.

He resolved to call Jack and his mom later in the day to come clean with them, to explain the situation and his role in Jack's condition. He would accept the ramifications of the truth, but they needed to know Jack had little time left. Darian would continue to search for a cure, but in all honesty, he didn't know where to look. He needed more information. Anything he tried now would constitute an unlikely guess.

He had failed them.

He pulled himself from his trance and focused on Clair. "How's that sweet little girl of yours?"

"She's growing like a weed. I can't believe she's already ten." She flipped around a framed picture of her daughter, who looked like a young version of Clair, all smiles in a yellow dress and pigtails.

"She's beautiful."

"Thanks, Darian." She looked at him with one eyebrow lifted. "Are you ready to settle down, maybe have a child of your own?"

"I thought you were already married!"

She blushed and chuckled. "I know a really nice girl from my church that I think you'd like."

He wondered if there was an unlimited supply of women from Clair's church looking for mates, or if she always had the same girl in mind. Before he could respond, the intercom buzzed. "Saved by the buzzer."

Clair grinned. "He'll see you now."

Darian swung the door open and strode into Wickersham's office. He had no idea why his boss had called the meeting, but he felt a little like he used to when called to the Warden's office in the orphanage for fighting.

Bright light flooded through the windows behind Wickersham's desk.

He squinted as he trekked his way toward his boss, who slouched behind his massive oak desk and fiddled with his bright red tie.

"Welcome, Doctor Beck. Good to see you. Please take a seat." Wickersham brushed a few imaginary particles of dust from his charcoal suit as he talked.

Darian didn't budge. He kept a scowl planted on his face like a danger sign. "I'd rather stand."

"Well, suit yourself." Wickersham leaned forward, resting his chin in his hands, his eyes smiling.

Darian assumed the rest of his face tried to follow along, but only so much free movement remained after the plastic surgeries.

"I've interrupted your good work because of an exciting development. A powerful benefactor of your research wants to meet with you and hear an update in person. This is a great opportunity for me... I mean for you, to sell EBF-202. Millions in funding may be on the line."

Darian listened to the words, but it took a moment for them to register. This was the last thing he'd expected to hear; he'd assumed the worst, that maybe Wickersham had removed him from the project.

As the initial surprise thawed, he started to heat up. "Who's the mysterious benefactor?"

"I can't say right now." Wickersham drummed his fingers on the desk.

"Does he know about Jack?"

"No, of course not." Wickersham's eyes widened. "That's our secret. There's no need to mention that until we see how it all plays out with the tennis instructor. We need to focus on the drug's positives. We'll stress the incredible possibilities behind the treatment, and the improvements from the first version."

"The treatment has a long way to go. I still can't stop it from overdeveloping the brain. We've lost all the canine test subjects but one, and Jack's not doing well." Darian leaned against the desk, his shoulders folded downward. He had invested so much of his life into this research, and made tremendous strides, but at what cost? If they hadn't injected Jack, everything would be different. But they had, and now the truth and Jack's life hung precariously by a thread of Darian's making.

"You're being too hard on yourself! One of the dogs is still alive. You've collected valuable data from the tennis instructor. I have confidence that you're just one more small breakthrough away from a viable drug."

Darian snorted and glanced away from Wickersham. *What does it matter anyway?* He was going to confess the truth to Jack later that afternoon, and there would be repercussions. "What do you want me to do?"

Wickersham hesitated.

Darian imagined a weasel running in a sphere deep within his brain.

"Nothing, except clear your schedule for Saturday night. My assistant will be making a presentation for you. It'll focus on the right things. The benefactor wants something quick and snazzy, not a bunch of jargon and technical stuff. I'll take care of the whole thing."

Darian clenched his hands into tight fists. *This is my project!* Then he noticed the time on the wall. *The computer simulation should be finished by now.* He sighed. "Great. Anything else?"

"Nothing else, but this meeting is of the utmost importance. It's in your best interest to make a positive impression. I would hate for your funding to be pulled and your research stopped before you help the tennis player... or anyone else."

Darian detected the threat in Wickersham's voice and knew it to be real. He could be pulled from the project. He wasn't far removed from going back to the ghetto. Everything could be taken away from him, but right now, he didn't care about any of that.

He spun and left without saying another word, leaving the door open behind him. He hoped for a miracle and dreaded the truth.

CHAPTER 21

Without warning, Aunt Jackie swerved the Silver Bullet to the side of the road, jumped over the curb, and screeched to a stop.

The car behind them veered into oncoming traffic, honking the horn as the driver skidded past them and missed the back bumper by inches.

Aunt Jackie flipped him the bird.

Tom began to see a pattern.

They'd ridden from the apartment in silence. The Waylon Jennings songs had driven most of the thoughts from Tom's mind, and the ones that lingered worried him too much to speak out loud.

Aunt Jackie popped the trunk. "Okay, boys, this is the end of the road." She swung out of the car with a slight groan, leaving the driver's-side door open and the motor running.

They were a hundred yards away from the main entrance to Kykuit, the state park that housed the old Rockefeller estate.

The boys tentatively followed her. "Aren't we going to go in?" asked Tom.

She grabbed a blue vest from the trunk and slammed it shut. The badge clipped on the front read *Tour Operator*. "Only I can pass through the gates. You boys will have to go in through the side entrance."

Jack huffed. "Can't you drop us off near the cemetery at least? We're more than a mile away!"

She smiled mischievously, turned, and jumped back into the car. Before they could react, she slammed the door shut and sped off, leaving the brothers behind with confused expressions on their faces.

"She's one weird bird," Jack said. "Which way to the cemetery?"

A secret tunnel in the cemetery led to the Fourteenth Colony's covert headquarters in the state park.

Tom pointed. "If we head east, we'll run into it. Let's get going." He headed off at a slow jog. He wanted to sprint to the cemetery, but Jack couldn't keep up. He had started teaching tennis at the Club on a part-time basis again, but he was still recovering.

Jack jogged alongside his brother. "Why'd she drop us off so far from the cemetery?"

"I don't like it." Tom frowned. "She wants to talk to Rachel first, without us there."

He increased his pace. His mind whirled as he tried to figure out what type of stew Aunt Jackie was cooking, certain he wasn't going to like the taste.

The brothers reached the aqueduct that ran along Sleepy Hollow Cemetery ten minutes later. They found the gap in the chain-link fence and scooted inside, then carefully made their way to the oldest part of the cemetery. The grounds were well cared for, trees healthy and pruned, and grass green and freshly mowed. Flowering plants splashed the landscape in abundant color.

They followed an uneven gravel path into the oldest part of the cemetery, their feet crunching against small white pebbles. This area, though still well groomed, remained bare of color—no bouquets decorated these ancient gravestones. The neatly designed rows of the cemetery's newer section contrasted with winding paths around ancient trees and even older rock formations in the older section.

Jack hesitated as they neared a sharp turn, and grabbed Tom's arm a second before a chipmunk bounded out of the nearby brush and skittered across the path.

"That critter sure made a ton of noise for something so small." Jack smiled. "I guess I'm jittery."

The brothers hurried along the path, took a sharp left around a wide oak tree, and continued as the path narrowed. They reached a small "T" and veered right off the main path.

Tom led the way, and within seconds stood before the flat tombstone of Samson Burr, who died in 1845. Tucked behind a rock formation, the stone marker could only be seen by someone standing directly in front of it. Still, Tom glanced around to make sure they were alone as Jack leaned down and pressed the "o" in Samson.

Nothing happened.

"This is the correct tombstone, right? Shouldn't it open to the tunnel?" Jack looked at Tom, mouth open. "What did Aunt Jackie do?"

Tom leaned down and jabbed the "o."

Nothing happened.

He balled his hands into fists. Pressing the "o" should have triggered a hydraulic hinge and revealed a hidden staircase into the tunnel that connected to the Fourteenth Colony's headquarters. But with Aunt Jackie involved, none of the things that should have happened were happening.

"Rachel has this place wired. She only admits those she wants," Tom explained. "Maybe Aunt Jackie has pull with her, but why would she take us here and not let us in?" He scanned the nearby surroundings and spotted likely hiding spots for video cameras.

"I'm going to kill that old bat," Jack grumbled. "I can see my hands around her wrinkled throat. She's old. It wouldn't take much."

"We can't force the stone up. We'll need another way in." Tom groaned. "Maybe we can sneak into Kykuit. We don't have time for this!"

His internal clock raced. They battled against time they didn't have. It could take hours to sneak into Kykuit, even if they figured out how to do it.

Jack silenced Tom with a look and a wave of his hand. "Someone's coming, and he's a lot bigger than a chipmunk."

CHAPTER 22

Maggie opened her eyes. *Something's wrong.*

She managed to lie still and shut them tight, wading through a swirling, drug-induced fog. She counted to ten, the numbers fuzzy at first but gradually clearing.

Her memory returned in flashes—the note, the crumpled drawing of Jack's face, and....

And Cooper.

With a rush, everything else returned in stark detail and she gasped for air.

Cooper brought me here. I'm under his control.

Her mouth turned dry and a tremor shook her body. She cracked opened her eyelids just enough to catch a glimpse of her surroundings, a large bed surrounded by soft sheets. Soft, yellow light brightened the dark room.

She shut her eyes again and listened, expecting to hear voices. She felt *his* eyes watching her, and a cold chill washed over her body. Frozen in terror, her breathing came in shallow, rapid gasps. The sound of her racing heart filled her head like water crashing over a waterfall, so loud she feared the noise would give her away.

I am not a weak woman. That floated up to her consciousness from somewhere deep within, bobbing up and down on the current of her thoughts. She had no idea how long she'd laid unmoving, but her confidence slowly returned.

Maggie opened her eyes and turned her head from side to side. She expected to see Cooper staring down at her, but breathed deeper when she saw no one. The sting from the bruise on her cheek sharpened her thoughts.

I am not a weak woman.

She sat up. She *was* alone, breathing deeper still, until the waterfall receded. Her fingers lingered over her plush robe, sure it had cost more than she earned in a week. Everything in the room was soft and expensive—the bed large and the sheets made from high thread-count cotton. The furniture looked well made, and the room stretched farther than the entire length of her apartment.

Bile rose in her throat as she resisted the urge to throw up. Something unhealthy about the richness of the room hit her hard. It felt unclean, though not in the literal meaning of the word. The place was spotless, but unclean in a spiritual sense. For the first time in her life, she believed Satan lived on Earth. Even worse, this was his room, and he'd be back for her soon.

She shook her head and chased the idea—a bad thought, a defeatist thought—from her mind.

I am not a weak woman.

She scanned the room more carefully this time, noting no windows and two doors. *I have to find a weapon.* She swung her legs off the bed and wobbled a little as she stood. Her head swam in circles at first, but the dizziness passed and she straightened herself. The soft carpet fibers bristled against her toes.

She bobbed her way to the bathroom door, still under the influence of the drugs Cooper had used to sedate her. She hesitated before opening it. Maybe *he* lurked behind that door, just waiting for her. Worse yet, maybe that door was a portal to hell.

Another negative thought she banished from her mind.

She steeled her nerves and touched the metal plate. The door slid sideways into a pocket in the wall and revealed nothing more extraordinary than a bathroom. Cooper didn't lurk behind the door.

I am not a weak woman.

She gazed into the largest, most elaborate bathroom she'd ever seen, with a huge claw-foot, stand-alone marble tub, and a shower stall with ten stainless steel showerheads. Two large mirrors, two marble pedestal sinks, and a five-foot-tall cherry wood medicine cabinet stood on the left side of the room.

She swayed toward the medicine cabinet and kicked a stainless steel stool that had three fluffy towels on top. *There has to be something in here I can use as a weapon.*

As a methodical person, she attacked tasks in orderly ways. First, she opened all the drawers in the medicine cabinet and found a few toiletries, some lotions, and a few basic first-aid medical supplies. She inspected each bottle, hopeful to find something she could use, but found nothing. Her search became more frantic as she studied the shower and the toilet—still nothing.

She leaned against one of the pedestal sinks and saw her image in the mirror. Her mental message changed. *I am a strong woman. I will figure this out.*

She straightened her posture. *What would happen if I killed myself?* She wasn't contemplating the afterlife, comfortable that her soul would live on when she stopped breathing, and would find her Paul again. No, her thoughts centered on Cooper and her boys.

What would he do if I defied him and killed myself?

He might move on, find a different woman, leave Tom and Jack alone.

It was possible, but she knew better. He wouldn't let her win. He would punish her boys. He would seek them out and, if he didn't kill them immediately, find some other way to make their lives miserable.

She couldn't take that risk.

I'm going to have to kill him before he kills me.

Maggie lifted her eyes and barely recognized the stranger in the mirror. The bruise on her cheek flared red and angry, but the vacant look in her eyes troubled her more than her puffy skin. *Bruises heal.* She took a clean white towel and washed dried blood from her cheek. The white cotton turned red.

I am a strong woman.

She pounded the mirror with her right hand, and the thin plastic film bent against her fist. She glanced at the top of the mirror and noticed the tiny camera lens. It wasn't a mirror at all, but a thin video screen. She pulled the robe tighter around her chest.

She used to love small moments of privacy—in the bath on Sunday nights, drawing the Hudson River alone on the shore, in the back pew at church. She glanced at the camera and wondered if she would ever feel that again.

A rattling sound of plates and glasses, rolled on a cart, broke the silence.

An unfamiliar, cheerful male voice called out, "Brunch is ready!"

She sighed, splashed water on her face, straightened her robe, and walked into the bedroom.

A young, athletic looking man stood stiffly behind a pushcart of food with both of his arms clasped behind his back. Upon seeing her, he smiled, his teeth white and straight and his short blond hair neatly parted to the side. "My name is Terry. I've brought brunch for you. Where would you like me to set it up?"

Maggie glanced around the large room. Her blank expression made it clear she had no preference.

"How about if I set it up on this table?" Terry pointed to a nearby wooden table and nodded. Careful not to turn his back, the attendant set up plates of food on the table while keeping on eye on her. "We have French toast, Canadian bacon, strawberries, and orange juice. I hope you like it." Steam spiraled up from the French toast.

She sensed an opportunity and scooted toward the young man, stopping only a foot away from him. "You have to help me. I'm trapped," she whispered.

His eyes narrowed and turned to stone, but the fake smile never left his face. "I'm sure we will become close friends and you'll be happy here. I'll be back to take the tray later. The closet has a full wardrobe for you, with all the latest fashions." He airily pointed to an open closet door.

"I don't want the latest fashions. Don't you understand? I'm a prisoner here!"

"We'll talk later. You should wear something pretty. He'll come to visit you later in the day."

Terry backed away from the table and toward the door, his hand resting on a thin black baton that hung from his belt. Without saying another word he placed his palm against a glass sensor by the door. It turned green, the door opened, and he left her alone.

She looked down at the table, and all her favorite foods for brunch stared back at her. *How could he have known that?*

She lifted the plastic knife and stabbed it against her palm. It bent too easily to work as a weapon.

I am a strong woman, I am a strong woman, I am a strong woman....

CHAPTER 23

"Come on, Jack, they can't find us here. We can't compromise the tunnel." Tom yanked his brother's arm and they raced back to the main path, kicking up dirt in the process.

When they cleared the "T," they almost barreled into a hulking security guard who marched toward them. He swung a baton in a wide arc and swayed as he moved. A tad shorter than Tom, he had wide shoulders and massive arms that bulged against his black, short-sleeved shirt.

His small black eyes narrowed, and his one bushy unibrow bunched together on his broad, square face. "What are you guys doing here?"

Jack smiled. "We're visiting our dead aunt."

The big man spat tobacco juice in a gross, brown flying missile that narrowly missed Jack's sneakers. "Where're your passes?"

"Tobacco chew is bad for you. You might want to give it up," Tom said, trying to sound as helpful as he could. "It's loaded with toxins."

The guard's pitted face turned into a sneer and his left eye twitched. "You're a funny one." He spit another glob of chew. This time, it splashed on Tom's sneakers. "You're not supposed to be here. Looks like it's time for a beat down." He smacked the baton into his hand.

Tom never participated in jujitsu competitions. Since middle school, he had been in exactly six fights, five of them connected to Jack's kidnapping. He'd won four of those and once, in seventh grade, an upperclassman made the mistake of picking on the skinny, brainy kid. Fighting was more about determination than bulky muscles, and he was plenty determined.

Adrenaline raced through him as he studied the behemoth to determine the man's weaknesses. *He looks slow. All those bulky muscles probably make him awkward.*

Before he could make his move, Jack rushed past him and recklessly raced headlong toward the giant. Tom tried to grab him, but Jack darted forward before he could reach him. Tom knew the baton was electrified, and he was sure Jack didn't.

The colossal guard swung the stick and whacked Jack on the shoulder. Fifty thousand volts shot through him and his shoulder sizzled. He moaned and crumpled to the ground.

The security guard smiled as he shot another gob of tobacco onto Jack's shirt.

"You shouldn't have done that," Tom growled.

"I'm gonna do worse to you!" A vein pulsed on the pitted man's forehead. His left eye twitched sporadically as if it were sending out Morse code.

Tom cautiously circled the hulk, body tensed to spring.

The guard lunged forward and swung the baton in a looping arc with his right hand.

Tom caught his arm at the wrist and shoulder and brought it down hard on his left knee. The elbow dislocated.

"Ahheee!" the guard screeched as he dropped the baton to the ground.

Tom shot his right leg into the man's midsection, knocking the wind out of him.

The guard doubled over and gasped for air.

Tom delivered a roundhouse kick flush to the side of his head—like hitting concrete.

The big man spun to the ground. Struggling to his knees, he spit again, but this time, it wasn't tobacco; the thick red goo was blood.

Tom retrieved the baton. "I warned you." He blasted the giant in his tree trunk-sized neck.

The hulk went down in an unconscious lump. The scent of burned flesh filled the air.

"Are you all right, Jack?" Tom helped him up.

Jack shrugged off his hands and tottered back and forth like a seesaw. "I had him right where I wanted him." He managed a grin.

"Really—leave the security guys to me next time. You're still recovering, and I'm the black belt, remember?"

"If I had a tennis racquet, I would have flattened him." He steadied on his feet.

"Next time we've got to remember to bring one. Come on, let's move before someone else comes along."

Tom led the way back to the tombstone. "Maybe Rachel didn't open the tunnel because she had spotted the guard."

Jack pressed the "o" in Samson, and this time the stone marker responded with a hydraulic hiss, lifting up a quarter of an inch.

Jack smiled. "I guess we're invited in."

The tunnel, originally built as part of the Rockefeller estate as an emergency escape path for its wealthy owners, worked as a secret entrance into the Fourteenth Colony's headquarters.

Jack climbed down the hidden staircase with Tom following close behind. The familiar musty smell of the tunnel welcomed them.

"Watch your step," Tom said. "The stone can be slippery!" He recalled the first time he'd entered the tunnel four months earlier, when he slipped on these steps and tumbled down the staircase into Mary. Luckily, he'd twisted his body under hers to avoid injuring her. He cracked a rib in the process, but it was worth it, even if she *had* called him an oaf.

As they reached the last step, Jack pointed to the words "The Fourteenth Colony" scrawled in red spray paint on the concrete wall at the entrance to the tunnel. "Do you think Dad wrote that?"

"I think so. It matches his handwriting from those letters he'd give us on our birthdays."

"I like your addition."

Tom had drawn the thirteen stars of the original colonies in a circle, with a larger fourteenth star in the center. It had become the unofficial symbol of the movement.

Tom had to stoop as he traveled the cramped passageway. His fingers brushed crumbling concrete sides fixed with dark spots of concrete patch, and his head bumped against exposed white lights hung on a cord along the top right side of the tunnel to light their path.

"I miss Dad," Tom said as he headed down the tunnel. "I wish he would have told us about the Fourteenth Colony."

"We were too young when he died. I'm sure he would have wanted us to join."

Their sneakers squeaked against the concrete floor.

"Tom, you know Mary's going to find out about Mom from Aunt Jackie. You'd better think of something to tell her. She's not going to be happy that you haven't called her yet. She can be awfully tough if you make her angry. Just ask David." David was Jack's best friend and Mary's older brother.

Tom had fallen in love with her from the first moment they'd met. He knew how tough she could be, having spent a lot of time with her over the past four months. He couldn't imagine his life without her, even if she did drive him crazy. He only wished she felt the same way, but she had other priorities.

CHAPTER 24

Tom stood stiff with anxiety. Time inched forward as he studied the heavy steel door, noticing for the first time scratches by the hinges and a small dent toward the bottom. He waited for someone to let them in, feeling as if he had to sit for a test he was woefully unprepared to take. He had walked through this entrance dozens of times over the past four months, but he felt different this time.

His mother was missing, and Mary would be angry with him.

Mary changed his world, made everything vivid. She added texture and meaning to everyday activities. Even breathing improved around her—she smelled like cinnamon and roses. He wanted only her happiness and for them to spend time together. It didn't matter what they did, as long as they did it together.

He hadn't realized it before, but he would be lost without her, and now she would be angry with him because he was an idiot. He should have listened to Jack. If he could go back in time, he would have called Mary first, but given that time travel was beyond his reach, he waited by the steel door like an inmate on death row.

The metal latch sprang open and echoed like a gunshot, and Tom flinched. Jack whacked him on the back, and they somberly entered the secretive group's headquarters.

As usual, it took his eyes a moment to adjust to the harsh white light after the relative darkness of the tunnel.

"Damn, that's bright," Jack whispered, even though he wore sunglasses.

A warning light went off on Tom's mental dashboard, but he ignored it. Concern about his imminent collision with Mary filled his mind.

When his vision cleared, he took in the familiar concrete cellar with long tables made from old, cracked wood, each piled high with new, high tech computer monitors and equipment. A half dozen people hunched over keyboards working diligently. They barely glanced up to see the brothers.

Mary stood just inside the doorway, waiting for Tom with her hands on her hips. Her long, wavy red hair tumbled below her shoulders. Her brilliant green eyes were ringed with red and sparkled with a moist sheen.

He had never seen her cry before, and a grapefruit-sized lump formed in his throat. Without uttering a word, she rushed forward and flung her arms around his broad shoulders, and he melted into the embrace. His death sentence had been lifted at the last second.

Mary squeezed him. "It's awful, but we're going to get her back, Tom. I know it."

"Of course we will." His assurances rang false, like a poorly tuned piano, and he clutched her tighter.

After a long moment, she pushed away, and new tear tracks ran down her cheeks. She wiped them away with her sleeve and blushed, which turned her normal cream-colored skin a bright shade of pink. "Aunt Jackie and Rachel are upstairs in Rachel's office. I'm supposed to bring you straight up."

"You know Aunt Jackie?" Jack said.

"Of course I do." Mary swung an elbow hard into Tom's stomach. The blow caught him by surprise and knocked the wind out of him. "Next time you call me right away!" Raw emotion rang through her voice.

Tom stammered three different apologies, hoping one of them would be good enough.

Jack chuckled at his helplessness and pushed him in the back.

Mary led them up a short metal staircase to a wooden trap door. She pressed her palm against a glass screen, the light above the trap door turned green, and she shoved it open.

The trio entered the ground floor of an old, abandoned carriage house. Tom liked the old building. He appreciated its utility and how the beams and wood joints were fashioned together. Most people saw an old oak barn built in the mid 1800s, with sawdust spread haphazardly along the floor where spiders and their immense webs ruled the day. Tom saw a beautifully crafted puzzle of wood, expertly formed together to create a functional space. Even the musty smell mixed with the pungent oak lifted his spirits.

Jack lowered the trap door behind him. It formed a perfect seam with the floor, impossible to detect unless you knew where to look. A gouge in the wood served as a handhold.

Mary led them to the east end of the building to the false wall, which blended into the rest of the structure almost perfectly. Almost.

Tom noticed the imperfections. The color of the wood was a shade darker than the rest of the carriage house, and probably most telling, the wood beams fit together perfectly—too perfectly for the rest of the structure, and given the tools available in the mid 1800s.

Mary crouched low at one end of the wall and placed her palm against a small glass plate. The sophisticated screen read Mary's DNA and flashed green, and a hidden door sprung open. Its modern, stainless steel hinges hissed as the door swung inward, granting them access to Rachel's office.

The simple narrow room had no windows. Rachel sat behind a massive antique oak desk and studied one of three video monitors that competed with two perfectly pruned bonsai trees for space. In her sixties, with long brown hair streaked with gray and pulled back in a ponytail, she exuded an understated confidence and authority. Her dark brown eyes, usually welcoming and bright, now darkened with worry.

Aunt Jackie sat on the opposite end of the room, on a couch near two small chairs and an oval cocktail table, her arms crossed against her chest and an angry scowl drawn on her face.

"Aunt Jackie, how nice to see you again," Jack said. "I'm sorry we're late, but we had an unpleasant meeting with a security guard in the cemetery." Jack pointed to a series of video feeds projected on the long exterior wall. They changed frequently, but the middle feed stayed fixed on the tombstone from the cemetery.

"Too bad the taser didn't hit you on the head. It could have jolted some sense into you. Naturally, Tom bailed you out." She smiled at Tom.

One feed showed the "T" where the brothers had fought off the security guard, who hadn't yet moved.

Jack's jaw clenched. "If you had dropped us off by the cemetery, we would never have had any problems, you old bat!"

Aunt Jackie stood, knees bent and hands held flat and tight in a martial arts ready position. She looked like a gray-haired, miniature ninja dressed in a blue tour vest and beige blouse. "I'm not too old to teach you a lesson, racquet boy! Come and get some!" She inched her way toward Jack.

He waved his arms and backed away from the approaching ninja. "I wish I had taken that taser."

Tom jumped between them. "Stop it! This isn't helping! We need to focus on Mom."

Rachel stood. "I'm sorry I couldn't open the tunnel when you first got to the tombstone, but the security guard might have noticed. Stop this bickering. We need to work together to rescue Maggie."

Jack tore his eyes from his aunt. "Where do we start?"

"Let's start with the letters and the pictures. There has to be a clue as to this man's identity in that file. From there, we can assess the situation and make a plan to save Maggie and bring her back." Rachel's usually soft voice sounded firm and definitive. "We start with the first note Cooper wrote. I am sure it's the key. The logo embedded in the paper has to be connected with the resort where Maggie was staying when they met. If we can figure out the name of that resort, it will be our starting point. The resort must keep records. If we can retrieve those records, we can crosscheck the family names and find a Cooper that fits. We know he's rich, has blue eyes, and is white."

Tom agreed. The only loose end they had was the original note. Cooper probably never imagined she would keep it. Maybe if they pulled on the loose end hard enough, everything else would unravel.

Mary squeezed his arm. "I've scanned the logo into my computer, and I'm running it through as many databases as I can think of. We should discover something soon."

"Which years should we check?" Jack asked. "When did Mom meet this monster?"

"Maggie was young when she met Cooper," Aunt Jackie said. "You can tell from the way she drew that first sketch of him. I traveled out of the country from the end of 2011 until 2014. She must have met him then. We need to focus on those years."

Rachel nodded and turned to Tom. "In the meantime, you should continue to go over the letters and photos and see if you can find any other clues. I'm throwing out some feelers with people I know to see if anyone's heard anything. Bring the folder to the basement and look it over down there. Call me the moment you come up with anything."

Tom reached for the manila folder on the cocktail table, and his hand shook. It looked like a simple folder, but he could almost see the evil rising from it.

CHAPTER 25

Jackie watched as the whirl of the door's metallic gears locked and sealed the room. "I don't want them involved in this. Maggie's been protecting them their entire lives. I can't have them facing Cooper. She wouldn't want them put in such a dangerous situation."

"You underestimate them. Jack's been contributing to us since he was fifteen. Tom saved his life only four months earlier. He handled himself extraordinarily well in an extremely dangerous situation."

"Anyone can be lucky once." Jackie scoffed.

"He's a gifted person, both mentally and physically. You saw how he handled the guard in the cemetery." Rachel paused, pressed her palms together and brought her fingertips to her lips. "I wonder how the guard knew to search for them in the old part of the cemetery. They don't patrol that part of the grounds often."

Jackie brushed aside the implied accusation. "They're still just boys. I'd be better off on my own."

"Maybe twenty years ago, but age catches up to all of us."

"There's still some life in me, and I know what needs to be done. Cooper has to be put down like a rabid dog, and I intend to do just that."

"You need help. Besides, there's nothing we could do now to keep them out of it. I'm not going to lock them up. It has to be their choice.

They're old enough. How many targets did you take out by the time you were seventeen?"

Jackie crossed her arms again and shot Rachel another searing glare. She had lost the argument, but she didn't have to like it. If she found a way to ditch her nephews and still get Cooper, she would take it.

They were her charges now. Rachel could go screw.

CHAPTER 26

Darian raced on old Bessie, his body sweating and his conscience clear as muddy water. The Beatles's *Hey Jude* filled the room.

The computer simulation had finished, and the events played out on the monitor in front of him. He saw only darkness and death. Under each scenario, Jack's brain continued to develop, the strain increasing against his skull until the computer pronounced him dead, dead, dead. Based upon the analysis, Jack had four days, perhaps five at most.

George strolled into the lab, a worried frown replacing his usually congenial expression. "I assume the computer analysis came back negative."

Darian nodded at the screen. "Under the best case assumptions, he has until Tuesday. Tuesday!" He pumped his legs furiously.

"Darian, you've done all you can do. EBF-202 will eventually save millions of lives once we figure out how to stop it. *You* will save millions of lives. We've learned a great deal from Jack already."

"I don't think he's going to see it that way. How do I explain his condition to his mother and brother? Do I tell them how much we've learned from him? 'Sorry he died, but someday we'll save a bunch of lives. Thanks so much for playing!'"

George moved in front of him. "What are you going to do?"

"What I should have done originally. I'm going to tell them the truth—that I tried an experimental drug on him and can't stop it. Now it's going to kill him. They only have a few days left to get his affairs in order. He deserves that much." He stopped pedaling and hung his head. Sweat rolled off his nose.

"He would probably have died already if he hadn't received the treatment. He only had a slight chance of pulling out of that coma by himself. You're being too hard on yourself."

"No, I'm not!" Darian pounded the handlebars with his fists. "His mom should have been given the choice. I should have given *him* the choice. I could have done it. I had hours to do it."

"Just think this through. A scandal could sidetrack the drug indefinitely, and everything you've worked for would be wasted. The drug works. It promotes brain growth. It will cure Alzheimer's and senility. The applications are endless. We just need the agent that stops the growth. As it is, the growth rate has slowed. Lassie is stable. Don't throw all our work in the trash. There must be another way."

"I'll keep your name out of it." Darian narrowed his eyes. "You won't get into any trouble."

"That's not what I meant and you know it." George's face flushed red and he stormed out of the lab.

Darian sighed. He knew George wasn't worried about himself, and he shouldn't have suggested it. George was a good man, a better man than he was. Anger and frustration had made him say it. Ten years removed from the orphanage and he still acted like an angry, forgotten child.

Will I ever change?

Darian dismounted from the bike and eyed his cell phone on the desk. Though not more than twenty feet away, it still felt like an impossibly wide chasm to cross.

George was right: if he told Jack about EBF-202, the drug might never be developed. All the good and promise behind the treatment would be wasted. Jack's life—and death—would be wasted. The dogs and the time invested, all wasted. He might get tossed back into the ghetto, back to the overpass where death lingers.

The distance to the phone grew even more daunting, and then he remembered the Warden and the ice cream and the moment he learned his mom had passed away. He didn't have a chance to say goodbye. She had already been *disposed of.*

The chasm shrunk to a few feet and he broke out in a cold sweat. His Beatles t-shirt clung to his body as he reached for the phone.

CHAPTER 27

Jack spent hours reviewing the letters and gruesome photographs with only a headache to show for it. The more he matched the words and the pictures together, the more he thought he understood the monster behind these murders. He felt Cooper's anger and hatred and, worst of all, the thrill he got when he sensed his victim's fear. When he closed his eyes and let his imagination roam, a picture of a man's face started to form—grainy around the edges, turquoise eyes jagged.

The feeling became so intense he started shaking. His imagination had run amok. *How can I see the bastard's face?*

He had to move. Sitting still and thinking suffocated him, so he walked toward Tom at the end of the table.

Tom methodically waved a specialized ultraviolet light across one of the notes. From his tight lips and narrow eyes, Jack could tell he was spinning his wheels. "How're you making out?"

"This is useless." Tom tossed the light on the table. "This Cooper is too smart to leave any evidence behind. Maybe if I analyze the paper itself, I might find the manufacturer. No one writes these days, and fine cotton paper must be rare. If I can figure out who made the paper, then maybe we can retrieve a client list or develop a lead."

"It's worth a try," Jack said, even though he couldn't see how it would pay off. Still, Tom needed a puzzle he could solve or this thing would swallow him whole. He was strong, but he had limits, and Jack saw the strain on him.

"How could someone take Mom?" Tom turned toward him, eyes wide and moist. "She wouldn't hurt anyone. I just don't understand it. How could she have kept this secret from us? We could have protected her."

"Don't go negative. We're going to rescue her. We'll do whatever it takes to get her back."

"She still makes my lunch, Jack. I tell her not to, but she leaves a sandwich in the fridge every day." Tom rubbed his eyes. "She's sacrificed everything for us."

Jack shook him by the shoulders. "We *will* find her, and when we do, Cooper is going to wish he had never been born."

Mary joined them. "Rachel wants us upstairs."

A distinctive-looking man stood stiff and straight next to Rachel's desk, nervously stroking a neat white goatee that contrasted with his dark skin. Sweat glistened off his clean-shaven head. He looked uncomfortable in a button down, long-sleeve shirt that hung loosely on his rail-thin frame.

Jack noticed his hollow eyes shift around the room as if he were seeing ghosts. They were eyes that had seen too much bad in the world and expected the worst at every corner. Jack knew those eyes. Lately, he had seen them in the mirror.

Mary closed the door behind them.

"This is The Professor," Rachel began. "He's an expert psychological profiler. I've asked him to review the letters and give us his best profile on Cooper."

Jack had heard rumors about The Professor, but had never seen him. The preeminent profiler in the early 2030s, The Professor had enjoyed a number of major successes. He took down the Ben Franklin Killer, who was credited with 32 deaths via electricity. Beside each victim, he left a small kite and key as his unique calling card. As a purely intellectual pursuit, The Professor had profiled each founding father, and had exercised poor judgment in publishing his findings, not all of which were flattering. The Originalist government had branded him a traitor and forced him into hiding.

Aunt Jackie leaned back on the couch and murmured, "What crap."

Jack smiled. The old bat was a handful, but she was honest. It wasn't hard to figure out where you stood with her.

The Professor smiled reluctantly, as if unaccustomed to making the simple facial expression. "We don't have a large sample of writings, but I think we have enough for me to work up a simple profile."

He pressed a button on a remote control, and the video feeds from Rachel's computer vanished. One large screen with the fourteen letters and the first note displayed on it took their place.

"First, the handwriting offers us some informative clues." He clicked another button and perfectly formed letters appeared highlighted and enlarged. "The letters are all neatly-formed, consistent block letters. That indicates a bright, orderly mind, one that is able to effectively departmentalize different parts of his life. The subject likely appears to be a well-adjusted, successful man, but we know better.

"The signature is also instructive." The letters vanished and all fifteen signatures appeared on the screen, each nearly identical. "He developed an elaborate signature early in his life, and the signature stayed consistent through the years. This shows classic signs of narcissism. He obviously thinks quite highly of himself."

The signatures disappeared and particular phrases took their place. "From his word choice and writing style, I'm sure he was born and raised in the Northeast—most likely a big city like New York, Boston, or Philadelphia. He went to school at an Ivy League institution. You might check them out as a lead. From his comments in the letters, it's clear he feels entitled to success, that it's his birthright. He probably did better his first two years than the last two, and finished somewhere between the middle and top-third of his class. Once the workload got tougher, he would have grown disinterested."

"How could he have fallen in love with Mom when he was so young?" Tom asked.

The Professor frowned. "He says she belongs with him, but he never says he loves her. He knows, at least in his subconscious, that he has no real feelings for Maggie. He thinks she's well below his station in life and has no genuine interest in her. It's obvious from the letters."

He pressed a series of buttons, and numerous phrases appeared on the wall. "It's a shame you never went to college," and "I don't know how you can live in such a small house," and "It's unfortunate Paul can't provide for you" were just a few.

Jack had noticed the tone and disdain dripping from the letters.

Tom sighed. "If he has no real feelings for Mom, then why stalk her for so long? Why not just take her earlier?"

Jack heard the desperation and futility in his voice. Math and the physical sciences couldn't help Tom here, and that threatened to bury him.

The Professor stroked his goatee. "The duration of most stalking events is one and a half years or shorter. Longer ones have been recorded, including some exceeding forty years, but those are rare. I don't think the subject is a classic stalker. His personality would more likely be diagnosed as a malignant narcissist."

The Professor paused at the blank stares around him, and continued in a somewhat less confident voice. "Malignant narcissists are extreme psychopaths who enjoy inflicting pain on their victims, and they possess a grandiose opinion of themselves. The subject clearly enjoys hurting women. Maggie rejected him when he was young. This hurt him. He wants to hurt her back and keep hurting her.

"He has combined those two feelings—his desire to repay her for rejecting him as a youngster, and his desire to hurt women in general—and the two have become inseparably intertwined in his mind. He's delayed going after Maggie for so long because terrorizing her thrills him. When he captures her, he'll lose his pretense for causing such pain in the other women. That scares him. Without Maggie, the reality that he's nothing more than a monster who enjoys hurting women will come to light."

"So he's using Mom as an excuse to butcher those other victims?" Tom asked.

"Exactly. But it's more complicated than pretense. Sending the letters and photos to Maggie provides the subject added excitement. He doesn't consciously understand it, but he feeds off punishing her."

The diagnosis didn't surprise Jack. He had gotten the same feelings when he reviewed the file.

The Professor continued. "Each letter is laced with subtle and explicit threats to those close to Maggie." The screen filled with dozens of threats. "He goes out of his way to mention specific developments in their lives, even including pictures of her sons. Again, he's making it clear to her that she cannot hide from him. He uses the threats like a dagger to inflict pain on her, revealing his sadistic tendencies. I believe he would have fulfilled his threats if Maggie had ever gone public with the letters."

"What about the victims? Who would mutilate people like that?" Tom blurted out.

"The women are all Maggie substitutes, with the possible exception of this one." The professor pressed a button, and all the photographs appeared side-by-side on the wall, with one enlarged over the rest. "This particular victim is different in physical appearance than the others. Her hair is lighter and she seems older with more muscle tone. Also, her wounds are similar, but the subject took less care hurting her.

He was less precise, as if she wasn't as interesting to him as the others. She's dressed and posed the same way as the other victims, so it's impossible to say why he killed her. Maybe his blood lust was heightened to an uncontrollable pitch and a more suitable Maggie substitute was not available."

The Professor paused. "All the other victims resemble Maggie when she married in her early twenties. His view of her is childlike. The victims never age. The injuries are similar in style but become increasingly violent over time. He cuts these women. It's hard to tell in the photos, but I think he removes their hearts. It's likely he keeps a collection of them. He's symbolically looking within these women to determine why she rejected him. He cannot understand it. He rips these women apart, looking for some secret he cannot fathom."

"What a monster," Mary whispered.

"Yes, he is indeed a monster, but don't be fooled by that nomenclature. He's very smart and shows no remorse for the hideous acts he has performed. He has likely never stayed at one job or profession for long. He bores easily, and when the learning curve becomes laborious, he moves on to something new, fooling himself into believing that he's too important to waste his time on any one task.

"In reality, he's unwilling to work hard and afraid that he might fail. He has no close friends. I doubt that he's married, unless the marriage is one of convenience. He's in good shape and enjoys some thrilling sports, but the risks involved are all containable. I would think something like mountain climbing, but not skiing. Most people find him attractive and charming. He has no problem manipulating people to achieve what he wants."

"How long does Maggie have before...?" Rachel shrunk in on herself.

The Professor's right eye twitched. "It's hard to say exactly. I would have a better guess if I could study the latest letters. I understand that he showed more rage in the recent ones. Taking Maggie suggests that he's under some external strain. He feels a certain loss of control in his life, some kind of stress from expectations placed on him by others close to him, perhaps a parental figure.

"Malignant narcissists often have one domineering parent. Those circumstances create incredible pressure, pressure he fools himself into believing will be relieved by grabbing her." The Professor hesitated for a moment, as if pulling together his thoughts from different compartments in his mind. "He will not hurt her immediately. He thinks she loves him but has been unable to express it. If she resists him, he will anger quickly. At most, she has a few days."

"And if she doesn't resist him?" Mary's voice cracked.

The Professor sighed. "He's at what we in the business call a *Shatter Point*—the point where his mind will splinter into a million shards as a result of stress. Once it shatters, he'll lash out. If she cooperates with him, he'll realize he doesn't actually love her. He desires a fictional version of her from his childhood. He wants the girl that rejected him. That will cause him to shatter. It might buy her an extra day or so, but he *will* shatter. He's a very dangerous man."

Stunned silence filled the room.

Aunt Jackie broke the tension. "When I put a bullet in his brain, will he die like anyone else?"

The Professor assessed her for a few moments, a spark of curiosity replacing the hollow look in his eyes. "Do not underestimate him. Show him no mercy."

Mary's phone pinged, and she checked the screen. "I have a hit on the logo."

CHAPTER 28

Charles Sheppard hovered his hand over the chessboard. His fingers fluttered and settled on his queen. He slid the piece diagonally to Rook Three.

Jacob Benjamin sat across from him and clucked his tongue. They were in Charles's luxurious penthouse apartment on the Upper West Side of Manhattan. He glanced at his opponent with steel gray eyes and a wrinkled, thin face. "What's on your mind, Charles? You're certainly not thinking about the match."

Charles smiled. "Have I played so poorly?"

Jacob moved his knight. "Checkmate. Now tell me what's troubling you."

Charles rose from his seat and strolled to the balcony. The real estate agent had said he could see five different airports from here. *Why would I care,* he'd thought at the time.

His gaze lingered over Central Pepsi Park, an oasis in the middle of the city. "What do you know about Gabriel and Moses? The two intrigue me. How do they work together?"

Jacob slid to Charles's side. "They've been partnered for ten years. Originally, Isabella White brought them together. She was Moses's sister and Gabriel's lover. I'm sure you've seen her from the file. She was a rising star in the ghettos before disappearing six years ago."

"Yes, she seemed like a real force. She could have united the ghettos if she hadn't vanished."

"We'll never know, but the two have done well without her." Jacob, ever the pragmatist, shrugged. "Most people believe Moses is the brains behind the operation while Gabriel supplies the muscle."

"That's what I was told, but I don't believe that's right. Moses does most of the talking, but it seemed like Gabriel called the shots. I used an obscure quote from Winston Churchill and Gabriel caught it. Still, there's something special about Moses I cannot put my finger on."

"Trust your instincts." Jacob placed his hand on Charles's shoulder. "You have an extraordinary gift for reading people. Either way, we need to work with them. They have become the most influential ghetto leaders. If we can forge a working relationship with them, much can be accomplished."

"They have serious misgivings about Peter. I can't say as I blame them. I don't know him well, but his disdain for the lower classes seems plain. If he becomes president, they think his election will trigger a violent response from all the ghettos."

"We have time before then. Politicians can be persuaded."

Charles's secure mobile rang. "Hello?"

"Bacchus, it's Merlot. We have a serious problem. Homeland Security is going to sweep the Westchester Ghetto and grab Moses and Gabriel soon, maybe as early as tomorrow."

A few months earlier, Charles had organized a group of powerful business people into a loosely formed organization to support change in America. He'd persuaded them that it would be best for everyone to reinstate fairness in the country, give the middle and lower classes a real chance at success, and bring the country back to its true roots. They called themselves the Wine Merchants. Each member used a different grape variety as a code name, except Charles who went by the Roman god of wine.

"I can't believe they would sweep into the ghetto. It would be a very dangerous operation," Charles said. "Are you sure?"

"Apparently they have a man on the inside. He's in their Inner Circle, whatever that means, and knows all their hiding places."

"Who authorized the operation? *I'm* the Secretary of Domestic Priorities. Ghettos fall under my domain! I should have had advanced warning about any plans to move against a ghetto."

"I'm not sure. My source heard it from the Vice President's team. His chief of staff might have authorized the sweep, or it could go all the way to the top. I've got to go. That's all I know."

Charles glanced at Jacob. "Merlot called. We have a big problem." He relayed the details of the call.

"The timing could not be worse for us, Charles." Jacob tented his fingers and brought them up to his chin. "They are important to us, but this makes them too risky. Everything we've worked for could be jeopardized, including the Fourteenth Colony. We'll have to find another way. You'll have to distance yourself from them, and we'll need a cover story, some reason you went to visit them, if they talk."

Charles leaned against the metal balcony, his mind spinning fast. A mischievous grin spread across his face. "We need them. Maybe this problem provides us with an opportunity."

"This is too risky. You could be compromised."

"I've taken bigger risks before. It was risky for me to see them in person, yet I went." He glanced at Jacob, but his older companion didn't understand him. He needed to take these risks. With every risk, he confirmed his commitment to action. Each risk pushed him farther along the path.

He'd made no alternative plans, no secret identities or hidden wealth to fall back on. If discovered, he would be doomed, but without that pressure, he was lost. He thrived on it, inhaled it... needed it. His poor biological parents demanded it from him. Those people who worked at his company's factory line in Pennsylvania required it. All the risks he took were calculated. Still, he wanted everything on the line, or he was afraid he would retreat and abandon those who relied upon him.

"If they are taken, Homeland Security will brand them as terrorists and we will never see them again," Charles said. "But if we save them, we gain months of goodwill and trust in one stroke. Time is running out for us. Either we push for change or events will overwhelm us."

"Even if we save them, they might not trust us. The timing is too close to your first meeting. They'll believe it's a setup."

"You're right." Sheppard rubbed the face of his antique Rolex for luck. "We'll need something else, something indisputable to earn their trust."

CHAPTER 29

Terry had told her to wear something pretty, so Maggie sorted through the fashionable clothes that hung in the closet and found a simple white cotton dress—custom made with soft, luxurious cotton and expensive lace around the neck. The dress draped wonderfully in long smooth lines, but she fought hard against the urge to rip it to shreds. At least there was no pink.

Something odd about the label caught her attention. Bringing it close to her eyes, she saw a faint red stain—a micro-spot of blood.

Her hand trembled. The dress had been bought for one of the other girls, one from the photographs.

Her legs started to buckle, and she raced into the bathroom just in time to throw up into the toilet.

Maggie glanced at her image in the bathroom video monitor. A stranger stared back at her. She splashed cold water against her face, leaned against the counter, and considered remaining dressed in the bathrobe, but a little voice in her head told her that was a bad idea. That little voice had kept her out of trouble, found a way to survive, found a way to make enough money to feed her boys.

How many of the other women wore this bathrobe?

Her skin crawled. That was a bad thought, negative, terrifying. She drove it from her mind and slipped into the dress. At least she felt whole in the dress, adult even, if she tried hard enough. It restored a measure of her dignity—not a big measure, but something to build on.

I am a strong woman.

She had found a wide array of makeup options in the dresser during her earlier search of the bathroom. She glanced back at the stranger in the mirror. She could hide the bruise with a little make-up. The puffiness would still be there, but she could conceal the redness.

She turned from the sink. *Let him see it. Maybe it will slow him next time.*

She returned the bedroom knowing that she needed to be careful.

Cooper had displayed a volcanic temper as a boy, and it would surely be worse now. The photographs proved it. They showed the work of a madman.

Cooper appeared at her doorway as if her thoughts had conjured him from some evil hiding place. He beamed a wide smile, his impossibly blue eyes twinkling. He cradled a gift in his hands as if it were the most valuable item in the world—as if it were a newborn. He strolled gracefully into the suite of rooms, like a dancer. "That dress looks lovely on you. You are more beautiful than ever."

She smiled. *I hate you!*

She steadied her breathing. "Thank you. You're too kind."

He waved his hand toward the couch in the living area. "Let's sit. We have much catching up to do."

Maggie nodded and inched her way toward the couch as if the world tilted under her feet and one misstep might cast her off. To steady herself, she focused on Cooper's throat, but he was too strong for her to choke the life out of him. *Maybe if he were sleeping....*

Cooper reached the couch first and waited for her to join him, the smile never leaving his face. When she got within arms reach, he held out the gift. "I've brought something for you."

Her hands trembled as she took the present. Pink wrapping paper encased the box, with a large green bow on top.

Cooper bounced to the couch, elegantly sitting on the end, and patted the seat next to him. "Come, sit and open your present. The gift is only a token, but I'm sure you'll enjoy it."

She stiffly joined him, sitting as far away as the couch allowed. The box felt heavy in her hands.

He bounced his legs boyishly, his smile widening to the point that it looked almost painful.

She unwrapped the present, careful not to rip the paper. An old habit; she hated to waste wrapping paper. She fleetingly considered stuffing the paper down his throat, but she needed to be smarter than that. Instead, she let the paper fall to the floor.

"Well, open the box, Maggs." Cooper's smile lost a little of its genuineness as his legs bounced to an even faster tempo.

She opened it and found a complete set of French drawing pencils and a new English sketchpad.

"Do you like it?"

She stared at the pencils. *Pencils are sharp. I can stab him in the throat with a pencil.*

"I like them very much. Thank you, Cooper." An idea flashed in her mind. She smiled and batted her eyes shyly. "I've started to dabble in calligraphy. If it isn't too much to ask, do you think you might be able to bring me a pen? I know they're expensive."

Calligraphy pens are sharper and stronger than pencils. The best are diamond tipped. A good calligraphy pen would make a reasonable dagger.

"Of course I can." He tenderly reached for her chin. She flinched, and his smile vanished as quickly as a flash flood.

She thought she smelled sulfur, and rolled her head back and feigned a dizzy spell.

"Are you all right, Maggs?"

The sulfur smell receded. "I'm just so tired, and a little dizzy."

He clenched his hands into fists. His jaw tightened and his eyes narrowed. "I told that doctor not to give you too much of the sedative. I told him I wanted you alert for my visit! He's going to pay for this!"

She stammered weakly, "I'm sure it's not his fault. Everything is so overwhelming. I just need a little rest." *Touch me again and I will bite your ear off!*

Cooper stood, a deep scowl on his face marring his good looks. "Of course, Maggie. I'll come back when I can." He kicked the discarded wrapping paper on the floor on his way out of the suite.

Please bring the pen so I can stab you in the heart.

CHAPTER 30

Mary led Jack and Tom back into Rachel's office.

Rachel and Aunt Jackie sat on the couch, and The Professor studied the letters on Rachel's computer with a sour expression.

"So what did you uncover?" Rachel asked Mary as Tom shut the door behind them.

Mary slid behind Rachel's desk. "Let me show you." She tapped on a keyboard and the video feeds on the wall vanished, replaced by a single image. "This press release was published in *The Patch,* which is a small local newspaper in upstate New York on August 22, 2013. At the bottom you can see the logo."

She highlighted the symbol, identical to the one from the stationary on which Cooper had written the first note. Mary watched their reaction to the short article. Having a photographic memory, she had no need to review the document again.

"According to the press release, a fire on the property killed one of their employees. Apparently, the main lodge was heavily damaged. The resort said they would rebuild the lodge, making it better, modernizing, expanding, et cetera."

"Did you find out anything else about the fire?" Rachel asked.

"Just these two short articles." Mary added two other pages from *The Patch* to the wall. "The first one simply reported the fire and the one casualty. The second is dated April 2014 and announced that the lodge had been fully reconstructed. A local zoning issue required the resort to post a notice in the paper. A reporter for the newspaper got credit for the article, but it reads like another press release with similar wording and style as the first one."

"Who died in the fire?" The Professor studied the newspaper articles intensely, his arms folded over his thin chest.

"Neither the article about the fire nor the press release mentioned the victim by name. However, I did find a short obituary in a local newspaper close to the resort, dated two days after the fire." The obituary appeared on the wall above the other articles. "A man by the name of John Grant died the same day as the fire. The obituary indicates he worked as a stable hand, but it doesn't say where he worked when he died. The days match up too closely to be a coincidence. I bet he died in that fire."

Jack turned toward Aunt Jackie. "Didn't you say Grandpa worked with horses? Have you ever heard of this guy?"

"This is the place. It has to be." Aunt Jackie's skin turned ash-white.

"Tell us what you know, Aunt Jackie. Don't hold back information from us."

"We need the data," encouraged Tom.

She tugged on her ear and sighed. "I've heard the name before. I was overseas at the time, but your grandfather had a good friend named John Grant. He died in an accident before I returned."

The Professor spoke, his voice heavy and dark. "The subject had already developed a strong attachment to Maggie by the time he gave her that first note. He signed it 'Your Special Friend,' but he has no ability to truly make any friends."

He stroked his goatee tenderly as a cherished pet. "It's impossible to tell with the limited information we have, but I wouldn't be surprised if the subject started this fire. If John Grant was a friend of Maggie's father, perhaps he wanted to show her how powerful and important he was. He would have been young to exhibit that level of malice, but there are other cases of children doing similar things."

"Great," Rachel muttered. "Mary, did you access their records so we can cull through them and find out the true identity of Cooper?"

"I've hacked into their systems. They have a sophisticated encrypted living database, but I found a back door and snuck in. They keep all their client lists off the servers on separate drives. Apparently they don't trust their electronic security to keep them safe. Everyone's worried about hackers these days." She shrugged. "I tried my best, but there's nothing I can do."

Rachel added, "This type of resort would keep those records on the property in a secure location."

Aunt Jackie pushed herself off the couch with a grunt. "Looks like I'm going on a road trip."

"Terrific," Jack muttered.

"Jack and I are coming," Tom said.

"Me too," Mary added.

"This may be dangerous, Mary. You should stay here and see if you can find anything else out through the computers." Tom tried to smile, but his expression withered under the glare she shot his way.

"The files might be encrypted on a separate drive, and you'll need me to retrieve them." Her hands flew to her hips, and her stance defied Tom to say another word about the matter.

For once, he made the smart decision and remained silent.

"Better break out the armory," Aunt Jackie said. "Everyone's going to be prepared. I've brought my own."

She slipped a thin but powerful looking old handgun from her bag—well oiled and glistening.

CHAPTER 31

"Aunt Jackie, I thought you sold insurance after leaving the circus," Jack said. "Something tells me that's not true."

Aunt Jackie smiled. "Who would have told you something like that?"

"You did!" Tom added. "You said you sold policies."

He felt as if someone had knocked the wind out of him. His family kept surprising him. Every time he dug, he unearthed family secrets—first the Fourteenth Colony, then his mom's situation with Cooper, and now Aunt Jackie's strange past. *What am I going to find next?*

"Oh that. I said I *traded* policies, my dear. I never said anything about insurance. *Policies* have nothing to do with insurance."

"Unbelievable," Jack grumbled.

Rachel placed a metal case on top of her desk. "Jackie's experience will come in handy." She popped it open and removed a sleek black pistol. "This is the latest advancement in weaponry. It acts much like a traditional gun, but instead of bullets, it shoots poison darts. The tips are razor sharp and will penetrate most types of armor."

She pointed to a small dial on the handle. "There are three settings. Three is the strongest and will kill the target immediately. Two should knock the average person unconscious for about five hours. One disables the target for an hour or so. The gun contains twelve darts."

"Poison darts?" Aunt Jackie snorted. "You must be joking! We're going to face serious people with real guns!"

Rachel scowled at her. "This weapon is as lethal as your gun. The people at the resort are innocents in all this. This way there will be no hesitation by those who are not as comfortable with killing as you are."

"I think they're an improvement over that relic," added Mary.

"Speaking of relics, Jackie, your pistol has to be over thirty years old," said Rachel. "Don't you think it's time to retire it and try something modern?"

"Never. Excalibur has never failed me. We're a team. I don't need anything *modern.* That's the problem with the world. Everybody wants the new thing, something that makes life easier. The new generation could learn a thing or two from the old ways."

"Your gun has a name?" Jack chuckled.

Aunt Jackie glared at him, and Jack shriveled under the strain.

"Well, I think it's important to keep up with technology," Mary said, interrupting the awkward silence. "The dart pistol will be good for me."

She tapped on the keyboard. The documents vanished off the wall and a wall-sized satellite view of the Lake Country Resort took their place.

"This is the resort. The place is huge, with a golf course, lake, lodge, individual houses, and several other buildings. Its size gives us an advantage. Three roads lead onto the property, all heavily guarded, but the golf course is not watched. We can take this service road along the edge of the course, cross through the grass, and head to the lodge up here." Mary pointed to the largest building toward the middle of the property.

Tom snuck a worried look at his diminutive aunt. "How far is it between the course and the lodge?"

Mary frowned. "A little over two miles separate the course from the lodge at the narrowest point."

"Do you think you can make it?" Jack glared at Aunt Jackie. "We're not going to be able to stop for oxygen."

The old woman bristled. "I'm in better shape than you, racquet boy! Just make sure you keep up."

Mary hid a grin with the back of her hand. "There's a summer ball tonight, so the lodge will be busy."

Aunt Jackie glanced at The Professor. "What about you, shrink? Are you saddling up? We might run into someone who needs psychoanalyzing."

"The Professor will stay behind," answered Rachel, glowering at her. "He'll continue to look into the letters and photographs. We'll try to determine the identities of some of the victims and start to develop a better profile of Cooper."

Jack's phone vibrated and he checked the screen. Doctor Beck called for the third time in the last half hour.

The doctor will have to wait.

He tucked the phone back into his pocket.

CHAPTER 32

Darian sat with his legs crossed on the tiled floor, a tablet at his side. He stroked Lassie's soft yellow fur with a gentle hand, and she wagged her tail and settled into his lap.

"We've been through a lot together. You're the last of my test subjects, the only animal I haven't managed to kill." His voice faded as he completed the thought.

Lassie settled even deeper in his lap, nuzzling her head against his thigh.

"I've taken more blood from you than a vampire, and I'm surprised you don't glow in the dark after all the imaging I've done of your brain. Still, you haven't complained."

Lassie barked once, as if she understood him and agreed.

He scooped up her head in his hands and kissed her on top. "I don't understand why your brain has stopped developing. You're the key to EBF-202, and I need to understand. Jack only has a few days left now."

He showed her the tablet. "This is a full analysis of your blood. There must be something here that makes you different from the rest. Can you just point it out to me?"

Lassie raised her head, looked at the computer, glanced at him, and dropped her head back on his lap with a sympathetic whine.

"I'll take one last vile of blood and a brain scan." He stopped petting her. "But if I can't figure out the secret, I'm going to have to put you to sleep and autopsy your brain. It's the only procedure I can think of that might give me the answer. Maybe I can create a drug from your gray matter. I know it's a lot to ask, but I can't just give up on Jack. He should have his whole life ahead of him. I can't be the one responsible for his death."

Lassie looked up at him, growled, and bit him firmly on the thigh.

CHAPTER 33

The Silver Bullet sped north with Aunt Jackie behind the wheel. She swung the car around slower moving traffic, traversing the highway like a downhill slalom course.

Tom sank his nails into the armrest and sucked in his breath a few times as she narrowly whizzed by cars, tractor-trailers, one speedboat, two tour busses, and an entire motorcycle gang. He was shocked the car could move so fast.

He reconfigured the radio. He couldn't shut it off completely, but he managed to lower the volume. Old-time country music gently wafted through the speakers. He had tried to change the station once, but when Aunt Jackie growled at him, he jerked his hand away from the controls, fearful she might bite him.

The music was still too loud for Jack, mumbling in the back seat next to Mary, who typed on her tablet, lost in her binary world.

Tom tore his eyes off the road and scrutinized his great aunt. *Was she really an assassin?* "So, Aunt Jackie, what exactly did you do with these *policies*?"

She grinned. "I guess you're old enough to know. I worked for the government when I was younger. As a circus performer, I traveled abroad without raising suspicion." She glanced at him. "Did I ever tell you what they called me?"

"Yes, Aunt Jackie, a million times. You were the Sorceress of Secretariat." Tom knew she was trying to distract him, but he wanted to learn more about her prior life. "Getting back to your other job, did you work for the CIA?"

"The Sorceress of Secretariat," Aunt Jackie repeated, ignoring Tom's question. "In some places in the world, they still talk about my performances. There's a Danish museum that runs a five-minute video of my most famous performance. They used to paint my costume right onto my skin. Nothing separated me from the horse or from the audience."

"I'll never sleep again," Jack muttered from the back seat.

"Seriously, Aunt Jackie, that's too much information," Tom said. "Tell me about your other job."

She gripped the steering wheel tighter. "I worked for the government, Thomas. There are agencies you don't know about. When I came home, I took more sophisticated jobs from them. I did things that needed doing."

"How many policies did you cancel?" He wasn't sure he wanted to know the answer. He still had a hard time imagining his diminutive great aunt as a killer, but as the day grew longer, it became easier.

She shrugged. "More than I can remember."

"Did Mom know what you did?"

"Maggie knew enough. That's why she came to me. If anything happened to her, she asked me to protect you boys from Cooper." She huffed. "I guess I screwed that up."

"How could you kill those people?" The question spilled out on its own. Tom understood killing in self-defense or while protecting a loved one, but premeditated murder was something altogether different.

Aunt Jackie stared intensely out the window. "The country had enemies that had to be dealt with. America was different back then. We stood for something—freedom, opportunity, democracy." She shook her head. "That was then. Now the country serves only the rich and powerful, but things will change back. They always do."

"How about for the Fourteenth Colony?" asked Jack from the backseat. "Have you ever canceled a policy for Rachel?"

Aunt Jackie glanced in the rearview mirror. "That's none of your business, sonny boy."

"This is our exit, Aunt Jackie." Tom pointed at a rapidly approaching turn off. "Watch out for the blue car in the right lane."

"What did you say, Thomas?"

"We need this exit!"

Aunt Jackie jerked the wheel to the right, screeching the tires, and slid the car onto the exit ramp at the last possible moment. "You don't have to shout."

The blue car slammed on its brakes to avoid the Silver Bullet, but the unmistakable sound of bumper smashing into bumper sang out as a truck rear-ended the blue car. Tom spun to see the pileup on the highway. Three cars and the one truck had twisted together by the time the Silver Bullet turned off the exit.

Mary navigated Aunt Jackie down a small gravel service road just wide enough for the car. Branches scratched against the Silver Bullet's sides as she had difficulty keeping the car in the middle of the path. When they reached a small widening, Mary directed her to swing the car onto the grass.

When everyone tumbled out, Jack bent and kissed the ground.

Aunt Jackie swung her leg back to kick him, but Tom held her back at that last second.

An almost full moon shone through the clear night sky, providing enough light for them to make their way. Mary led them along an old deer path, past a small stream, around a massive rock outcropping, under a canopy of tree branches, and toward the golf course.

When the manicured fairway came into sight, Tom grabbed Mary by the waist. "Wait!"

The group froze.

He released her and squatted low, swinging his head left and right.

"What's wrong?" Jack asked.

He pointed at two tiny red dots spaced fifty feet apart, sparkling in the dark. They originated from small black boxes thirty feet in the air, affixed to oak trees.

"Those are heat sensors. They've probably installed them around the entire edge of the golf course. They use infrared technology to register any large heat sources that cross the line. That way, they can ignore the small critters and focus on the heat signatures of the larger animals. They can tell deer from bear from humans. If we cross it, security at the resort will know."

"We can still send in Aunt Jackie. She's so small, they'll think she's a raccoon," Jack joked.

Tom shot him a look.

Aunt Jackie stomped down hard on his foot, and pulled Excalibur from her bag. "Can't we shoot the darn things? They won't be able to register anything with a bullet through them."

Tom waved her off. "No, we can't. We would have to take out two of them, and that would definitely be suspicious. They'll know we're here."

There must be a way around them. We need the element of surprise.

He dropped his backpack and rummaged inside. "Got it!" He withdrew a small plastic bottle.

"That's genius, Tom," Mary said.

"What's genius?" Jack asked.

Tom lifted the small bottle. "This is a petrol-based flammable that burns super hot and bright. If we dose one of these loose branches, we can create a torch that will burn out in a few seconds. The heat sensors will be blinded. It will look like a quick flare on the video feed, something these sensors are prone to do. With any luck, they'll think it's a simple malfunction."

Tom scanned the nearby forest. "These sensors are programmed to sense heat sources below them. If I can climb a nearby tree and toss the lit branch so it falls from above, then it will appear like an instant flare-up. The branch should burn bright enough and long enough for us to scoot to the other side without them detecting us. The key is to find the right tree."

He pointed to an oak fifteen feet from the sensors. "That one will work. The sensors detect heat in a band twelve feet or so wide. That oak is far enough away and tall enough that I can toss the branch by the sensors. They'll probably come out and inspect them eventually, but they might not treat it as an emergency. It should buy us time."

Jack found a dead branch and handed it over.

Tom dosed it with the fluid and scampered up the oak tree. When he climbed into position, he lit the branch until it burned white hot, and tossed it high in the air. It landed in the middle of the invisible sensor line.

Tom jumped from the tree.

They huddled together and raced across the imaginary line as one, the light from the burning branch temporarily blinding them.

As they reached the manicured fairway, Tom heard bleating in the distance. "What the heck is that?"

"Sounds like sheep," Jack answered.

"The golf course was designed after a Scottish links style course," Mary explained. "They imported the sheep to make it seem authentic."

"Of course they did," snickered Jack.

All that wealth, thought Tom. *No wonder Mom thought she couldn't tell anyone about Cooper. But now we know, and his money won't protect him for long.*

CHAPTER 34

Reaching the lodge was easier than Tom had imagined.

They trekked across the deserted golf course and used the GPS in Mary's phone to find the starter's station near the first tee. The resort used the latest in living computer technology.

Mary needed a direct line into the hotel's computer systems, and the computer at the small wooden hut served as her portal. More worried about external threats than anything that might originate on resort grounds, the resort staff had left the computer unlocked.

Mary hacked the username and password without difficulty, and injected a cancer through the resort's computer as if it were a vein leading to the hotel's blood stream. Once the resort's system recognized the foreign body, the cancer multiplied and mutated at a faster pace than the resort's defenses could contend with.

Mary now controlled all the security video feeds, heat sensors, and security personnel communications from her tablet. With a wide grin on her face, they piled into an unused golf cart and motored toward the lodge.

The main building resembled a nineteenth century hunting lodge on steroids, with a soaring inverted v-shaped portico, dark brown cedar shingles, large two-story windows, and a steep hunter green tiled roof. Well-placed spotlights lit the three-story building. Two armed guards patrolled the front of the lodge, and a solitary guard, dressed in black, circled the exterior toward the back.

Tom parked the golf cart behind a maple tree.

Mary studied her tablet. "There's no mention on the system where the offline records are kept. My best guess is the general manager's office. It's the largest office on the third floor in the back corner." She pointed to a dark window in the corner of the wooden building. "The ball should be in full swing. Everyone's attention will be in the ballroom, which is on the other side of the lodge."

Aunt Jackie squinted at the building. "Leave the guard to me." She nodded at the lone gunman on patrol.

"Why don't we just send him to the pool instead?" Mary typed on the tablet. "Apparently there's an emergency by the pool house. We should have plenty of time to reach the door before he comes back."

The guard hesitated, checked his mobile computer, and moved away from the lodge toward the pool.

Aunt Jackie eyed the tablet through slanted eyes. "Where were you when I needed help in the business?"

Tom led them at a slow jog to the back door, staying in the shadows. Their feet crunched softly on the grass. After Mary unlocked the door with her computer, he inched it open and, upon seeing an empty hallway, led the small group inside.

Flickering sconces lit the hallway, casting orange light off the wood paneled walls. A live jazz band played in the ballroom, their music loud enough that no one would notice the little noise Tom and the others made. He held the door open as they darted inside the back staircase.

"The video cameras are on a five-minute loop," Mary said. "We can go without being seen, but we won't be able to spot security coming at us either."

Tom raced up the two flights of stairs. At the top, he glanced at Jack. "Are you ready, brother?"

"Whatever it takes."

"We go on three." Tom started the countdown. "One... Two...."

Jack flung open the door and charged into the empty hallway, gun held out.

"I thought we were going on three!" Tom grabbed Jack by the arm.

His brother shrugged him off. "I'm the oldest. I'm first in."

Mary unlocked the general manager's door. A variety of animal heads hung on the walls of the vast office, most big game. Mounted on plaques, deer, moose, elk, zebra, bear, and a lion all stared down at them menacingly, but also a number of birds of prey, like owls, hawks, and one stuffed eagle. A giant black bearskin rug covered the center of the floor. At the far end toward the windows stood a massive desk fashioned out of logs that looked as if Lincoln might have used it as a country lawyer.

Mary shuddered. "Who would want to be surrounded by these dead animals all day?"

"A creep," Aunt Jackie answered. "I'm going to wait outside and keep a lookout." She glided from the room, pistol in hand.

"Okay, so where do we look?" Jack asked.

"Anywhere something seems out of place," Tom said.

Jack gravitated toward the wet bar in the corner while Mary searched the desk.

Tom studied the room, looking for a good hiding spot. He started with the interior wall as the most likely place, and strolled over to investigate.

The animal heads created an unsettling jigsaw puzzle. He examined the plaques closely. A grizzly bear head hung at eye level caught his attention. The oak plaque read, "Momma Grizzly—April 9, 1910." Momma grizzly bears were famous for their protective instincts, and the lodge originally opened in 1910.

Too many coincidences.

The plaque appeared too large and rectangular for the animal's head. Tom glanced at the hardwood floor. Scuffs at the base of the plaque created fine grooves lighter in color than the rest of the room, as if many shoes had stood in this spot over the years to study the fierce creature.

He smiled and felt around the edges of the plaque for a lever. After an unsuccessful pass, he studied the face again. *Come on, this has to be the right plaque.*

He concentrated on the face, his attention drawn to the teeth. There were thirty-nine in all, and he remembered reading that a full-grown grizzly should have forty-two teeth. This one had lost a few over its life. The front left incisor, smoother and shinier than the rest, had an empty space behind it. He reached in and pulled on it. A spring twanged and the plaque swung from the wall.

"I've found the safe, but it's not what we thought it would be."

Hidden behind the plaque was an antique gun safe made from heavy, hunter green steel, with the name Remington inscribed in gold at the top, with a round dial and stainless steel latch.

"Where's the electricity and the computerized locking mechanism?"

Mary searched the web and found a hit. "It's an antique. It opens on a simple three-number combination. First spin of the wheel goes around twice to the right, second once to the left, and the last stops straight at the final number to the right."

Jack sidled over to Tom. "How do we break in?"

Mary studied her tablet. "They used to use dynamite back in the day, or a trained safecracker who could hear the tumbling mechanism behind the steel. When it clicked, that would be the right number."

Tom kicked the wall in frustration. "Great. The damn thing is so old it's more secure than it was a hundred and fifty years ago. We'll never crack it."

"Not so fast, brother. Sometimes, we have to try something besides math and science." Jack slapped him on the back and removed his earplugs. "My hearing has improved over the past few months. Let me give it a go."

Tom held his breath as Jack placed his ear against the cold steel. Jack slowly spun the dial, inching it forward, stopping and going as he went. On the second try, he twisted the latch and swung the door open.

Just as the safe unlocked, the door to the office crashed open. A hulking security guard stood in the doorway, and he didn't look happy.

CHAPTER 35

Jack froze at the sight of the giant security guard and wondered where Aunt Jackie had gone. Before he reached for his dart pistol, her scratchy voice came from behind the enormous guard.

"Move!"

The bear-sized man staggered forward into the room. Blood dripped from his face as he tenderly held his right arm in his left hand.

Aunt Jackie slammed the door shut behind her, shot her foot out, and crunched the back of the man's left knee.

He went down hard on his face in the center of the bearskin rug with a screech. "Help me! She's crazy, that one is!"

Jack stared at her openmouthed, his eyes threatening to pop out of his face and roll on the floor in shock.

She grinned. "I would have killed him, but you all seem squeamish about that sort of thing."

Twang.

Mary shot the guard with a poison dart in the back.

"Nice work," Aunt Jackie said. "Have I told you how much I like you? If only Jack could find someone like you."

"There's no time for that, Aunt Jackie," Tom blurted out, his face reddening.

"Now that's a safe." She whistled and pointed Excalibur at the Remington. "None of that modern crap."

Mary stepped in front of Jack to examine the safe to look for the off-line records.

When he turned to help, a sharp pain split his head and his skull nearly exploded as a fuzzy vision of a face flashed across his mind—a face with deep blue eyes, a perfect tan, and a bright smile.

He focused hard on the face and seeped inside the image, like water soaking into a sponge. As the pain grew more intense, he shook and fell to his knees. His mind filled with thoughts, images... rage. An infant and a stern old woman scowled at him. Other faces stared at him also, expecting answers, decisions. He fell deeper into the image and hazy visions of his mother filled his mind, which filled him with anger and desire and hate. The world turned dark and he collapsed to the floor.

Jack woke to find Tom and Mary's concerned faces pinched tight and hovering over him.

"Are you all right?" Tom asked.

The pain in his head had subsided into a dull ache. "We need to return to the city, Tom. He's close to his shatter point. I sensed him."

"How could you do that?"

"I don't know. These feelings just come to me. This one was intense. I practically saw his face. He's just barely holding on to reality. We have to hurry." He couldn't explain these visions without sounding silly. Tom viewed the world through a black and white scientific prism, whereas Jack had experienced a kaleidoscope of color.

"Mary has what we need," Aunt Jackie said. "There's no sense lingering. Let's move."

She tenderly squeezed his arm. It surprised him.

Tom helped him to his feet. "I'm going to call Doctor Beck, Jack. I don't like these headaches."

"After we get Mom back." He had the uneasy feeling it would be too late anyway. His phone buzzed, but he didn't need to check the number to know it was Darian.

Tom drove as Aunt Jackie sat in the passenger seat and fell asleep, snoring loudly.

Jack grunted from the back. "I can't believe I'm saying this, but turn up the volume on the country music. She sounds like two dogs fighting."

The old records were coded, and Mary tried with no luck cracking it. As the car rolled down the highway, her typing grew louder until Tom thought she might break the keyboard.

"Argh!" she moaned. "I can't break this code without a key. I need the name of one of the guests and their resort number. If I have that, everything else will follow. Without it, the files are useless." She pounded the armrest.

Aunt Jackie woke from her uneasy slumber. "Call Rachel. Maybe she can help."

Mary hit the speaker button and dialed Rachel from Aunt Jackie's secure phone. "We're on our way back. We're all fine. The trip was successful, but I can't break the code for the files. I need the name and number the resort uses for one of the guests."

"Does it have to be an old guest or can it be a current one?" Rachel asked.

"An old one would be best. One from our timeframe would be great, but if I had a recent one, I could figure out the correct format and hack back from there. It will take longer, but it'll give me something to work with."

"Okay, I'll speak to Bacchus about it. The resort seems to fit his crowd. Meet me at the safe house on the Upper West Side. I'll make sure you have clearance to pass the checkpoints. We'll regroup there."

Tom pressed down on the accelerator. He didn't have a premonition like his brother, but he felt time running out just the same.

Cooper gripped the phone. "Do you like the roses, Lori? They're Juliet Roses. I had them flown in from England. Their distinctive peach color should match the rug in the foyer perfectly."

"I threw them in the trash. They're no good."

"Why? I thought you'd love them."

"No, they're too dark. As usual, you...."

He let the phone fall away from his ear and lost track of his wife's complaints as he began to wander around his sanctuary. No one else knew about his safe place in Greenwich Village. Connected to an old apartment building where the poet E.E. Cummings had once lived, his sanctuary was hidden in the basement behind a false wall, where the original wine cellar once stood.

A few people knew he owned the abandoned building. His mom asked him about it once, and he waxed poetically about the connection to Cummings and Dylan Thomas and other nonsense. She didn't really buy it, but she stopped asking about the place, which was all he wanted.

He circled among the wine racks. Digital candles flickered at exactly the same rate and intensity as the candles in the monastery at Mont Saint-Michel in France. The light danced off the glass mason jars—seventy-two of them.

He wished he could remember every Maggie and the moment she had died, but only a dozen stood out over the years: the first one, of course, and some of the young ones. It wasn't his fault. They weren't extraordinary.

He lifted the nearest jar from the rack on which it sat, and the heart inside sloshed to one side. He glanced at the bottom of the jar at the photo attached to it. Yes, he thought he remembered this one. *Didn't she have an accent?*

His wife's voice interrupted his reverie. "When are you coming home? We've got a baby shower planned in two days, and you have to be home for it. You have to attend or—"

"Lori, I have to go. Mom's got this meeting planned with Chinese businessmen that I'm late for."

"Sure, do whatever *Mommy* wants. Just make sure you get home in time."

Click.

He put the jar back, looked at the plain wooden box that sat on top of the oak table, snapped open the bronze latch, and peered inside. Three shiny new calligraphy pens rested on red velvet. The light sparkled off their diamond tips.

He sighed and surveyed his sanctuary. The racks were only a third full.

CHAPTER 36

Darian leaned back in his chair and studied Lassie's latest brain scan and blood reports. Her brain development had stalled right after all the other dogs had died, three months ago.

He had designed EBF-202 to dissolve in the bloodstream, but in the other test subjects, including Jack, the drug never fully dissolved. EBF-202 worked better than EBF-101, partially breaking down in all the subjects. However, enough residue remained to fuel brain development even at a reduced pace, until the pressure on the cranium damaged the brain and the patient died.

Lassie was different. Small traces of EBF-202 lingered in her blood system, but her brain resisted it and she remained stable. The secret must be right in front of him. If he could just see it and understand it, he could save Jack, but it hid from him, taunting him, making him feel helpless.

If self-loathing were an Olympic sport, he would have been a gold medalist.

How hard can it be? Jack is depending upon me.

A tsunami of guilt whipped through his mind. Four months had past since Jack's initial treatment—four months to figure out the secret, four months to tell Jack the truth, four months to do something, *anything*. At first, he'd rationalized he would discover the cure and tell Jack about the treatment with the resolution in hand.

Why worry him over nothing?

Over time, the lie became so large he couldn't confront it. Now, when he finally summoned up the courage to tell Jack, he couldn't reach him.

Darian bashed his forehead on his desk in time with *(I Can't Get No) Satisfaction* by the Rolling Stones. When the song ended, he started toward his small refrigerator and the needle full of EBF-202.

Perhaps it's time.

Vanessa sauntered into the lab without Darian noticing. *He's working and worrying himself to death*, she thought. *Tonight, I'm going to take him away from his troubles. He needs fun. We need fun.*

She cleared her throat at the doorway, and Darian shut off the music. She held a picnic basket in one hand and a bottle of California Cabernet in the other. She swayed toward him, her white lab coat parting down the middle, a string of pearls shifting loosely around her neck.

She spoke in a flirtatious, lilting voice. "I hope you didn't forget about our date tonight, Doctor Beck. I have something special planned for us."

Darian smiled, but it looked forced.

He forgot about the date.

Jack's plight so consumed him lately, he had no room for any other thoughts. Every one of their conversations ended with Jack.

"I'm not sure I will be good company tonight. I'm running out of time. The answer is right here somewhere, and it's making me crazy." He clenched his hand into an angry fist and pounded his thigh.

She sighed. "I understand, but it's late and you need to eat, Doctor. You'll be of no use to anyone if you starve yourself." She placed the picnic basket on the floor and bored her eyes into his to drive the point home.

He relented. "Dinner is a good idea. I feel a little lightheaded."

She grinned, opened the bottle of wine with a soft pop, and poured two glasses. She busied herself by opening the picnic basket and taking out various plastic containers of take-out Chinese food. She possessed many remarkable talents, but cooking wasn't one of them.

She frowned. "I forgot the forks and knives. Be a sweetie and grab some from the kitchen area."

He jumped from his chair. "I'll be right back." He bounded from the office in long, looping strides.

She tossed the knives and forks she had brought into the trashcan and surreptitiously removed a glass vial from her lab coat. She poured the latest mood-enhancing narcotic into both glasses of wine, swirled the red liquid into tiny whirlpools, and smiled to herself.

Darian needed to relax, and she would make sure he did.

Darian finished the remaining wine in his glass with a messy gulp. His mood had improved dramatically. Gone were his worries about Jack and EBF-202, replaced by visions of Vanessa, who let her lab coat drop to the floor. She wore a form fitting, low-cut red dress with spaghetti straps, and a skirt that ended at the top of her thighs. The lab filled with big band jazz compositions she played from her phone. It wasn't Darian's first choice in music, but he swayed against her. Her lips glistened with crimson lipstick, and her perfume lingered in the air like a soft caress.

When he began to trace his mouth and tongue along her neck, she pulled back, shook her head, and playfully scowled at him. "No, no, Doctor Beck. This place has too many windows. I have a better spot planned for us." She waved a card key in front of his nose as if he were a dog, and the key his treat.

"What's the key for?" He read the lettering—*Doctor Wickersham PHD's Office*. "You've got to be kidding me. Does that open Wicky's office?"

She nodded, took his hand, and led him down the hallway to the elevator. When the door closed, she pressed the button for the top floor. He nuzzled the back of her neck, drinking in her perfume and running his hands up her thighs.

"No one should be on the top floor tonight," she whispered. "There's a board meeting."

He didn't care.

The bell rang, the elevator doors opened, and they stumbled giggling into the hallway. He grabbed her hand and raced toward the corner office, skipping as he went. He flung open the door and shouted, "We've scheduled a very important meeting, Clair!"

The leather couch beckoned, so he flopped down while she unzipped her dress. The fabric cascaded gently to the ground, revealing a warm and inviting naked body. He clumsily ripped his Rolling Stones t-shirt over his head and tossed the rest of his garments around the office.

She pounced on top with a purr in her throat, and they lost themselves in the moment.

His heart rate soared as she moaned and clutched his shaggy blond hair. The leather burned his back, but he didn't care as his body shuddered with a blast of energy.

When they were spent, Vanessa laughed and stumbled her way to the bathroom.

Darian stood and had an almost irresistible urge to urinate in Wickersham's trashcan. He eyed it enthusiastically and started calculating distance and angles, when voices wafted in from the waiting room.

"That's odd. Clair left the door open. I'll scold her tomorrow." Wickersham's voice droned on from the hallway and became progressively closer.

Darian bolted into action. He grabbed his clothes, just remembering to snatch his boxers from Wickersham's desk, and raced into the bathroom a second before the office door opened.

Vanessa was already dressed when he lifted his finger to his lips. He wanted to laugh, but the distressed expression on Vanessa's face stopped him.

"I will save the presentations on an external disk for you, Coop. It shouldn't take more than a minute." Wickersham slurred his words.

"So, is Project Qing ready for launch?"

Darian pressed his ear against the door and strained to hear the conversation.

"Almost, Coop. The drug will make the population very susceptible to subliminal suggestions at the right frequency—just below the normal hearing range—but we haven't determined the best dosage yet."

"It also increases productivity, correct? We're not making a population of zombies that won't work for us?"

"That's the best part." Wickersham laughed. "'We can brainwash the ghettos *and* transform them into hard-working citizens at the same time. Some will even work themselves to death without realizing what they're doing."

Darian strangled his small pile of clothes, his hand aching from the pressure.

"And no one knows about the full effects of Project Qing except the project leader and us?"

"We have maintained total secrecy. We used some of the work done for the brain cancer vaccine, some of Doctor Beck's work on EBF-202, and new findings. All the teams on the project have discrete tasks. No one has a clue as to the whole project except Doctor Sanders."

Vanessa flung her arms around Darian's shoulders as he reached for the doorknob. Sweat glistened across his back and his nostrils flared as a crashing sound filled his head. He so wanted to strangle Wickersham.

She held him tight and whispered, "Not now."

"The Vice President is going to be well pleased, Samuel. I can see a new appointment for you—perhaps Surgeon General."

Wickersham chuckled, the voices faded, and the door to the office slammed shut.

Darian turned on Vanessa. "Did you know what Project Qing was about?"

She stepped backed and pressed against the sink. "I don't know the full scope of the project. No one does except Doctor Sanders."

"They're using my research to brainwash the people in the ghettos and make them into working robots." He struggled to grasp the ramifications of the plan. "I have to stop them."

She whispered, "Would it be so bad to have the ghettos more compliant? They need to pull their weight."

For the first time, she reminded him of her father. Her face was suddenly too perfect.

"I think it's time you understand who I am and where I come from."

CHAPTER 37

Maggie slept fitfully, her dreams unearthing a part of her past she would have preferred to leave buried.

Young and back at the Lake Country Resort, it was the year after she had first met Cooper. Thoughts about Mr. Cat had faded to the back of her memory. Cooper returned to the resort that summer, and although she tried to avoid him, he made it impossible. The stables were the only place he wouldn't follow her, but she could only spend so much time with the horses and her father.

He never mentioned Mr. Cat or the events of the prior summer. He started this vacation the same way he had the prior year—funny, friendly, charming, interested in her. He had grown taller, stronger, and more handsome. She convinced herself he was not responsible for Mr. Cat's disappearance. Maybe he'd taken the collar, but the cat could have wandered away on his own. He was a free cat, after all. She was foolish and young, and his eyes were beautiful and his smile appealing.

As the summer dragged on, signs of the volcano started to bubble up and her fear burst back to the surface. In early August, he started to talk about the end of summer and her living with him and his family. She said no, and he got angry. To avoid him, she stayed close to her father in the stables.

One night, late in the summer, her father came home shaken. A guest's prize colt had died inexplicably, and the owner would blame him.

She stormed out of their small apartment with her hands balled up in fists and stomped to the rose garden, where she waited for Cooper.

Sure enough, he appeared, a smug expression on his face. "I haven't seen you in a while, Maggs. You spend too much time in the stables."

"I know you had something to do with that horse, Cooper! You have to tell them so my father doesn't get fired."

He moved close to her, his face pinched together. "I'll tell them if you agree to come live with me and my family."

She imagined rivers of lava bubbling inside his head, the volcano close to erupting.

She felt heat flush her face as she stomped her foot. "I will not!"

He grabbed her by the arms, shook her fiercely and yelled, but what he shouted, she couldn't tell. The words sounded garbled, as if they had a hard time fighting through his anger. The world slowed as fear dulled her mind. She closed her eyes and became dizzy.

"Hey!"

Suddenly, John Grant shoved Cooper away from her and into the dirt.

"Don't touch her," John bellowed in his baritone voice. He worked for Maggie's father and was his best friend. Big, wide in the chest, shoulders, and arms, he loomed larger still as he rose to his feet and puffed out his chest. John had the sweetest personality Maggie had ever known, but this John looked and sounded angry. He even scared her a little.

Cooper stayed silent, dusted himself off, smiled sickly at John, and stalked away seething.

John peered down at her with concern etched into his face. "Are you all right, child?"

"I'm fine, John. It was no big deal."

"No big deal, child? I don't like the look of that one. Does your father know about him?" His big bushy eyebrows made a v-shape on his forehead as he crossed his arms against his chest.

"No. Don't tell him. Promise me you won't tell him! He'll get mad, and he'll be fired."

He frowned. "I promised your Aunt Jackie I'd help look after you. If I find him around you again, I'll have to tell your dad."

Maggie had heard that he planned on asking Aunt Jackie to marry him when she returned from her circus trip in Europe. He thought he had kept it a secret, but everyone knew.

Later, her dream world spun and she found herself thrown into a pitch-black night. She ran after her parents, who sprinted toward the lodge as smoke filled the air and flames lit the horizon like the noon sun. She stumbled to the ground and saw the ambulance and her father jumping in the back. Her mother wept.

"Who got hurt?"

Through the sobs, her mother managed to say, "It's John, sweetie."

Maggie twisted in her bed. She imagined a young Cooper watching her, smiling at her. A nauseous feeling settled in her chest, so she forced her eyes open.

Cooper stared down at her, a cold smile spread across his face.

CHAPTER 38

Rachel unlocked the Upper West Side townhouse, stormed inside, and marched passed Steven into the galley kitchen. The townhouse stood three stories tall with a basement that stretched under the middle of the adjacent street. A cutting edge wave jamming system protected the residents and made it impossible to trace cell phones or citizen cards, shielding the townhouse from prying electronic eyes.

She walked smartly and tossed her Cooper file on the kitchen table. "Charles, I need some help."

Charles Sheppard appeared on the staircase moments later, cupping a glass of Shiraz in the palm of his hand. "Yes, Rachel. You look lovely." He kissed her tenderly on the cheek.

The two were secretly married. The world believed she had died in an accident twenty years earlier, when she chose to run the Fourteenth Colony, a job she could not hope to perform as the public wife of Charles Sheppard. She'd had no choice. She saw the direction the country was headed and needed to act, and even though he'd argued with her, he couldn't help but be *Charles*—the exciting, visionary, celebrity businessperson who revolutionized the world one innovation at a time. The two roles couldn't coexist.

Rachel missed the little, everyday things that should have woven their lives closer together. She told herself the amount of time they spent together wasn't important, but the quality of that time was what counted. It was a lie. Sometimes, she imagined she had made a different choice, one where they fully shared the present. Regret was too big a word for how she felt. Still, going back wasn't an option, and even if she could, she would make the same choice over again.

"I need help with the search for Cooper. We're running out of time to save Maggie. We've stolen the records to the Lake Country Resort guest lists. The information is coded, and Mary is having a hard time cracking the code. She needs the name and number of one of the guests at the resort—hopefully an old client, but anyone would do. Otherwise, she's searching for a leaf in a forest of trees."

"From what you've told me, this resort is an ultra-luxury establishment." He swirled the wine in his glass. "I've never even heard of this place, but there's older money than what runs in my family. I can reach out to the Wine Merchants. One of them might know something."

"Please do, Charles. Maggie doesn't have much time." She squeezed his arm.

Charles walked to the kitchen to retrieve a secure phone, and saw the Cooper File on the table. Drawn to it, he flipped it open. The photographs tumbled onto the kitchen table, and he winced. He detested violence. Watching violent movies gave him troubled dreams afterward, but one of the photos caught his eye. His fingers trembled as he moved the photo close to his face.

"What is it, Charles?" Rachel moved beside him.

"Do you know who this is?" He lowered the picture.

"We've hadn't had any luck identifying the victims yet. That one stands out, though. She least resembles Maggie."

"She's Isabella White." Charles drained the last of the wine from his glass.

He needed a name and number. He was looking for a needle in a haystack, but if he found it, everything else might fall into place.

CHAPTER 39

Darian and Vanessa strolled through the grimy streets of the Upper Manhattan Ghetto. Most of the apartments had boarded up windows, garbage collected on the sidewalks, and an overpowering stench filled the air. She did her best not to think what caused that awful smell. Still, energy and life permeated the neighborhood—music and laughter floated onto the street, and a few open clubs teemed with activity and excitement.

He pointed to some of the buildings as they passed them. "The lucky ones who have a roof over their heads cram into these apartments. They should hold four people, but usually house ten or more. The plumbing often stops working, and forget about heat in the winter time."

She frowned. "Don't these people work? Shouldn't they have more?"

He kicked a plastic container. "These people work hard, some with multiple jobs, but there's no college for them. Even vocational school is a dream most can't realize. Only low-paying jobs are left for them. Without a minimum wage, they're beholden to factory owners, construction companies, or landscaping businesses. Wages are low and there's nothing they can do about it, but even a meager salary is better than nothing."

He pointed to a teenager who snuck out of the back door to a bakery carrying a handful of old rolls.

She whispered. "He's stealing. Shouldn't we do something?"

"I know that bakery. The baker unlocks the back door on purpose and leaves out the old bread. When I lived on the streets I used to do the same thing. The baker will never admit it, but he's giving back the best he can."

She watched the teenager fade into the darkness, and couldn't imagine Darian being so desperate. "How do things become better for these people?"

"Not from brainwashing them!" Darian barked. "They're good people. They have their own system of justice. It's harsh, but it works, for the most part. They just need opportunities."

He paused. They stood on the edge of the overpass.

Vanessa stood close to him. The mood-enhancing drug having waned, she trembled as she took his arm. "What are they all doing here? Don't they have a place to go?"

Four little groups scattered along the pavement living in cardboard boxes.

Darian led her toward a spot that seemed to hold some significance for him. "There's no place for these people to go. There are thousands of them in the ghetto. It doesn't take much to make someone homeless—they become sick, or lose a job, or... become addicted to drugs or booze or anything they can't afford. With no cushion, they become destitute in the blink of an eye."

He slowed his gait. "This is the spot where I thought my mom was about to die. I was nine." He glanced around as if death lurked nearby, about to take him.

She clutched his arm as a youngster approached them.

No older than ten, dirt stained the girl's face beneath matted and stringy hair. She struggled to move in shorts too big for her and a t-shirt too tight. She glanced up at them with beautiful, sad eyes. They were stunning. She was stunning.

"Do you want a date?" the girl asked, batting her eyes.

Vanessa gasped and turned away.

Darian squatted low and pointed toward a prone figure against the greasy, concrete floor under the overpass. "Is that your mom?"

The girl glanced back. "Yeah. She's sick and can't party tonight, but we need money, so I can. I know what to do."

Darian reached into his pocket and gave the girl all the money he had. When she took it, he shouted, "Go away! We don't want to be bothered by your type."

He dropped on the couch beside her and crossed his legs. His fine woolen trousers creased perfectly. *Why isn't she smiling? This apartment is better than any place she has lived in her miserable life!*

"Is the suite to your liking? You'll only be here for a short time. I have bigger plans for us." The words froze in the air from the frosty quality to his voice.

Maggie's lips twitched upward. "It's fine."

Cooper scowled. Fine was not the word he desired. *Perhaps she is overwhelmed.*

He looked away from her, and his mind flashed toward a conversation he had with his mother earlier in the day. "Don't be *overwhelmed* by events, son. I will help you sort them out."

The great Ethel Simmens will help me sort out events! Why doesn't she believe in me? I can sort them out on my own!

He snapped back to the present as his fingernails dug into the wooden box.

Maggie melted further into the armrest, her complexion turning paler.

He chased away his mother with a shake of his head. "Perhaps this will improve your mood." He handed the box to Maggie and noticed her trembling hands. *That's better.*

She flipped open the top and peered inside.

He sensed her excitement and his spirits improved. "They are the most expensive calligraphy pens on the market," he announced happily.

She lifted one from the box. Her hands quivered as the light danced off the diamond tip. "Thank you."

"It's a shame you married that loser. What was his name again?" He asked even though he knew the name.

Maggie tore her eyes from the pen. "Do you mean Paul?"

"Yes, Paul was his name—a common name for a common guy. He could never afford to buy you the things you deserved. Such a pity he died in a car crash." He clucked his tongue, enjoying himself.

She clenched her fist around the pen.

"I understand why you felt unworthy of being with me, but Paul? Really? And those sons of yours."

Her eyes narrowed. "My sons?"

"You shouldn't blame yourself." He smiled reassuringly. "They were corrupted by Paul's DNA, no doubt. The young one, Tom, has potential. He scored high on his tests, but just think what he would be able to accomplish with the proper schooling." He shook his head. "But Jack, only a tennis instructor?"

An irresistible urge to hurt her overcame him. It felt good to lash out.

She started shaking.

"I'll tell you a secret," he whispered. "I took a tennis lesson with Jack a year ago—a short one, only fifteen minutes before playing a match at the country club where he works. Still, he wasn't any good. Maybe his nerves got to him, but I think he should try something else with his life. Perhaps ditch digging?" He laughed.

Maggie dropped her gaze to his neck, unable apparently to look him in the face.

"You'll never be able to see them again, of course. They'll think you died, but I'll keep tabs on them. I wouldn't want any accidents to happen to them." He sneered.

Maggie's face twisted together. She reared her hand back and lunged for his neck, holding the shiny diamond tip out in front of her like a dagger.

He saw the tip rush toward him and yanked his head back against the couch at the last second. The pen missed the mark and jabbed into his thigh. He screeched and backhanded her hard across the face, sending her sprawling to the floor.

He wrenched the bloody pen from his leg. "How dare you!"

He snatched the wooden box and smashed it against her head, splintering the wood, and Maggie collapsed on the floor.

"I've taken you away from your miserable life, and this is how you repay me!"

He kicked her in the stomach. She groaned, and he kicked her again.

He thought of his pregnant wife and her growing belly and kicked her again, hard. She rolled over into a fetal position and whimpered.

He brought his foot up to stomp on her head but stopped himself.

"On further thought, your boys should know where you are. I think I'll invite them over." Pure venom dripped from his voice.

She tried to talk but had difficulty breathing. Pain fired through her ribcage and her lungs. "No, I'm sorry. I'll do anything," she squeaked, gasping for air.

He barely heard her, having already turned to limp out of the room.

Cooper faced his two most trusted and well-trained security guys, the

Peterson twins. They had helped him take Maggie from her apartment. "I want you to find Tom and Jack and bring them to me."

They nodded.

"I don't care if you hurt them, but bring them alive. Understood?"

They smiled.

He called them Tick and Tock—identical twins trained from an early age to be lethal and to do his bidding. They had certain vices. So long as Cooper kept them satiated, they did whatever he wanted with relish.

CHAPTER 41

Jackie stared angrily at Rachel. "I don't want to work with Gabriel and Moses on this."

Rachel frowned. "Why not? You've worked with them before."

Jackie wandered to the small bedroom window while Rachel sat patiently on the edge of the bed. She had poured herself three fingers worth of tequila and knocked it down in two noisy gulps. "It's not that I don't trust them. It's just not a good idea."

"They won't have any problem using lethal force. That should make you happy."

Jackie turned. "Once we find Maggie, I want to kill Cooper. I won't let Gabriel or Moses do it. I won't!"

"Cooper killed Moses's sister and Gabriel's significant other. They should have the first claim." Rachel leaned forward. "I don't understand. You know how these things play out."

Jackie sighed as she reached for the half empty bottle of Riazul tequila, and poured herself another healthy glass before settling next to Rachel. "I lied earlier. I knew John Grant. He was the love of my life. He died while I worked for the government and traveled around Europe in the circus. The government work was only a temporary assignment back then. I was about to come home when I got the phone call."

Her voice broke and she swallowed half the booze in her glass. "I'm such an old fool, beyond redemption. When I heard about John's death, I became so angry I couldn't come back. The world turned black for me. I committed to the government and was lost. Everything was lost for me."

"Everything?"

"I might have had a normal life. I wanted to marry, maybe have a family. I wanted those things with John. Cooper stole that life from me. After John, I wanted to hurt people. I've lived a life of killing and shadows and hate because of him."

Rachel squeezed her shoulder. "I never realized how you felt, but Gabriel and Moses know about Cooper and Izzy. Charles had to tell them. We need their help, for the Fourteenth Colony and for the country. They need closure, too."

Jackie glanced back toward the window and seemed to shrink into her sadness, into herself.

"It hasn't been all hate for you. You love Maggie and those boys. They know that. Besides, with Gabriel and Moses involved, Charles has to give you Steven. He's the best. He could prove invaluable."

Jackie lifted her glass and the rest of the alcohol slid into her mouth. "Steven has the look."

"The look?"

"The look of a killer. I know that look. I see it every day in the mirror." Jackie said.

She turned to face her. "Gabriel and Moses can be part of this. I can't stop that, but I'm going to be the one who puts a bullet in that monster's skull."

Steven had retrieved Gabriel and Moses on Charles's orders. One look at the photograph of Isabella White and the two came willingly.

Charles sat with Tom and the two ghetto leaders around a large round table in the basement. Rachel, Steven, Jack, and Aunt Jackie rested in the upstairs bedrooms.

Jack suffered from another severe headache. He looked terrible—drawn, tired, and weak—so Tom forced him into a bedroom for some rest, promising to wake him when something happened.

It had been a long day for everyone. Mary worked a computer toward the far end of the room. They waited for her to crack the code on her own, or with the help of a name and number from the Wine Merchants that hadn't arrived yet.

Wanting to break the tense mood, Charles talked about his favorite topic—the Knicks basketball team, which he owned. "I have an important decision to make. It will change the entire future of the world. Do I draft the point guard from the University of Phoenix or the power forward from Miami College?"

Moses and Tom were both Knicks fans.

Tom said, "Draft Walt Monroe from Phoenix. Statistically, point guard is the most important position on the team. Three of the last four champions had all-star point guards. With Monroe, we'll be the favorite to win next year."

Moses shook his head. "Walt is a great player. He comes from New York. I've met him, but he's not going to last long."

"Why?" Charles asked.

"I get these feelings sometimes when I touch someone. They're hard to explain. He likes to drive too fast. I'd be worried about his longevity."

Gabriel grunted. "I'd listen to him, Charles. Moses is never wrong about these things."

Moses shrugged knowingly.

The phone rang. Sheppard answered, talked briefly, and hung up. A smile spread across his face. "I've got a name and number. Five years ago, one of the Wine Merchants stayed at the Lake Country Resort as a guest of a family friend. The official resort name and number of his friend was Anthony 777."

CHAPTER 42

Shafts of sunlight streamed through the windows in Darian's studio apartment. Vanessa slept in his bed. Her body moved up and down to a steady rhythm.

His head pounded to a faster beat.

His tablet was open on the kitchen table and he held his mobile phone. Xavier Daniels was the Sheppard Group's representative on the hospital board. He was also the acting head of the Sheppard Group, in charge while Charles Sheppard fulfilled his duties as Secretary of Domestic Priorities.

He dialed Xavier's office.

A smooth sounding male assistant answered on the first ring. "Xavier Daniels's office."

"My name is Darian Beck. I'm a doctor at the New York Research and Teaching Hospital. I need to speak to Mr. Daniels immediately."

"Is this a private matter?" the assistant asked. He sounded worried.

"Yes, and the situation is grave."

"Please hold."

Darian waited, feeling like a heel. He hadn't lied exactly, but he knew the assistant had misunderstood him.

"This is Xavier," answered a breathless voice. "What's wrong?"

"I'm Doctor Darian Beck. I head a research team at the hospital. There's an emergency Charles Sheppard needs to know about immediately."

Silence hung on the line for a moment like wet clothes on a clothesline. "I thought there was a health emergency for someone in my family. This is highly irregular. We're on the hospital board, but there is a proper chain of command for these types of things. You should speak to the head of research."

Darian spoke quickly, before Xavier could hang up. "I don't know if Project Qing or EBF-202 mean anything to you, but the hospital is involved in secretive research projects with explosive ramifications. They're perverting science. I can't go to the head of research. He's in on it."

The phone line stayed open for ten seconds, then Xavier sighed. "I thought your name sounded familiar. I've heard of your project, EBF-202, before, but I don't know anything about a Project Qing. What's the problem?"

"I will only speak to Charles Sheppard about these matters. He needs to hear what I have to say. He can reach me at this number."

Darian disconnected the call and wondered how long it would be before government security personnel arrested him. He should have figured out something better to do, but he had no choice. His guilt over the role EBF-202 played in Project Qing overcame him and forced him to reach out to Sheppard, even if the odds of success were against him.

He hadn't noticed Vanessa's eyes opened. He turned to face her and she quickly closed them and began to stir, stretching and yawning like a cat.

He strolled to the foot of the bed. "I'm not sure what type of wine you bought yesterday, but my head's pounding."

"Mine too. It must have been bad somehow." She brushed hair from her face. "I didn't know you were from the ghetto. I just assumed... well, I don't really know what I assumed."

"I thought you deserved to know. Hopefully you see why Project Qing is wrong. Those people don't need to be brainwashed and made into some type of brainless working robots. They need a fair chance and an opportunity."

"I never thought about it like that before." She looked at the time projected on the wall and bolted out of the bed. "I've got to go. I'm going to be late." She padded into the bathroom naked.

Darian also glanced at the time. Ten minutes had past since he called Xavier.

I wonder if I'll have another ten.

CHAPTER 43

Charles watched as Mary faced the group in the basement, her voice clear and confident. "With help from Mr. Sheppard, I've been able to decode the guest registries from 2010 to 2014. There are two hundred and twenty-eight family names on the list." She handed them each a sheet of paper.

Rachel whistled. "This is quite a list. Some of the oldest and most powerful families in the country are on it."

"The Cooper we're looking for might not even be on this paper," Tom said. "He could've been a guest of one of these families. We still might not have the right name. On average, each probably had five different guests over a summer—that's another 1,140 people. The numbers start to add up."

"Tom's right," Mary answered tersely. "But we have to start with these names. Let's divide up the list among ourselves, research our families, and see how many Coopers show up. It's a distinctive name. With any luck, we'll find our man. Remember, we only have family names, so we must research the entire family tree—everyone who shares the same last name."

Charles's private line rang. He excused himself and left the main area for the small room next door. "Hello?"

"Charles, this is Xavier. I'm sorry to bother you, but something weird came up."

He plunked down in a leather chair and placed the list Mary had compiled on a table next to him. "Just weird, Xavier? That would be a relief right about now."

"I'm not sure how much of a relief this will be. I just received a phone call from a Doctor Beck. He works at the New York Hospital. He said something sinister is going on in the research department. Apparently two projects, EBF-202 and a Project Qing, have some type of improper behavior or misuse. I know he's the team leader on EBF-202."

"I've been briefed on EBF-202. The drug is very promising, but I've never heard about a Project Qing before. Did he elaborate on his concerns?" He lifted Mary's list and absentmindedly started to review it while talking to Xavier.

"He said he would only talk to you about it. He sounded serious, Charles. I looked into the name. Qing was the last great Chinese dynasty. The Opium Wars were waged under it."

"Terrific. Did he say anything else?"

"Just that the head of research at the hospital is in on it."

"That *is* weird. It sounds like something I'll want to investigate, but right now, other more pressing concerns are squeezing me." His eyes tripped on a name from the list. "Xavier, what's the name of the vice president's chief of staff?"

"Cooper Simmens. He's the vice president's younger cousin."

"How old is he?

"He keeps in good shape, but I'd say he's around forty or so."

"Do you recall what color his eyes are?"

"Sure, he was at the board meeting for the hospital last night. They're blue."

"Thanks, Xavier." Charles lowered the paper.

The Simmens family was one of the most powerful families in the country, which made going after Cooper Simmens hard and dangerous.

He felt his resolve buckle. He needed to take another risk.

CHAPTER 44

"What aren't you telling me, Charles?" Rachel stood close to her husband, alone in one of the upstairs bedrooms. "I know that look on your face."

A laptop lay open on the bed. "I was just doing some research."

She kept her eyes focused on him. "I can see the laptop, but I asked you what you're keeping from me. I've known you for forty years. You've never been able to keep a secret from me, and you aren't going to be able to do it now." She crossed her arms over her chest.

"Sometimes, I think you can read my mind." Charles sighed. "One of the names on the list caught my attention."

"Which one?" She tapped her foot impatiently.

"Simmens. The vice president's chief of staff is Cooper Simmens. He's the vice president's cousin."

Rachel's arms fell to her side. "That's not good. I've heard Ethel runs that clan with an iron grip."

Charles nodded.

Rachel frowned. "The Professor said Cooper would likely have a dominating parental figure in his life. Ethel would fit. Does he have blue eyes?"

Charles lifted the laptop. "This is a dossier on Cooper Simmens. It was risky for me to obtain it. Homeland Security vetted him before he became chief of the vice president's staff. "

He turned the screen so Rachel could see it. On the screen Cooper

Simmens sat behind a desk, grinning shrewdly, his deep tan contrasting with his white shirt and his sparkling light blue eyes.

She scanned the rest of his information. "He graduated from Princeton in the top ten percent of his class. That fits, although The Professor thought he would have done worse. He's forty-three years old. That's about right. Maggie is forty-one. It says he worked for the Simmens Group in their hotel division since he graduated from Princeton, a job like that would certainly let him travel freely. He's been the chief of staff for his cousin for the last four years."

She finished reading the rest of the report a few minutes later and handed the laptop back. "He's going to be hard to reach. The Simmens family employs heavy security. They don't only utilize Secret Service, but private guards also."

Charles closed the laptop. "I don't need to tell you that this is a very sensitive situation. Crossing the Simmens family is not something to do lightly." He brushed his white hair to the side of his face. "Cooper Simmens's cousin will likely run unopposed to replace the President."

"I don't care if Peter Perfect is the King of England," Rachel said sternly. "This is Maggie we're talking about. We've got to find a way to grab his cousin and make him talk. We don't have much time. It might be too late already."

He dropped the laptop on the bed. "Yes, of course you're right. We'll think of something. Give me a little bit of time. We need a way to grab him. We can't barge into the Simmens estate with guns blasting."

"Mary's going to find him on her own. It's just a matter of time."

"I understand. I'm working on it, and I *will* think of something."

Rachel moved toward the door and he grabbed her arm. "Another thing popped up this morning. A Doctor Beck called Xavier about research projects in the New York Research and Teaching Hospital. You know him, don't you?"

"He's the doctor who treated Jack a few months ago. Let's ask him."

They found Jack hunched over a computer screen researching names from Mary's list. "Jack, what can you tell me about Doctor Beck?"

He glanced up from the screen. "Doctor Beck's a good guy. I'm helping him in a brain trauma study. Why?"

Charles leaned toward him. "He called someone close to me and said he needed to speak with me. He said something about research projects. He made it sound ominous."

Jack pulled out his cell phone. "I have his number right here. You should call him. He's not the type of guy to make something up."

CHAPTER 45

Darian pointed to the computer simulation projected on the wall. Each variation ended with the screen flashing the same red words: "Subject Deceased." George and Brenda studied the results somberly. The analysis surprised no one.

"I'm almost out of ideas," Darian said wearily. "According to the computer analysis, Jack only has a few days left at most."

"Have you told him?" George asked.

Darian shook his head. "I can't reach him or his mom. I've left a dozen messages for them both, but so far, neither one called me back."

"What about Jack's brother, Tom? Have you tried him?" Brenda asked.

Darian stopped the computer simulation and the endless loop of death that depressed him. "Jack's an adult. I shouldn't have called his mom as it is, but if I don't hear from one of them soon, I guess I'll call Tom."

He leaned heavily against the stationary bike. "There's only one more thing left to try at this point. We need to put Lassie down and autopsy her brain. Perhaps we can learn what her body has done to stop her brain development. She could be producing a chemical that remains in her brain tissue, one we can't register with the other tests. It's a long shot, but it might work."

"But Lassie's so valuable to the ongoing research, Darian," George protested. "She proves EBF-202 works. If we put her down now, we'll lose out on months of valuable data, data that will lead to a breakthrough. As you said, the autopsy's a long shot. We're unlikely to gain useful information from it that could save Jack."

"We must do something, George. Jack's a human being. He's a great guy. It wouldn't be right to let him go without trying everything." Brenda's voice cracked.

George nodded. "Of course we should do the best for Jack! Bring him in, and let's try our best guess. We know EBF-202 breaks down in the body more quickly than EBF-101 did. We can try other drugs. It would be as long a shot as anything we could find out from autopsying Lassie now." George rubbed his face. "He only has a few days, and EBF-202 will eventually save millions of lives. If we delay the development of the drug now, we'll be sentencing thousands to death. We need to look at the big picture, too."

Darian's phone buzzed. An unfamiliar number flashed on the screen, and his heart skipped a beat. He had spent most of the morning looking over his shoulder, sure a government agent would come for him, but until now, nothing had happened.

He waved at George, cutting him off, and took the call. "This is Doctor Beck."

"I am Charles Sheppard. I understand you want to talk to me."

Darian's mind spun. He never thought Charles would actually call him. "How do I know you're Sheppard?"

The voice chuckled into the phone. "I guess we're going to have to meet for you to be certain. There's a black sedan parked by the employee exit to the hospital. Go to the car."

He nervously glanced at George and Brenda. "Now isn't a great time."

"If you want to see me, you'll have to get in the sedan. It'll leave in five minutes. The decision is yours." The call disconnected.

"What's going on?" George asked.

"I need to step out for a while. Think about what we should do here. If you can find an alternative treatment for Jack, then I'm game. Otherwise, start the autopsy in two hours if I'm not back by then." Darian removed a thin envelope from his back pocket and handed it to George. "If I don't come back by tonight, read the letter. It explains everything."

George took the paper without a word.

"I have to go." He slipped on his flip-flops and raced from the lab. As he reached the elevator, he spotted Vanessa in the distance coming toward him from the restricted Project Qing area.

"Where are you going?" she called out.

He hesitated as the elevator doors opened. "I'll be back soon." He darted into the waiting elevator and tapped the lobby button.

The black sedan waited for him on the street. As he approached, the passenger side window slid down, and the driver said, "Get in the back, Doctor Beck."

Darian opened the back door and jumped in. When the door shut, the driver locked it from the front.

"Where's Sheppard?"

A bulletproof glass partition rose between the front and backseats, the windows and the partition turning black.

An embedded screen in the back of the seat in front of him flickered to life as the car pulled away from the curb. The driver's grim face filled the screen. "There's a hood on the seat next to you. I'll tell you when to put it on. If you don't, you will never leave the car alive."

The screen went black.

What have I done?

CHAPTER 46

Maggie's subconscious churned up her past in a tornado of dark memories and deposited her in the midst of a dream. The powerful pain medication she took before going to sleep enhanced it, making it more vivid than a normal dream—the colors and textures sharper and the emotions more intense.

Battered and bruised, she lay alone in a hospital bed, and a couple of pillows in rough cases propped up her head. Though weary, her spirits soared. Paul had gone to the cafeteria, his coat draped over the chair in the corner of the room.

A large male nurse wheeled a bassinet into the room and smiled as he approached. "Little Jack needs his momma."

Jack's face had turned beet red as he angrily demanded his momma. The nurse rolled the bassinet next to her bed, and Maggie noticed a black and white stuffed cat tucked next to him with a note tied around the plush toy's neck.

"Did Paul buy him the stuffed toy?" she asked no one in particular. It would be just like him to slip out to the gift shop and buy his new son a toy, although why would he choose a cat? "Let me see the note."

The nurse handed her the toy, and her hand dug into its surprisingly soft fibers.

Dear Maggs,

I wonder what type of heavenly children we will have together. Of course, Jack will need to disappear.

Your Special Friend,

Cooper

Maggie glanced at the cat and noticed the collar—the same blue collar she'd made for Mr. Cat all those years ago. An old bloodstain marred the inside of the fabric.

She screamed and threw the stuffed toy at the door.

She woke with the scream still on her lips.

Terry leaned in close. "Are you okay?" He carried a tin tray containing a bowl of chicken consommé, tea, and a toasted baguette slice, and placed it on the table next to the bed.

She sat up and winced from the sharp pain in her broken ribs and the ache in her head. "I've been better."

He clucked his tongue. "That must have been a really nasty fall you took."

She glared at the young man. "You and I both know that I didn't take a fall."

"You should be more careful next time." He shot her a knowing look.

She felt a chill. *Is he trying to warn me? Will he help me?*

"Terry, be a dear and grab me my pencils and the sketchpad."

He returned with the pad and pencils.

While he arranged the food on the tray, she scribbled a quick note and furtively ripped it from the pad.

"Is there anything else you need right now?"

"I'm a little tired. Can you take back the pad?"

When he reached his hand out for the pad, she discreetly slipped her note into his palm.

"You should eat. Food will help you build up your strength."

She smiled weakly and nodded.

When Terry closed the door to the suite, he opened his palm and read the note.

Please call my boys to warn them. He's going to kill them.

He smiled, rolled the note into a ball, and popped it in his mouth. It always surprised him how easily he could manipulate the Maggies. Just give them a bit of hope and they always jumped.

CHAPTER 47

Vanessa strolled into her father's waiting room.

Clair sat staring sourly at her computer monitor, and glanced up from her screen with a forced smile on her face. "Good morning. Your father is waiting for you."

Vanessa paused at seeing the sadness behind Clair's eyes. "Why are you so upset?"

"A riot erupted in a Florida ghetto last night. The radicals turned over government cars and raided an armory. They say *communists* are to blame." She whispered the word *communists* as if it were bad luck to speak it out loud. "The military is sweeping in to round them up."

She shook her head and a frown replaced her smile.

"Communists? Yeah, sure," Vanessa muttered as she continued into her father's office. The government used an assortment of bogeymen to cover their harsh treatment of citizens, usually rotating between communists, artists, organic farmers, and liberals.

Her father perched regally behind his desk while George and Doctor Sanders sat facing him. As she entered the room, he enthusiastically waved for her to come close. "We've saved a chair for you."

Why are Doctor Sanders and George meeting together with my dad? And where is Darian?

She trudged toward the one empty chair, and both men stood politely. She greeted them with an empty smile and a nod of her head. With no other options, she sat in the chair and faced her father, donning a pleasant mask.

"I'm sure you're wondering why you were called into this meeting," her father said. "We are doing an important presentation tonight on Project Qing and EBF-202, and we would like you to attend." While unable to express much emotion with his face, he used his voice to emote a wide range of feelings, as a concert violinist might with his bow.

Over the years, she had become attuned to those nuances, and she sensed a certain level of giddiness laced with concern in her father's tone.

Hiding her surprise well, she smiled at the two doctors sitting next to her. "Will Doctor Beck be joining us?"

The pleasantness vanished from her father's voice. "Doctor Beck won't be attending the presentation. His behavior has become too erratic. This presentation is for extremely important hospital benefactors. George is taking over for Doctor Beck and will discuss EBF-202. You'll be at the meeting as an observer. It will give you a chance to understand more about the entire project you're working on. It was Doctor Sanders's idea to include you."

"Are you taking Doctor Beck off EBF-202?"

The temperature in the office dropped off a cliff as her father leaned forward. "That's not your concern. We will leave at 8 P.M. Let's meet in my office by 7:45. If you two doctors wouldn't mind, I'd like to speak to Vanessa alone for a moment."

They scooted out of the room, looking happy to be dismissed.

Wickersham somberly pointed at the couch. "Let's have a quiet conversation."

Vanessa cringed as she remembered the previous night—the last time she had been on the couch with Darian—but she reluctantly followed her father and sat next to him.

"Nessa, you know I always have your best interests in mind, don't you?" He spoke softly, as if she were still a child. He always called her Nessa when he wanted something from her. "You and I have developed certain rules of conduct over the years. I don't inquire about your personal relationships, and you respect my privacy as well, right?"

A pit grew in her stomach and all she could do was nod.

"Good. It's always been that way for us, but this time is different. Your... dalliance with Doctor Beck must end. He's a subversive. Yes, he's brilliant, and I understand that many women find him attractive, but he's dangerous and you will never see him again."

Her throat tightened. "You know about my relationship with Darian?"

He interlaced his fingers on his lap. "Nessa, these are highly secretive and important research projects. We have Doctor Beck under surveillance. Don't be so naïve. Homeland can spy on anyone they suspect might be dangerous. You would be surprised what they know about all of us."

"Why did you say that I'll never see him again?" She turned angry as she narrowed her eyes. "What did you do?"

He shrugged. "I would never *do* anything. I respect Doctor Beck. He's brilliant, but others who are interested in these research projects might think otherwise. I'm sure he'll be reassigned to another, less sensitive project."

"You're wrong about Darian." She considered arguing with him, but paused as she remembered the anxious look on Darian's face as he darted into the elevator in a hurry, and felt her blood turn to ice water.

"There are things concerning Doctor Beck's past that would shock you, dangerous personality traits. He's unstable. I will not debate you about this!"

He must have noticed the angry expression on Vanessa's face because he softened his voice. "Tonight's presentation is a big deal for your career. You're going to meet some very important people. The vice president and his chief of staff will be at the meeting. Forget about Doctor Beck. He can fend for himself. He was never good enough for you, anyway."

She wiped her true feelings from her face, put her mask back on and smiled blandly. She recalled a similar discussion she had with him when she was twelve. After she'd caught her father in an intimate relationship with a neighbor, he bought her a pony for her silence.

Ponies wouldn't work this time.

CHAPTER 48

Vanessa marched into the restricted Project Qing area and sought out Doctor Sanders, who sat in his office and studied his computer monitor while biting his lower lip. A half-formed plan swirled in her head like a gathering storm. She knocked softly on his open door.

In his late forties, he wore a thin gray mustache and a crew cut. His eyes scurried up to see her and then flickered back to his screen. He reminded her of a rat with quick darting movements.

"What can I do for you?"

There's no way he wants me at that meeting, Vanessa thought. *This is my father's doing. A handful of more senior researchers deserved to be at the meeting before me.*

She leaned against his desk and spoke with a tired, raspy voice. "I think I'm coming down with... something. Would you mind if I take the rest of the day off?" She coughed into her hand.

He glanced from the monitor to measure her for a moment, frowned, and leaned back in his chair. "Yes, you look a little under the weather. By all means go home, but make sure you come back by 7:45. This meeting is a great opportunity for you to understand the big picture." He pulled an antibiotic wipe from an industrial-sized box next to his keyboard, and started rubbing his hands energetically.

"Thank you, Doctor. I wouldn't miss the meeting for anything." She smiled weakly and left him in his office to review the latest draft of his presentation and bite his lower lip.

She strode from the Project Qing area clutching her cell phone in her hand, and started to speed dial Darian's phone, but hesitated.

If they monitor Darian, why wouldn't they monitor me?

She found an empty office, slipped inside, shut the door behind her, dialed him from an unused phone, and got his voice mail. She hung up without leaving a message.

Her head spun. *What do I do next? Darian wanted to reach out to Charles Sheppard.* She reviewed the history function on her phone. Last month, he had called Jack from her phone because his battery went dead.

Yes, here it is.

Darian had mentioned Jack knew Sheppard somehow. She dialed the number on the facility phone and waited anxiously.

Jack answered. "Hello?"

"Jack, my name is Vanessa. I'm a friend of Darian's. You've met me once. I'm worried that he's in trouble. Do you have a way of reaching Charles Sheppard?

"What type of trouble?"

"Serious trouble, Jack. I know he wanted to reach Sheppard, but I don't think he had the chance." Her eyes fluttered to the office door, as she half expected her father to barge in.

"Hold on a second."

She counted off the time and wondered if she had gone crazy. She could get in real trouble, but Darian was a good man, even if he was born poor. She couldn't stand idly by because her career would benefit. He needed help.

He'd help me.

"Hello, this is Charles Sheppard."

She spoke in one quick desperate breath. "Mr. Sheppard, I'm a friend of Doctor Darian Beck. He wanted to reach you and tell you about a secret research project here at the hospital. I think something terrible has happened to him."

"I will send a black sedan for you in twenty minutes. The car will wait for you in the parking lot. Don't tell anyone where you're going. I don't know who you can trust."

Vanessa nervously drummed her fingers against a wooden table in a plain interrogation room with a heavy steel door. She had no idea where she was.

The door opened and Charles Sheppard, accompanied by a medium-built man with an athletic gain and dangerous eyes, strolled into the room. Charles held his hand out toward her and greeted her warmly. "I'm Charles Sheppard and this is Steven. It's nice to meet you, Ms. Wickersham. I'm sorry about all the secrecy. The government has certain secret locations only authorized personnel are aware of."

She shook his hand. "Thank you for meeting with me, Mr. Sheppard. I didn't know where else to turn." She glanced toward Steven, her eyes lingering over the handgun at his side.

"You can talk freely in front of Steven," Charles said with a smile. "I wouldn't trouble yourself about the pistol. He could kill both of us in a few seconds without any weapons. But not to worry. He's normally a pussycat."

"Wonderful," she muttered.

"I understand you're worried about Doctor Beck's safety. Why?"

"Darian and I overheard a conversation at the hospital between my father and the vice president's chief of staff late last night. They mentioned a Project Qing. Are you familiar with it?"

He shook his head.

"One research team has secretly used Darian's research on EBF-202 to create a new drug that can brainwash people living in the ghettos. The drug makes them susceptible to subliminal messages and increases their work drive."

"Are you sure?"

"Yes. I'm on the project. The research is kept scattered with discrete assignments, but now that I know the objective of the project, everything fits. I'm sure we heard correctly."

"Are you positive the vice president's chief of staff was part of this conversation?"

"Yes."

"Interesting." He flattened his hands together and brought the tips of his fingers up to his lips. "Why do you think Doctor Beck is in trouble?"

"I overheard him calling someone in your office named Xavier Daniel this morning. Darian was anxious to talk to you about the ramifications of the research projects." She brushed lose strands of hair from her eyes. "He left the hospital in a hurry earlier today, and then my father called me into a meeting.

"A presentation is set up for tonight that I'm supposed to attend. The project leader for Qing will give a presentation, and there will also be a discussion of EBF-202, but Darian won't be giving the presentation. His assistant, George, will present on EBF-202. When I asked my father about it, he was vague, but he said that I won't be seeing Doctor Beck again—that important people are interested in his research, and he suspects Darian will be reassigned elsewhere."

Charles glanced at his Rolex. "Do you know who is supposed to be at this meeting?"

"I don't know everyone, but I'm sure the vice president and his chief of staff will be attending."

Someone knocked on the door and Charles inched it open.

A middle-aged woman appeared worried. "Mary has a name."

"Good." He smiled mischievously.

CHAPTER 49

After the sedan pulled to a stop, two men dragged Darian from the car, pushed him into a building, and shoved him down a staircase. He tripped on slippery metal steps and stumbled down a flight of stairs into a basement with stone walls, concrete floors, and fluorescent lights.

"Sorry about that, Doc. I should have warned you about those steps," the shorter of the two men said, skipping down the steps. "You won't be needing the hood anymore." He yanked it from Darian's head.

Darian groaned. He'd ripped his jeans and cut his shin on a sharp edge.

The taller one pulled out a revolver and pressed it to his forehead. "I wouldn't worry about your jeans." He chuckled. "Get up and walk toward that table." He nodded at a metal table with one stainless steel stool.

When Darian reached the table, the shorter man shackled metal chains to his wrists and tied them to a bar suspended from the ceiling, stretching Darian's hands wide, his arms fully extended. The height of the bar required him to balance precariously on the tips of his toes. Miserable, he could do nothing but hang.

"Relax, Doc, you're going to hang out for a while." The short man laughed. "You get that, Saul? I said *hang out*."

"Come on. Let's go, you maroon. How many times have I told you not to use my name? How many times?"

They left Darian alone.

Time ticked past slowly, and his shoulders and calves ached from the strain. To keep from going insane, he thought about Jack and his condition and made a mental list of every ailment that impacted brain function. When he finished, he started again.

By the time he had started the same list for the sixth time, a door opened and boots clattered down the staircase. He peered over his shoulder at an aged man, who wore a simple gray long-sleeved shirt and black pants, limping toward him.

The man breathed heavily as he walked. He smiled when he placed a small velvet pouch on the table and turned to face Darian. His short white hair and matching white beard contrasted with his dark outfit and narrow black eyes.

"Good afternoon, Doctor Beck." The interrogator dragged the stool toward him and removed a box cutter from his pocket.

Darian's eyes shot wide.

"Don't worry, Doctor. I'm not going to cut you. Just stay as still as possible." The interrogator sliced off his clothes. "That's better. You won't be needing those."

He circled Darian, his bad leg causing his foot to swoosh lightly against the concrete floor. "You've done a good job staying in shape. I'm impressed a researcher who spends so much time indoors maintains such excellent muscle tone."

A light sheen of sweat blanketed Darian's body even though the cool air chilled his skin.

"I have a hard time keeping the weight off." The interrogator patted his ample stomach. "But I'm pleased you're so fit. Good muscle tone makes my job much easier."

"You should try biking. I'd be happy to show you some great trails."

The interrogator chuckled. "That's very good, Doctor Beck. You should keep your sense of humor. It won't really matter in the end, but it might make the process more pleasant for both of us. I certainly enjoy a nice laugh now and again."

He untied the velvet pouch and removed a six-inch stainless steel needle, and held the instrument up for Darian to inspect. "It's just a simple needle. Beautiful, really."

He twisted the shiny implement in his hand, and the stark fluorescent light reflected off the thin spike.

Fear jolted through Darian as he strained against the chains. Sweat rolled down his face as his body swayed.

"Good. I see from your reaction you understand the excruciating pain I can cause with this simple needle. Most people don't understand at first. They expect all types of sophisticated devices." He took another step closer and looked up into Darian's eyes.

Darian smelled something sour, as if the interrogator had drunk milk that had gone bad a short time ago.

"They probably didn't teach you much about acupuncture in the fancy universities you attended. It dates back to ancient China, as far back as the second century B.C. during the Han Dynasty, when they first developed metal needles."

The interrogator frowned. "I know what you're thinking. Isn't acupuncture a way to alleviate pain? It can be used to cure a long list of ailments. I have studied them all. You would be surprised at the good I can do with this needle." He twirled the implement in his hand. "But as in all things, the good is shadowed by the bad. I like to focus on the flip side. Acupuncture was also first used as an effective means of torture. I think you'll discover the old ways are still effective."

"I've done nothing wrong. There's no reason for this. Why don't you let me down? We'll knock down some drinks and I'll tell you whatever you want to know."

He studied Darian's body. "I don't care what you've done or didn't do, whether it was right or wrong. The difference between the two is simply a matter of perception. That is none of my concern."

He moved swiftly and jabbed the needle into a nerve in Darian's stomach.

Pain shot through his left side. His leg felt as if it had burst into flames and he screamed. Visions of his mother under the overpass ran through his mind, and he screamed again.

The interrogator smiled and stepped back. "You're going to be fun to work on."

CHAPTER 50

Charles and Steven left Vanessa in the interrogation room and joined the rest of the group in the main basement chamber.

Mary started her presentation. "Based on our collective research, we uncovered two possible suspects." She clicked a button on a remote control and a picture of a round-faced man appeared on the brick wall behind her. "One possibility is Cooper Johnson. The Johnson family is listed on the guest registry. They made a fortune in energy seventy years ago. He's in his early forties, but he graduated from a southern university and grew up in Texas, which doesn't fit The Professor's profile."

She pressed another button and a series of press clippings flashed on the wall. "Thanks to Gabriel and Moses, we know when Izzy was taken. Johnson visited London negotiating an energy contract with a Saudi prince at the time. The British tabloids chronicled his activities while there. Apparently, he enjoys late night clubbing, getting sloppy drunk, and spending time with exotic models. It's not entirely impossible he had someone else take Izzy and kept her while he was out of the country, but from what The Professor told us, that would seem unlikely."

"That's not him," Jack said. "I'm certain he had nothing to do with Mom's kidnapping."

"I tend to agree." Mary pressed another button and Cooper Simmens's face appeared on the wall. "This is Cooper Simmens. Cooper is an old Simmens family name going back one hundred years. Many of the Simmens men are named Cooper, but he's the only one who uses it as a first name and fits the age parameters. He obviously has blue eyes."

When Mary finished her report on Cooper Simmens, Aunt Jackie asked, "How do we take him?"

"It's going to be tough," she answered. "We need to locate him first, and he uses a lot of security. The Secret Service protects him, along with private security hired by the Simmens family. When he's in New York, he lives in a penthouse apartment not far from here, but the apartment is virtually impenetrable."

"If I've learned anything over the years, it's that anyone can be taken out," Aunt Jackie grunted.

"Yes, but we need to take him alive," Tom explained. "Killing him will do us no good. He can't die before we find out where he took Mom."

Charles stroked the face of his lucky Rolex. "I think we might be in luck. I have reliable information that Cooper Simmens and the vice president have a highly secretive meeting planned for tonight. They're attending a presentation about covert scientific research projects. Security should be light. They won't want the Secret Service at the discussion, and they probably don't trust many in their private security detail to attend, either. They will primarily rely upon the secret location of the meeting for their safety."

"Sounds perfect, but we'll need the time and location of the meeting," Gabriel said.

"I'm working on a plan." Charles smiled.

Charles and Steven returned to the interrogation room with Steven carrying the thin Cooper File. "I'm sorry we kept you so long. I think we can help."

Vanessa sighed. "Great, because I don't know where else to turn."

Steven placed the Cooper File on the table. "The people who took Darian are probably the ones behind Project Qing."

"Do you think the vice president is involved?"

Charles shrugged. "I doubt he's involved directly, but I'd guess his chief of staff, Cooper Simmens, is behind the abduction."

He slid the Cooper File to her. "Take a look at these photographs. I think he's responsible for what happened to these women."

Vanessa began reviewing the photographs in the file, but stopped halfway through and closed the folder tight. "How many women did he tortured like that and kill?"

"At least twenty-four, but probably many more."

Her hands turned sweaty. "If he is capable of torturing those women, then Darian is in real trouble."

"I'm not going to sugar coat this for you, Vanessa. The situation is grim. Once he finishes questioning Doctor Beck, he will kill him. He also kidnapped Jack's mother, Maggie, two days ago. We think she's still alive, but as time slips by, our chance to rescue her diminishes. We need to capture Cooper Simmens and find out where he's holding Maggie and Darian, and we need to do it tonight."

"Can't you go to the police?"

"Without direct evidence implicating him in these deaths or Darian's kidnapping, what can we do?" Charles shrugged. "He comes from a powerful family. All we would end up accomplishing is warning him, thereby placing Maggie and Darian in further peril. They would become instant liabilities, and he would kill them immediately."

Her head dropped. "What do you want me to do?"

"Our best opportunity is to grab him during tonight's presentation. We need to track you to the meeting."

Steven removed a tiny perfume bottle from his pocket and placed it on the table.

"What's that?"

"This perfume is laced with a specific radioactive isotope which will allow us to track you," Steven explained.

"Is it dangerous?"

"It's harmless. The isotope evaporates in six hours. They will know if you're carrying any devices that emit signals of any kind. Plus, the transport will have a jammer, and so will the location of the meeting. But there's no way to jam the isotope."

She stared at the vial for a moment. "Won't they search me?"

"They will definitely search you, but they will never find the isotope. This technology is so advanced it doesn't even exist yet. They would need to know the exact signature of the isotope to detect it, which is impossible. Just apply the perfume like you would your normal fragrance an hour before the meeting."

"This is a dangerous situation," Charles said. "I would understand if you decline, but I don't see any other way to help Doctor Beck." He checked the time on his Rolex. "There's no time. We need your answer now."

CHAPTER 51

Maggie sat uncomfortably on the leather recliner. A knifing pain stabbed through her ribs, her head ached, and worse than that, her spirits had reached an all-time low. A vase with flowers stood on the table in front of her, her sketchpad lay on her lap, and her pencils lay spread out on the table beside her. To pass the time, she had sketched the flowers and tried to capture their life and colors, but she failed miserably. They appeared weak, tired, and lifeless, just like her.

I am a strong woman. The thought rang hollow, but she repeated it until she started to believe it.

Cooper appeared in the doorway. He had an unsettling way of moving shadow-quiet.

She forced a wide smile onto her face, trying to remember how she had smiled when she had first met him. Anyone who knew her would recognize the fake expression of happiness she now sported, but he didn't know her. He remembered a young girl in pigtails who liked pink and had the nerve to reject him.

He crept toward Maggie with an uncertain expression on his face, but his wide and wild eyes appeared combustible. He looked as he had when they'd first met—about to explode.

She shuddered.

He stopped ten feet away from her. "Why would you attack me?" He sounded immature, speaking in a boy's voice.

She had pondered how to answer that question all morning. She had to make up something good, an excuse he wanted to believe.

"I was so angry, Cooper." Her voice sounded feathery. "I keep thinking about all those years we wasted apart. You should have come for me sooner."

He furrowed his forehead. "You could have found me. I sent you the letters." He waved his arms. "I've given you all *this*. I gave you gifts. The next place will be better. You shouldn't have stabbed me."

The confusion and hurt in his voice was as plain as if he had written them across his face. He hadn't really changed from that little boy she refused so many years ago.

"I felt like I did when we were kids." She remembered to smile. "I so wanted to go with you back then. You should have taken me away with you, but instead you left me. I cried for months. I'm sorry. I'd never do anything like that again." She was a bad liar, but she did her best.

He ran a hand through his perfectly placed hair and his anger seemed to subside.

He smiled tentatively. "You can't do that again. I won't be pleased." His brilliantly royal blue eyes fired with malice.

The threat lurking behind his glare was real and dangerous. She wouldn't get a third chance.

Cooper studied a video feed of Maggie. She sat in the recliner, still drawing the same flowers she had been working on when he left her.

He didn't know what to believe. Her explanation made sense—she secretly loved him, and he could only imagine her anger at wasting those years, living a sorrowful life with that husband and her two children in poverty, when she wanted to be with him. Still, she could have reached out to him.

It wouldn't have been hard. She could have managed a simple letter or phone call. How dumb is she? I hate her!

Rage ravaged his mind. He tossed a file from his desk and imagined cutting her with the surgical tools and squeezing her throat.

"The Peterson twins are here to see you, sir."

He shut off the video feed and instructed his assistant to send them in.

The twins' wide shoulders swayed as they walked.

He glared at them. "Why haven't you apprehended Tom and Jack by now? I told you to take them yesterday!"

The twins shared a look and the more talkative of the two answered. Tick was slightly bigger than his twin, and his beard a touch longer. "They're off the grid. We can't find them."

"I don't tolerate excuses. Have you searched for their citizen identification cards?"

"We've searched for their cards and their cell phones. Both have gone missing. Either they destroyed them or they're jamming the signal."

"The system must be malfunctioning. Where would these boys find wave jammers? That's sophisticated technology. Have you gone back to their apartment?"

"Yes. They came home after we took their mother, but there's no sign of them in the apartment. The older one, Jack, didn't show at the club where he works, and Tom's been absent from his internship without an explanation."

"What nonsense!" Cooper pounded his desk. "I pay you both plenty to do these tasks for me. I want them taken by morning. Failure is *not* an option!"

Tock edged closer to Tick, looking nervous.

"Yes sir," Tick said.

Cooper waved at them to leave. They had never disappointed him before. *How could Maggie's sons get their hands on a wave jammer, and why would they use it? Why is everything so difficult?*

He heard a sound in his head and for a few heartbeats he thought he had started hearing *voices*. Then he realized his assistant had called him, when she repeated her message. "Samuel Wickersham is on the line, sir."

"Put him through."

"I am so sorry about this Doctor Beck situation, Mr. Simmens." Wickersham sounded apologetic, worried, a little scared maybe.

"I don't want Sheppard to find out about Project Qing. That would be a costly mistake. You will pay dearly for that mistake."

"The interrogator assures me he has told no one about Project Qing. He's very confident of it."

"For your sake, I hope he's correct."

"I understand, sir. Everything will be in order." Wickersham spoke quickly as if any delay might be fatal. "The applications for both projects are impressive. I'm sure you'll be pleased by the presentations."

"I'd better be," Cooper snarled before he hung up.

He glanced at his long list of messages: Ethel needed to speak to him, Homeland Security wasn't sure where Moses and Gabriel had gone, his publicist wanted a statement about the Florida Ghettos, his wife called.... The list stretched on and on.

He ripped it to shreds. A sharp pain knifed through his head and fragmented his thoughts into a million pieces. He shut off the lights, dropped his head to his desk, put the video feed of Maggie back on his computer, and pulled at his hair as he spied on her in silence.

Violent, bloody visions filled his mind, and he started to kick the bottom of his desk until the wood splintered.

CHAPTER 52

Steven surveyed the small group before him: three teenagers, two untrained ghetto leaders, and one senior citizen who might stretch to five feet tall when she stood on a stool. A motley crew if ever one existed, but they were willing and had proven themselves in the past. They were not the team he would have preferred, but he could do a lot worse.

He had grown up in the Philadelphia ghetto a lifetime ago, and had signed up for the armed services with a friend's identity when only fifteen. After starting in the infantry, he moved to Special Forces within eight months. Two years later, he transferred to a special unit so black the summer sun couldn't lighten them.

He never officially left the super secretive black ops unit. No one ever left. The unit never officially existed, but when he turned thirty he had had enough, so he vanished.

For the first time in his life, he worked for someone he believed in, someone he respected, but it scared him. Following orders was easy, but working for Sheppard had become difficult. He found himself vested in an outcome he could not control, one he wanted but feared would prove too elusive in the end. Somehow, Sheppard had breathed life into a heart he thought long dead, and he couldn't go back now. He had a team, and they had a mission.

"We have an informant on the inside who will wear a tracking device to the meeting."

"Who is the informant, and can we trust him?" Aunt Jackie asked.

"For the informant's safety, only I'm aware of his or her identity. I have no reason to distrust the informant, but he or she is not a professional and is, therefore, unreliable. We'll take an unmarked van to the meeting and devise a strategy once we assess the meeting place."

"How tight do you think security will be?" Tom asked.

"I expect it to be light, but I'm sure a handful of heavily armed private bodyguards will be at the meeting. You should expect the worst." Steven worked a tablet to flash a picture of Cooper Simmens on the wall. "Our mission is to capture him alive and limit the number of casualties." He glanced at Gabriel. "We don't need any unnecessary fatalities. Once we detain him, we will use him to find Maggie. After—"

"After that we kill him," Aunt Jackie said. Gabriel glanced at her, and their eyes locked.

"We will need to be quick and decisive, but we discharge our weapons only if we must. With that said, the bodyguards will use lethal force. You should all respond accordingly."

He opened a hidden door in the brick wall and revealed a large walk-in closet that contained a small armory of assault rifles, pistols, Kevlar vests, explosive devices, and an assortment of other neatly stored weapons.

Moses whistled. "That's a nice collection of toys you've got."

Steven frowned. "I know you all have various levels of training. We should keep the weaponry to a minimum. Simple and effective is all we need."

Tom lifted his dart pistol. "I'm fine using one of these."

Jack and Mary agreed with him.

"Those will be fine, but I suggest you use the medium setting at least. I don't trust anything lower." Steven glanced at Moses and Gabriel. "If my information is accurate, you both prefer these AK-5000s." He pulled two assault rifles off a rack on the far wall and handed them to the ghetto leaders.

Aunt Jackie pulled Excalibur from her bag. "I'm good with this one. Excalibur has always worked for me in the past."

He nodded and removed a specially designed pair of sunglasses from a crate, then tossed them to Tom. "These glasses use the latest penetrating sound wave technology. They project images from the other side of walls. Their range is limited to fifty feet, and the images won't appear razor sharp, but they will indicate the location of hostiles and the outline of the room. They take a little getting used to but will be helpful for a mission like this one."

Tom squinted at the eyewear. "They don't seem large enough. Where's the sound wave equipment?"

Steven nodded. "You're right, Tom. They work remotely. The van has the serious equipment. We'll need someone to operate the gear and warn us about dangers outside the range of the glasses."

All eyes in the room turned toward Aunt Jackie.

She bristled. "Don't look at me. I don't need sonar to do a little killing. I'm going in with or without the bat goggles."

"I'll operate the equipment," Mary said. "I'm the most capable person to handle the advanced equipment, and I'd rather not shoot anyone if I can avoid it."

Tom and Mary huddled close together in the interrogation room, knees rubbing against each other. They were finally alone.

He smiled. "You've been a star. I don't know how to thank you. We'd never know this monster's name if it weren't for you."

She squeezed his hand. "Maggie means a lot to me. I'd do anything to get her back, and you've been pretty spectacular yourself."

"I just hope we have time."

"The Professor said we should have a few days. We're going to save her, I'm sure of it."

"I can't imagine what she's going through." He shuddered. "What if this guy reaches the shatter point before we find her?"

"That's a negative thought, and we won't have any of those. You know what Maggie says about negative thoughts." She playfully wagged her finger at him.

"Negative thoughts lead to negative results," he said. His mom had told him that dozens of times over the years. "You know there's no scientific evidence proving that hypothesis."

"Not everything needs to be proven to be real."

He frowned. "Do you ever wonder if the Fourteenth Colony and all this effort is worth it? Maybe we should leave the country to the

Originalists. When we get Mom back, we could all move somewhere else, somewhere we can have a fairer chance away from this fight."

"This is our country, Tom. If we don't fight for it, who will?"

"Our odds of success are so low. The Originalists control the government, Homeland Security, the advanced technologies, most of the money, and the military. How can we overcome all those advantages?"

"Stop doing that!" She shot him a sharp look.

"Doing what?" He slumped downward, his face drawn.

"Using math and probabilities to analyze everything! Fairness and doing what's right count, too. Countries are governed by the will of their people. Throughout time, powerful governments have failed because of greed and excesses. We have a way forward. We just need to renew the social contract our country was founded on."

"It seems like we shredded the social contract decades ago." Tom sullenly looked into her eyes. "So we can't move to Fiji?"

"How about you kiss me instead?"

He didn't need to be asked twice. His lips eagerly found hers as he folded into her warmth. He tasted honey and cinnamon and felt alive, truly alive, but the kiss lasted only a few seconds.

Jack cleared his throat in the doorway.

Tom pulled away from Mary and felt his face redden.

Jack grinned sheepishly. "Time's up. We need to go." He tossed two facemasks at his brother. "Don't worry, the masks have holes for your mouths so you can continue in the van." He wiggled two fingers through an opening in his mask and made smooching sounds.

"Very funny." Tom moved toward the door but paused. A bolt of worry shot through him as he looked at his brother.

When did he become this bad?

Jack leaned awkwardly against the doorframe, his hand shaking, his face ashen, his eyes hollow and distant.

"Are you okay?"

Jack glanced back at him. "We'll do whatever it takes to get her back. Right, brother?"

CHAPTER 53

Vanessa studied her reflection in the shiny steel elevator doors. Her beige silk blouse fit perfectly and tucked neatly into her light gray slacks, but her thoughts returned to the perfume. The scent reminded her of roses—not her typical fragrance. Would her father notice?

What do I say if he asks me about it?

She shook those doubts from her mind and thought back to the first day she met Darian. She had jumped into this elevator with him inside. It was only her third day working in the lab, but she'd already heard much about the young, handsome, funny, and sometimes available young researcher. The women in the lab talked about him with such reverence and desire, she knew she must have him.

At first, he was the new glittery toy everyone else wanted and therefore she must possess, but the relationship changed as the months passed. Her feelings for him transformed until she *needed* to be around him. She felt *better* near him. He brightened her life with color for the first time, and she would not go back to a gray world without him.

When the elevator bell rang, she strolled toward her father's office with her head high and her shoulders back. It was 7:44.

Wickersham, Sanders, and George already waited anxiously for her. All three men wore suits and ties, although the differences were stark.

Her father wore an Italian pinstripe suit with a solid red tie and matching silk handkerchief folded perfectly in his breast pocket. The bold hues contrasted deeply with the charcoal suit. Gold cufflinks held together the sleeves of his French cuffed shirt. The hand-tailored outfit looked as natural on him as a bathing suit on a swimmer.

The two other doctors wore ill-fitting navy suits, checkered ties, brown belts, and scuffed black shoes. Both were so similarly dressed she wondered if they learned how to dress like that in medical school. They looked uncomfortable, as if counting the minutes before they could undress and slip back into white lab coats.

"You look lovely, Vanessa." Her father greeted her warmly, but she heard a touch of anxiety in his voice. "I think we should be going. The limo is waiting for us outside."

The black limo idled in the parking lot. With everyone inside, the windows darkened. "The meeting is at a secret government facility." He turned to face Sanders and George. "I guess I'm at liberty to tell you whom we'll be meeting at this point. We will be presenting in front of two special guests. The first one is Cooper Simmens. He is the vice president's chief of staff."

"Haven't you mentioned him to me before?" Vanessa forced a smile, keeping her tone neutral. She wished she had never heard of Cooper Simmens, and certainly wished she had never seen those photographs.

"Yes, dear. Coop is an old friend of mine. We go way back. I'm sure I've spoken about him a number of times." He paused for dramatic effect and stared at Sanders and George as if he was announcing the winner of an Academy Award and they were the expectant audience. "And the second guest will be the vice president himself. He's very interested in these research projects, so it will be important to be upbeat and quick. He doesn't have patience for long explanations or lots of scientific jargon."

The color drained from George's face.

Sanders chomped down on his lip so hard he drew blood.

The limo stopped in front of an old industrial building in southern Manhattan. The driver held the door open, and the small group filed out. They followed the driver through thick glass doors into a dark lobby.

He turned to face them. "I have to search you." He retrieved a plastic wand from a wooden table and approached Vanessa with a sly smile on his face.

Her eyes focused on the wand, and her chest tightened as if the perfume wrapped around her like a tight belt. They had told her that the isotope was undetectable and she had nothing to worry about, but could she trust them? Maybe other technologies existed they knew nothing about?

"Just raise your arms out to the side."

He hovered the wand over her body and unnecessarily brushed against her legs and arms. She held her breath, and when he finished, she exhaled.

After he searched everyone else, they all piled into the elevator, which stopped on the third floor.

Designed as warehouse space, the floor's open layout had unfinished concrete floors and walls, exposed metal support beams, twelve-foot ceilings, and harsh white lights dangling from electrical cords fixed to the ceiling.

The driver gestured at a door on the east end of the building and strolled with looping strides. The clatter of their shoes against the concrete echoed in the quiet. The door led to a long rectangular room with plush carpeting, dark wood paneling, a long mahogany table with a dozen chairs, and framed pictures of Originalist politicians on the walls—a typical high-end boardroom.

"Please wait here," the driver said. "The vice president should be here shortly." He shut the door and left them alone.

Her father busied himself by examining the drawings on the walls.

Vanessa settled herself at the end of the table.

George and Doctor Sanders fidgeted with their tablets, making sure everything was in order.

Soon the door at the end of the room swung open, and three men strode in—a beefy security guard wearing a black suit, shirt and tie, followed by Cooper Simmens and the vice president.

Her father rushed forward to shake their hands.

The vice president looked skittish, his eyes flashing around the room as if he had more important things to do.

Vanessa stayed glued in her chair. Uncertainty and doubt froze her in place as her heart galloped and fear gripped her.

For a moment, she worried she might pass out.

CHAPTER 54

Steven parked the van at the corner of a narrow one-way street. "Based upon the isotope, our informant just entered that building." He operated sophisticated surveillance equipment and zoomed in on an industrial building two hundred feet away toward the middle of the block. "That building must be our target."

Mary fired up the penetrating sound wave equipment, and a green holographic image of the building floated in the center of the van. "The third floor is our goal. Three men appear to be guarding the elevator and front staircase, and three more guard the rear staircase. A cluster of people are in a large room on the east end of the third floor. The rest of the building is empty."

Steven pointed to the main floor. "One man patrols the lobby, and based on the surveillance cameras...." He nodded at the video feed of the front of the building. "...two others are standing out front."

Mary rotated the holographic image in a circle. "The front door is our only way in."

"What if we use the roof?" Gabriel said.

Mary brought up a satellite view of the building. The structure was twenty feet taller than any of its neighbors.

Steven shook his head. "The roof won't work for us. We would need a helicopter or climbing gear. We don't have either."

"So we go in the front," Aunt Jackie said.

"We'll have to, but the layout is problematic. We need to dispense with all three men at the entrance before they alert their friends upstairs. If the other six know we're coming, we'll never gain access to the third floor. The two teams will easily hold us off until reinforcements arrive. We'll need the element of surprise."

He nodded at the man in the lobby. "He's the problem. I'll take him out with a high-powered rifle, but I'll need a diversion to sneak into position."

He pointed to a sedan across from the industrial building. "If I can reach this car here, I'll have an angle to take out the inside man, so long as he approaches the doors. The doors are made of heavy glass, so even with the high-powered rifle I'll need him within a few feet of the entrance. Someone else will have to simultaneously take out the other two guards before they notify the rest of the security detail. The key is creating the right diversion."

"What type of distraction do you want?" Tom asked.

"It must be something that won't put them on notice."

A second black limo pulled in front of the building, and Steven zoomed the cameras in tight. A well-dressed driver wearing a black suit stepped out of the car and held the door open. From his gait, it was clear he had military training. Two men exited the limo and entered the building with the driver trailing close behind. He reversed the video feed and zoomed in on their faces. The vice president and his Chief of Staff had just arrived.

"Hello there, fellas." Gabriel snarled.

They watched the three-dimensional, sonar-produced version of the building and saw the three men enter the boardroom on the east end of the third floor.

"I'll go," Aunt Jackie said. "They won't suspect me of anything."

Steven shook his head. "Maybe, but we need to draw the inside guy to the doors so I can have a good shot."

"I'll go with Aunt Jackie," Mary offered. "I'll pose as a call girl, and Jackie can be my handler. I'll make the guard come to the doors." She flipped her hair away from her face and smiled seductively.

"Aunt Jackie's going to be a pimp? That's hard to believe," Jack said.

"You'd be surprised at what I did for our country back in the day, sonny boy. I can play the role of a pimp just fine."

Steven sized Mary up for a moment. Undercover work, even for only a few minutes, could be tricky. If they didn't believe her, the entire operation would be blown, and she'd be in real risk, which he might not be able to protect her from.

Still, no other ideas came to mind. "Okay, Mary and Jackie will go in together, but at the first sign of trouble you both run."

"Mary will do no such thing!" Tom sputtered. "She's staying in the van!"

"Why? Don't you think I'm attractive enough to make the guard interested?"

"It's not that! It's just too dangerous." He instantly regretted his outburst. There must have been a smarter way to object to the plan. He scanned the group and got the sinking feeling he had already lost the argument.

"Nonsense. I won't be doing anything dangerous. Aunt Jackie will take out the guards after Steven shoots the man in the lobby."

"What could go wrong?" Tom grumbled.

Steven rummaged through one of the storage bins in the back of the van, which contained extra clothes. He retrieved a low-cut, black dress and tossed it to Mary, who dressed, applied thick make-up, and mussed her wavy red hair.

Finished, she turned to the group. "How do I look?"

"Great," Jack said.

Everyone nodded in agreement except Tom, who felt numb.

"Here's the plan," Steven said. "Mary and Jackie will approach the guards, create a diversion, and I'll get into position. I'll need no more than thirty seconds. Mary will draw the inside guard out toward the doors." He looked at her. "Drop your cell phone when he's within three feet of the glass and stay down. That will be our sign, Jackie. I'll shoot the inside guy, and you take out the two outside guards. After the guards are down, you guys join us and Mary will return to the van."

He glanced at the two women. "Does that sound workable?"

"We'll do it. Don't worry about us," Aunt Jackie said.

"Good. Once the outside guards go down, we won't have much time to reach the third floor." He pointed toward the holographic image of the industrial building. "Jackie, Tom, and Jack will go up the front staircase, and I'll take the back with Gabriel and Moses. At my signal, we charge onto the third floor. I'll move a second before Jackie's team does so they can have the benefit of the diversion. Try to finish the guards quickly with as little noise as possible. Once we secure the third floor, we'll improvise a way into the boardroom. Are we all in?"

Everyone agreed.

Steven and Jackie left the van.

Jack elbowed Tom in the ribs as Mary started to follow them.

Tom stopped her with a squeeze of her arm. "You look fantastic, irresistible."

"Really? I don't feel fantastic."

"I'd empty my bank account to spend time with you."

"You don't have any money." She punched him in the arm.

"I meant it as a compliment."

"Thanks." She pecked him on the cheek, searched his eyes for a long moment, and when he said nothing, she left.

"You are hopeless. Do you know that?" Jack groused.

"What?"

"She probably wanted you to tell her that you *love* her." Moses chuckled.

"Sometimes, you have to speak from your heart," Jack added.

"Oh," Tom mumbled, feeling like a slug.

CHAPTER 55

Brenda glanced around the deserted laboratory, and a chill swept through her. She could count on one hand how often she'd been alone in the lab over the last two years. Quiet and empty, it took on a surreal quality.

Two hours after Darian left, she had turned to George and suggested they start the autopsy as Darian had dictated.

George shook his head. "Wickersham called and said we could not proceed with the procedure. He thinks Lassie is too important. He didn't give me an option." He shrugged and turned away.

Technically, the autopsy required Wickersham's approval. Darian would never have asked, but George followed rules.

She'd read something in George's eyes that worried her, so she left without saying another word and raced to the kennel, determined to perform the autopsy on her own. When she reached the holding area, her access card wouldn't work. On the third swipe, she realized it was fruitless and returned to the lab.

George had given her a hard stare when she returned. He clearly knew more than he told her.

Alone now, she floated in the lab and drifted among the desks and the equipment. *How are we going to save Jack?*

The major difference between EBF-101 and EBF-202 was the dissolving agent Darian and George had created to break down the drug in the brain's fatty tissue. It worked, but not completely. George believed he had discovered a better agent, but the new drug had to be combined with EBF-202 *before* adding it to the bloodstream. Designed as a psychoactive drug to sneak past the blood-brain barrier, EBF-202 was hard to reach after injected into the patient. Once administered, there was no practical way to specifically target the drug.

Darian had focused on finding a blocker that would prevent EBF-202 from working generally in the bloodstream. EBF-202 operated as a targeted growth hormone for brain cells. There should be some way to block it from stimulating that growth, but so far, he had run into a brick wall.

Brenda strolled past Bessie and toward Darian's desk. She spotted his notebook tossed on top and shook her head. No one else used notebooks anymore, and this one was worn, its corner bent, doodles etched into the cover. Darian kept his journal secret, functioning as a type of diary. He usually carried it with him, but he'd left in such a hurry, he must have forgotten to take it with him.

She reached for it without thinking and flipped to the last page. He had scrawled a message on it: *Look to the brain?* A crude picture of a seesaw had been drawn next to the message.

Look to the brain?

Brenda latched onto the idea like a life preserver. *What things killed brain cells?*

She started her computer. Dozens of agents killed brain cells: various drugs, alcohol, cortisol from stress, trauma, certain proteins, dehydration, elevated testosterone levels, chemotherapy, radiation.... The list stretched on and on.

She leaned back in her chair. *Which one would Lassie have come into contact with?*

Lost in an ocean of possibilities, she had a raft, and so long as Jack lived, she would paddle. She just wished she knew which way to go.

CHAPTER 56

Mary tumbled from the back of the van, feeling awkward in the short dress and unsteady in four-inch pumps a half size too tight.

"You've got to really sell it when you go undercover," Aunt Jackie said. "Think like a hooker. You're desperate and you're selling yourself. Let's see you walk."

She stiffly wobbled forward a few steps.

Aunt Jackie handed her a flask. "Take a long sip."

She looked at it questionably, but when Aunt Jackie shoved it toward her, she grabbed it and tipped it back. Tequila burned her throat.

"Take another pull. It'll help you loosen up."

She lifted the flask again and swallowed another mouthful. The alcohol warmed her body and numbed her a little.

"Okay. Remember, you want to attract these men. You're not headed to some geek technology convention. Sway your hips and copy me." Aunt Jackie led her toward the industrial building, her hips swaying aggressively from side to side.

Mary had to smile despite the situation. She hoped Jackie didn't dislocate a hip.

After a few steps, she felt more comfortable and got into a rhythm as they reached the guards.

"I'm lost. Either one of you big, strong men know where Bleecker Street is?" Jackie added a lilt to her voice Mary had never heard before.

They ignored her and leered at Mary. "I think you've found the right place. What's your name, sweet thing?" the taller of the two men asked.

Mary placed her hand on her hips and smiled seductively. "They call me Sugar."

The shorter guard chuckled. "You certainly are sweet."

"We're not giving anything away for free here, boys," Jackie said. "We might have a little time before our next appointment if you boys want to party."

"Quiet down, you old crow." The taller guard shoved Jackie off to the side.

Mary peered into the lobby. "Who's the handsome man inside? Why is he so shy?" She stepped toward the doors and beckoned him forward with a wave of her hand and a long, lingering lick of her tongue. She felt foolish, but she needed him to come close.

The shorter guard banged on the glass. "Take a look, Ralph. She can't hurt you."

Ralph cautiously stepped forward, but he was still five feet away, too far for Steven.

The guard banged the glass again. "Don't be such a stick-in-the-mud. Where would she hide a gun?"

Mary pursed her lips and bent at the waist. Her chest practically sprung free from the tight dress as she playfully tugged on the fabric.

Come on Ralph, come closer.

He crept toward the glass, a sick smile twisting his lips.

That's right. Four feet, three feet, two feet....

She dropped her cell phone. "Oops." She bent low to pick it up.

Glass exploded around them, and Ralph flew backward.

Thump, thump.

Both guards were down. The shorter one had been shot in the head and the taller one in the chest. The taller one moaned.

"Old crow, my ass." Jackie stepped on his chest and shot him between the eyes.

Gabriel and Moses dragged the two guards inside.

"Good work," Steven said. "We need to move. We have five minutes at most before security inside the building realizes something's wrong."

Tom squeezed Mary's shoulder. "You were great, but you've got to go back to the van." He considered saying more, but the right words stuck in his throat. As hopeless as he was, he realized this was the wrong moment to tell her he loved her for the first time.

Jackie handed her the flask, and Mary nodded, turned, and woodenly headed back to the van. The sway had vanished from her hips and blood had splattered across the front of the dress.

Jack tugged on Tom's arm and they raced to the front staircase. They took the stairs two at a time and reached the door to the third floor in no time.

Jackie huffed her way, sweating profusely. She looked unsteady when she joined them.

Tom used the enhanced vision and got a read on three men on the other side of the door. "I'll take the guy on the left," he whispered. "Jack, you shoot the guy on the right, and Jackie takes out the man in the middle."

Tom's heart raced and adrenaline jolted through his body. Time crawled until Steven's voice rang in his earpiece. "We go in three, two, one."

Tom kicked the door open and charged, dart pistol in front, Jack and Aunt Jackie close on his heels. The three guards swung their heads around to see the commotion, and he shot the guard to the left in the back before the man had a chance to turn.

Aunt Jackie blasted the man in the middle with a clean shot to the head, but when Jack pulled the trigger, his target dodged to the right and the dart missed.

As the guard leveled his assault rifle, Tom leaped forward and grabbed the barrel of the weapon. He yanked the gun up and a volley of bullets ricocheted off the ceiling. Sweeping the guard's feet, they both fell hard to the floor, hands still locked on the assault rifle. The security guard twisted on top of Tom and head-butted him hard, connecting with his nose, which began to spurt blood like a fountain.

Tom released the gun and the guard grinned, then fell backward with a *thump.* Jack had shot him in the back of the neck. He fell to the side unconscious, still clutching the assault rifle.

Jack helped him up.

"Thanks, brother."

"Why are you thanking him?" Aunt Jackie grumbled. "That was *his* man."

Jack threw his hands out in frustration. "The guy jumped out of the way!"

"I told you to aim for his chest," Aunt Jackie growled.

Jack pointed to the man Aunt Jackie plugged, the bullet hole visible in his forehead.

She shrugged. "I don't miss."

Steven, Gabriel, and Moses raced over. Gabriel limped as he ran.

"Are you okay?" Tom asked.

"Moses shot me."

"I said I was sorry," Moses said sheepishly. "The gun went off by accident."

Tom peeled off his mask and blood smeared across his nose and cheeks.

Steven tossed him a rag. "We made more noise than I had hoped." He scanned the boardroom with a worried expression on his face.

CHAPTER 57

Mary studied the three-dimensional holographic version of the industrial building. Her heart thumped in her head and she held her breath when she saw the jumble of bodies by the front staircase. She breathed only when three figures stood to one side. She could make out Aunt Jackie—half the size of the other two.

Her concentration was so intense and focused on the gadgetry that she hadn't notice two armed men sneak up on the van. She discovered them only when they yanked open the backdoor of the vehicle, and she screamed.

Two eerily similar faces smiled back at her.

Tick darted into the van and smacked her with the back of his hand. The momentum from the blow propelled her against the side of the van, and she fell awkwardly on her hip.

"Shut up," he snarled.

Tock pointed to the holographic image. "Looks like our targets are on the third floor."

Mary lunged for the system's controls and managed to slap the power button before Tick caught her by the waist and tossed her to the floor. She fell hard and groaned.

"She's a live one," Tick remarked.

"We'd better take her along. I love a good hostage."

Tick grabbed her by the hair and pulled her out of the van. "If you scream, I'll shoot you." He pressed a handgun to her back while he wrapped his left arm around her neck.

"Come on, brother, stop playing with the hostage and let's collect these boys. We can have *fun* with her later."

CHAPTER 58

Jack glanced at the door that led to the boardroom, and the air in his lungs froze. *Cooper is here.* He felt the evil bastard's presence like a bad cold, and clutched the handle of his dart pistol, anxious to meet the monster who stole his mom.

"The room should be soundproofed" Tom said. "I'm sure they have sound-soaking paint, double walls, and the latest fiberglass insulation. It's possible they didn't hear any of the noise we made."

Steven removed a small transistor from one of the many pockets in his Kevlar vest and clicked a switch. The device turned green.

"What's that?" Tom asked.

"This is a transmission inhibitor. It prevents anyone within two hundred feet from using cell phone signals to radio out for help." Steven glanced at the boardroom. "I'm sure they have the latest in Beacon technology, which will eventually outpace the inhibitor. The Beacon searches for different signals until it finds one. The inhibitor will buy us some time, but not much. Come on, let's get within sonar range to view inside the room."

The group crept forward until they saw the interior of the boardroom through their goggles. Seven people stood clustered together behind a long desk. Three were armed.

Steven frowned. "They know we're here. The driver is in the center. The vice president and Cooper Simmens are on the ends, hiding behind hostages. This is going to get messy."

It appeared that Vanessa sat at the end of the table, and George stood in front of her. The vice president cowered behind them both.

"We need to disarm them without hurting any of the innocents. Sheppard ordered me to keep the vice president safe. His death would bring heat—too much heat for the Wine Merchants and the Fourteenth Colony."

Tom spun in a circle and scanned the floor's open layout. *There has to be something here I can use.* His vision lingered on the ceiling. "Do you have any smoke bombs in your vest, Steven?"

"Sure."

"This is warehouse space. They design it with a central air duct system in case there's a fire. The flames channel into the air duct like a chimney and away from the rest of the floor."

He wandered toward the center of the floor and pointed to a grate in the ceiling. "This duct will be fireproofed and lead into the boardroom. If we toss in a smoke bomb, the air circulation will carry the smoke to the boardroom."

"That's brilliant," Jack said.

"I like it." Steven handed Tom two small, round, plastic devices. "Just squeeze them until the device flashes red and toss them down the air ducts as far as you can. We need the air current to carry the smoke to the boardroom. We don't want to smoke ourselves out."

Tom took the devices. "Got it. I'll need to stand on someone's shoulders to reach the grate."

As the broadest, Gabriel agreed to be the human ladder.

The rest of the group headed for the boardroom.

Steven stood next to the boardroom door. "Once the smoke fills the room, I want to move fast. We'll be able to see through the haze with our sonar vision, so that gives us a big advantage. I'll take out the driver, and in the confusion, we'll disarm the vice president and his chief of staff. It looks like they're both holding handguns, so be careful."

He swept his eyes over the team. "The objective of the mission is to take Cooper alive. There's no need to kill anyone."

Aunt Jackie huffed.

Tom saw Steven flash the *go* sign, and climbed on Gabriel's wide shoulders. He pulled off the metal grate and dropped it to the concrete floor. It made a louder clatter.

Peering into the duct system, he found three smaller shoots that led from the main channel. *Which one leads to the boardroom?*

All three were similar, but a cool breeze came from the one farthest to his left. Then he noticed the extra insulation, which confirmed his choice. He squeezed the smoke bombs, waited for them to turn red, and tossed them as far as he could down the left shoot. When the devices detonated with a soft pop, he dropped to the floor and raced to the boardroom with Gabriel at his heels.

By the time Tom burst into the meeting room, Steven had already taken down the driver and disarmed the vice president and his chief of staff.

Wickersham writhed on the floor in pain with a miniature taser in his hand.

Vanessa sat at one end of the table next to George, who stood behind her, his face ash white.

Jack slumped in a chair, holding his head and groaning, stricken by another headache—from the looks of him, a bad one.

The sonar vision switched off, and the world turned gray with swirling smoke.

All waited for the haze to dissipate but Aunt Jackie, who cursed and quietly slid from the room.

CHAPTER 59

It took a few minutes for the smoke to clear, but when it did, three figures appeared in the doorway. Tick held Mary with his arm across her neck and a handgun pressed hard against her temple.

Tock stood on his right, his assault rifle level.

"Throw down your guns or I shoot her," Tick said.

Tock snickered next to him and swept the barrel of his rifle across the room, pausing for a moment on Cooper.

Steven hesitated. His mission was clear—make sure the vice president remained unharmed, protect Gabriel and Moses, and then recover Cooper. He knew what he should do. The scene played out in his mind: he should shoot Tock; Tick would kill Mary; and he would have enough time to kill him afterward and complete his objectives.

It was simple enough, except nothing was simple now that Sheppard had breathed life back into his stone heart. He liked Mary, and sacrificing her was no longer acceptable.

He cursed to himself and tossed his pistol on the table. Everyone else dropped their weapons on the floor while he focused on the twins.

One's eyes darted around the room, his grip on the gun tight. Sweat glistened on his knuckles. He looked scared and nervous.

The other appeared cool and calm, but heat smoldered behind his eyes.

Steven knew that fire; the man wanted to kill and eagerly anticipated what might come next.

"Kill them! Kill them all!" Cooper shouted.

The twins shared a glanced, and Tick's heart sank. He didn't enjoy killing. He only wanted to take the boys. He even hoped to find a way to let Mary go. He'd let other hostages go before without telling his brother. They could do other things to make money.

Their uncle was a florist, and Tick liked flowers. If he could kick the addictions that roiled him, he could think clearly, plan something concrete.

Then he saw his brother's eyes, and everything became clear. His heart plummeted.

Tock was the quiet one, but he was born to kill. He enjoyed it. Now he wanted to kill again.

The energy drained from Tom's legs and he almost fell to his knees.

How could this happen? She's supposed to be safe in the van.

The world tilted on its axis and time stopped. Sweat froze on the back of his neck. He hadn't even told her he loved her yet.

He stared at the gun pressed against her temple. *They're going to kill her.*

Panic raced through him. He tried to shove aside the despair that raked him, but the pistol was a .44 caliber weapon. A bullet fired at that range would pierce her skull, rip apart her brain, and escape through the other side along with much of her head. She would die in a heartbeat.

He stripped the mask from his face and let it fall to the ground. *This is my fault. I shouldn't have let her come.*

"Let her go," he pleaded.

He didn't know what else to say. He poised to jump, but it would be pointless—the distance was too far. Possibilities and probabilities swirled in his mind. There had to be a way to trade places, but nothing computed—all his intelligence, useless. Every scenario ended the same way. Still, he would try. He had to try.

He bent at the knees.

Aunt Jackie silently glided behind the twins, her pistol held steady. She looked like the shadow of death.

One twin shifted his weight and moved into a shooter's stance, his eyes glimmering eagerly.

The other twin increased the pressure around Mary's neck and held her still as his finger tightened on the trigger.

When the sonar glasses shut off, Aunt Jackie knew something was wrong. She had worked too many jobs not to trust her instinct now, so she slipped from the room and hid in the shadows.

It didn't take long for the twins to show up. They moved like mercenaries—confident and well trained as they dragged Mary with them.

When they entered the boardroom, she slid behind them, silent and ready. She knew what she had to do.

She leveled her gun at the head of the one holding Mary. She couldn't kill them both. Maybe when younger she might have been quick enough, but that was another lifetime ago.

Still, she had no choice. She loved the boys, and by extension, she loved Mary. It was her job to protect them. *It's the one job I've been trained to do. The one job where I can't fail.*

Faces flashed through her mind in a *whoosh*—names she hardly remembered. In the past, she'd always felt a wave of anger before pulling the trigger. Sometimes, she believed she was born angry.

She felt no comforting fury now. This was her one chance at redemption. After all the hate and killing, she would act out of love. A peace she had never experienced before filled her with strength.

Can this one selfless act save me after all I have done? Will I see John again?

She had started to think about him more often.

She narrowed her eyes and squeezed the trigger.

The bullet exploded through the one twin's head, and the other twin spun.

Jackie swung Excalibur at him, but he moved too fast and peppered her with bullets. Ice-cold needles pierced her body.

She smiled as she collapsed to the ground. She expected pain but felt none.

Steven flicked his wrist, and the handle of a throwing knife dug in the center of the remaining twin's back.

Tom lunged forward and reached the assailant before he turned, grabbed him around the shoulders, and drove his head into the wall. Plaster chipped as Tom rode him down to the ground and smashed his head into the floor again and again and again. He lifted the man's bloodied head for a fourth time, but Mary stopped him.

He shuddered angrily as she wrapped her arms around him.

Jack raced to Aunt Jackie's side and cradled her head in his hands. "You're going to be fine, Aunt Jackie." He gently peeled off her mask. "We're going to get you to a hospital."

She coughed up blood. "Don't be stupid, sonny boy. It was bound to happen sometime. Every circus ends eventually." She smiled and tried to sit up, but she didn't have the strength and fell back into Jack's hands, still clutching Excalibur.

"Do you know what they used to call me, Jack?" She smiled thinly.

Jack shared a helpless look with Tom. "The Sorcerer of Secretariat."

She smiled. "The Sorcerer of Secretariat. I wish you had seen me. They still talk about me."

"I bet you were great."

"You don't know this, but... I quit the circus when you were born. Maggie was sick and I took care of you for four months until she recovered. That was the best four months of my life."

She coughed again. More blood this time. "I should have quit the business for good back then, but I was afraid. So much hate and killing. Those were the only things I was ever good at. I should have been braver."

She smiled with only the edges of her lips. "Don't tell Thomas, but you've always been my favorite." She coughed again and spit blood from her mouth as she scowled at Jack. Her eyes focused sharply and she grabbed his shirt. "Make sure you kill him, Jack. You'll never be free of him until he's dead. Some people need killing. I'm counting on you, sonny boy."

As life left her, Jack felt her love for him in a wave of emotion that blew him back as if a dam had broken. He shook and tears tracked down his face.

Gabriel grabbed Cooper Simmens by the suit jacket and lifted him off the ground. "So you like killing women, do you?"

"I don't know what you're talking about," he sputtered. "I have a family. You're crazy."

Gabriel slapped him hard across the face and sent him sprawling to the floor at Moses's feet.

Moses grabbed two handfuls of hair and pushed him down hard on the floor. He held him for a moment and looked up, his face ashen. "He's telling the truth. It's not him."

CHAPTER 60

Terry glanced at the video monitor and saw Maggie sitting in the leather recliner, drawing. *How boring*.

He daydreamed about her demise and longed for the climax with childlike anticipation. Lately, Cooper had let him do more of the end work. He liked the feel of the surgical instruments—the cool steel in his hand, the look of panic on the woman's face. Cooper always strangled the last bit of oxygen from them, but he always smiled as Terry inflicted some of the punishment.

Terry knew it was his destiny to hurt people and had known it from an early age. He'd fought against those urges for a long while, but Cooper saw through his exterior. He understood the real Terry and had freed him to be his true self.

Most of the time, he lived an exciting, interesting life traveling with Cooper as a member of his staff with no specific responsibilities. His official title, *Butler*, sounded old fashioned, but old was in right now, and he loved the way it rolled off his tongue.

As butler, he enjoyed an elevated status over Cooper's other personal servants, and was supposed to *manage* them when he wasn't finding the next Maggie. He reveled in his role as supervisor and used his leverage to blackmail legions of servants—cooks, maids, drivers, assistants, and others. He caused all types of pain, some physical, but more often emotional and mental. He yearned to go back to that life, hating the *Maggie Times*, as he called them.

The Maggie Times were dead time. As the one responsible to keep the latest victim safe and secret until they had their way with her, he hated watching the latest Maggie, tending to her needs, befriending her. He wanted to dominate the other members of the staff, but everything Maggie-related had to be done secretly, and he simply didn't get the opportunity.

He surveyed his sparse room—just a bed, one dresser and the video monitor. During the Maggie Times, he spent all his time focused on the latest Maggie. The nightclubs, fancy dinners, and gallery openings all vanished.

He sighed. The worst part of the Maggie Times was the oppressive sameness of it. *How boring!*

This Maggie bored him worse than the others. All she wanted to do was draw, draw, draw. Luckily, the Maggie Times had dwindled in duration over the past few years. What started as a month had shrunk to a week, and the last time, only three days. This Maggie would never last, but he fretted over Cooper's busy schedule packed with events and meetings. Set to leave town in the morning, he wouldn't return for weeks.

Terry would be stuck in this prison for a month, and he couldn't take that. He had to make sure tonight was this Maggie's last.

He held a glass vial filled with a potent psychedelic drug he'd stolen from the pharmacy. Multiple warnings about side effects and proper dosage amounts peppered the outside of the bottle. He barely glanced at them, and dumped the entire contents of the vial into a freshly brewed cup of chamomile tea.

Maggie had given him the idea for it. She had fire. No one else had stabbed Cooper before. Terry liked that spirit, but he needed to give her spirit a boost. Cooper would return soon, and by the time he arrived the drug should already be working.

Lately, Cooper's mood had been erratic, quick to anger. Hopefully tonight would be more of the same. Hopefully tonight Terry would have a chance to use the surgical instruments.

Maybe he'll even let me take out the heart.

Terry lifted the tray and his spirits buoyed. One way or another, tonight would be stimulating. He needed Cooper to return to cut his Maggie Time short, and Terry had already made plans to dispose of her body.

CHAPTER 61

Jack tore his eyes from Aunt Jackie and studied the chief of staff, who lay on the floor. Tears streaked from his light blue eyes and his body trembled with fear.

"How do you know? It has to be him," Tom said. "If he's not the right Cooper, then what are we going to do? We don't have any other leads. Mom is running out of time. Aunt Jackie is dead. It can't all be for nothing."

Moses is right. We don't need the chief of staff. Jack couldn't say exactly how he knew, but he was certain of it. His wasn't the face that haunted his mind's eye, but the monster *was* in the room, and he stood next to Steven.

Jack ripped off his mask, rose to his feet, and pointed at the vice president. "He's the Cooper we need. He's the man we want."

"What are you talking about? I'm going to be the next president." The vice president sounded indignant and his face turned red.

Tom looked at Jack warily. "Are you sure?"

"You're going to have to trust me, Tom. There are times when you've to go with your gut. I'm sure!"

Jack watched Tom's face twist with doubts. He could almost hear him perform calculations and probabilities in his head.

Finally, Tom nodded. "If you say so, I believe you."

Tom turned and faced the vice president. His mind made up, he narrowed his eyes and inched his way toward him.

Steven leveled his handgun and aimed the weapon steadily at Tom's chest. "Don't come any closer, Tom. We can't take him on a hunch."

The vice president shifted behind Steven to use him as a shield, resting one hand on Vanessa's chair. She tried to push away, but he held the chair in place.

"Jack's word is good enough for me," Gabriel growled.

"Stand down!" ordered Steven.

Everyone in the room froze.

"I thought we needed someone named Cooper," Moses said. "The vice president's name is Peter."

"His full name is Peter *Cooper* Simmens," Mary said. "Everything fits The Professor's profile. He finished in the middle of his class at Princeton. He's three years older than Maggie. He floated around different business divisions of the Simmens Group for years before he became a senator from New York. He became Vice President after serving only three years in the Senate. Ethel Simmens is his mother. I should have seen this before."

"That's not enough." Steven kept his gun pointed at Tom, but it looked heavy in his hand. Indecision had crept into his eyes.

Tom had never seen that look on him before, and wondered if Steven could pull the trigger.

Jack growled, "I know it's him! I've seen his face. You have to believe me."

"You're nothing but a bad tennis instructor! How dare you accuse me!" The vice president's voice cracked as his eyes danced around the room. He hooted shrilly and pulled at his hair.

Tom slid closer. "How do you know Jack is a tennis instructor?"

Steven lowered his gun. As an expert interrogator, he now knew the truth. Peter *Cooper* Simmens was the Cooper they needed.

He nodded at Tom. Sheppard had ordered him to keep the vice president safe, but Steven had seen the pictures. He knew Maggie and felt the worry from the boys. He would not protect this monster.

His days of being a soldier were over. When he left the government, he thought he needed to take orders from someone else, someone better. Now he had Sheppard, a man he believed in, and his orders remained meaningless. He'd have to sort out his own decisions from now on.

His hand trembled. He was more scared than he'd ever been.

Steven spotted movement from the corner of his eye.

The chief of staff lunged for a handgun only a couple of feet away on the floor, and grabbed it before anyone else in the room reacted.

"Look out!" Vanessa shouted.

The chief of staff leveled the gun at Moses.

Gabriel dove at his friend and pushed him out of the way. Moses went flying, but the chief of staff discharged the weapon and shot Gabriel in the back. He went down hard.

In a heartbeat, Steven leveled his gun and blasted the chief of staff in the head.

"Gabe!" Moses rushed to his friend's side.

CHAPTER 62

Maggie watched as Terry entered the suite carrying a tin tray with a freshly brewed cup of tea on it, whistling a happy tune and bouncing on his toes as he walked.

"I thought you might like something hot to drink." He smiled as he placed the tray on the small table beside her.

She needed to know whether he would help her, and didn't have much time left. Cooper's volcano was bubbling up, and the next time they were together, one of them would die. She needed to warn her boys, and Terry was her only chance.

"Did you contact my sons?" she whispered.

He smiled. "You should drink the tea." He handed her a full mug; steam circled above it. "I've added sugar the way you like it."

She took the mug. "What about my note? Did you reach my boys?"

He nodded. "Yes, Maggie, I sent them a text message explaining everything."

She studied the expression on his face. She had raised two sons mostly by herself. They were good boys, but they had spun a yarn every once in a while, and her finely tuned truth meter suspected he was lying. "What number did you send the message to?"

His eyes flickered. "I sent the text to the number on file. I think it was Jack's number. Now drink the tea."

Maggie's truth meter blared.

He's lying to me. He won't help me.

Anger swelled up in her. "You know what Cooper does here, don't you? How many women have you helped him murder?"

His face turned frigid as he leaned toward her and spoke through gritted teeth. "I don't know what you're talking about. Why don't you drink your tea? It will make you feel better."

Sensing danger, Maggie disarmed him with a smile. After working many years at a high-powered law firm, she'd learned how to disarm volatile, stressed-out attorneys.

How hard could he be?

"I'm sorry. I'm under so much stress. I know you're helping me and would have nothing to do with such nastiness." She glanced at the porcelain mug and inched it toward her mouth.

He relaxed and his smile returned.

Something is amiss.

Maggie lowered the mug and peered inside. "What type of tea is this? It smells unusual."

"It's chamomile. I'm sure it will help you rest." He tried to sound sweet, but he balled his hands into fists and clenched his jaw tight.

He's too interested in the tea. Why does he care so much if I drink it?

She glanced at the cup again. "I think there's something swirling in the tea."

"There's nothing in that mug."

His face turned red, and when he leaned close to examine it, she thrust the cup at him. Hot tea scalded his face, and he squealed.

Maggie grabbed the tin platter from the table and bashed it against his face, knocking him backward and toppling him to the ground. She jumped from her chair, raced to the bathroom, and slammed the door shut.

What am I going to do now?

CHAPTER 63

Gabriel moaned as Jack and Moses removed his shirt and peeled off his armored vest. A nasty bruise had developed on his back, but only the tip of the bullet peeked through the armored material. It had held.

Cooper cackled. He rubbed his manicured hands through his perfectly feathered hair, and muttered gibberish.

Cornered, he couldn't understand how they had found him, how they could have caught him. Rage ripped through him.

I am Vice President of the United States! What are they? Nothing. Inferior stock.

He shuddered, furious. Animal instinct warned him that he was in trouble, and he fought hard to keep himself together.

I have superior genes.

He snapped out of his fog, furious yet lucid. "I used to go by Cooper when I was young. I always liked that name better, but Ethel preferred Peter, and Ethel always gets what she wants."

"How could you hurt all those women?" Mary asked.

"Those women were nothing. I took them away from a miserable life and gave them everything. They were lucky to be with me. They had a moment in the sun instead of a lifetime in darkness."

"You killed them!"

"They had to die. They were no good. They deserved to die. I needed to understand why... why Maggs refused me. The secret should have been inside them. It was their fault."

He brushed his hair, straightened his tie, and smiled. "But I never found the reason. No matter how hard I searched or how much I hurt them. Now I understand. Maggs was the problem all along. *She* was the defective one!"

A wild fury grew inside him. "I hate her! She has to die, has to die, *has to die!*" He lowered his head and stared at the floor, half-expecting a trap door to spring open at any moment and for him to fall through and plummet to hell.

The maniac started muttering to himself.

Tom leaped over the table and landed at his side. "Where's my mother?"

A wicked smile graced Cooper's face. "I like hurting your mother. I've always liked it."

Tom slapped him hard across the face, and blood trickled out of his mouth.

"You will never find her." The words floated in a slow, high-pitched, singsong voice. "Never ever find her." He closed his eyes tight and clamped his hands over his ears.

Steven pulled a five-inch hunting knife from his vest and held the blade to his throat. "Tell us where she is."

Cooper twisted his face furiously, and laughed uncontrollably. He pulled at his hair and stumbled backward against the wall, searching the room frantically, as if seeing people who weren't there. "I don't want children! Why am I never good enough? Mom!"

He twisted and stared at the wall behind him. "Stop staring at me! I don't want to be President. Who are all you people? You have no right to be here. Make your own decisions! Stop asking me! Go away,

Grandfather, and leave me alone! I'm not weak! I killed you! I killed all of you!"

Steven glanced at Tom. "I can't interrogate him like this. He can't separate real from unreal. I tried questioning someone else in the same condition a long time ago. It was useless. I had to slit his throat in a mercy killing. Even drugs won't help." He lowered his knife from Cooper's throat.

Cooper tore the fine cotton collar of his shirt and scratched at his face, breaking the skin. Blood trickled down his left cheek as he turned and faced Tom straight on. He seemed to look right past Tom—through him.

"Help me!" He spun away and stared at the wall, sobbing. "Why won't you live with me and my parents? I don't want any of it. I just want you!"

He twisted and laughed again. "Tick! Tock! Tick! Tock! What's wrong with me?"

He continued spouting random thoughts and jabbing at things not there. He pulled out his hair in chunks, twisted in place, and clawed at his face.

Finally, he collapsed on the floor and shook violently.

Tom turned toward Jack, whose face clouded with uncertainty. "He's reached the shatter point, Jack. How are we going to find Mom now?"

"Maybe I can pry the truth out of him." Jack sighed. "Something is wrong with me. It's more than sensitivity to light or noise. I've been seeing visions. At first, I thought they were daydreams, but they're more than that. That's how I knew he was the Cooper we needed, and what was in Aunt Jackie's bag, and that you'd been fighting with Mary. Even now, I see things from his mind—disturbing things—but they're hazy, as if hidden behind the insanity. When I touch someone, the visions sometimes become clearer, stronger. If I grab him, I might learn where he's holding Mom."

Tom felt as if the wind had been knocked out of him. He knew Jack needed help, but he didn't know his condition was this bad. "Is it dangerous?" He knew the answer but had to ask anyway.

Jack shrugged and stalked toward Cooper.

"Wait!" Tom stood in his path. "Those were the times when you got the worst headaches. You were unconscious for five minutes at the lodge. I can't lose you again."

He thought he had lost Jack four months ago when he lay in that coma, and a hole ripped opened in his heart that had never fully closed. He'd sworn he would never lose him again, but that hole tore open again; only this time the pain was even worse.

"I'm not sure I ever fully came back." Jack turned to face George, who stood at the right hand corner of the room. "Isn't that right?"

"Darian's been trying to reach you. There are still treatments we can try." He offered the right words, but his face told a different story.

Tears swelled in Tom's eyes.

Jack squeezed his arm. "You're a good brother. The best! I wouldn't trade you for anyone. This is our only chance to save Mom. I know she's running out of time. I feel it. We have to do whatever it takes to save her. I need to do this. You'd do it for me. You *did* do it for me."

Tom tried to breathe, but the air caught in his throat. All he could do was nod and step aside. His legs turned to liquid and he did his best not to collapse to the floor.

Jack wrapped his bloodied hands around Cooper's throat. Electricity jolted through him, the pain in his head intense.

He dove into Cooper's mind, finding a kaleidoscope of thoughts, one merging into another. Trying to sort through the fragments, he drifted among Cooper's visions, feeling rather like he was in a raft circled by sharks. He searched for Maggie, and found her face, but she swam away from him—just under the surface. He concentrated on her image, and bits of memory flashed into his mind—she was in their apartment, and a note fluttered to the ground.

Jack groaned as his head split open, but he increased his concentration and bore down deeper. He experienced a sharp pain in his leg, as if someone had stabbed him, and then he caught something—a sign for a hospital.

Tom's voice, full of worry, floated on the sea of thoughts. The words sounded garbled, as if they came from the other side of a wall. He tried to hear them clearly but couldn't.

Then he saw Aunt Jackie's face. The collar of her shirt was open and the top of a horse tattoo peeked out. Suddenly, she looked young again and beautiful, but her voice sounded old and raspy, as she'd sounded before she died.

"Get going, sonny boy!"

Somehow he found the strength and pushed Cooper away.

Jack opened his eyes and his body shook. White-hot pain seared through his skull and pierced through bone. His words slurred together. "She's at the New York Hospital in the mental ward."

He looked at Tom through watery eyes. Tom's face fractured and the pieces scattered as rage flooded through Jack. He saw the women Cooper had ravaged—all of them. He felt Cooper's excitement and heard his sick thoughts. He tried to escape, to bury Cooper, but he couldn't. The feeling intensified and grew first white hot, then black, and....

CHAPTER 64

What now? Maggie scanned the bathroom.

Slam!

Terry must have left the suite. She breathed as deeply as her broken ribs would allow and tried to clear her mind.

I need time.

She stared at the closed bathroom door, knowing that it offered her no real safety. Terry would come back. She needed one last chance to kill Cooper. There had to be something, some way to keep Terry away from her.

She noticed a small, thin metal plate by the side of the door, and it hit her. Electricity operated the door, but if she opened the plate and disable the motor, it would slow him down.

She grabbed the nail clippers from the dresser and pried open one of the small and pointy attachments. *Good enough.*

Two Phillips head screws held the metal plate in place. Using the attachment from the clippers, she loosened the screws until the plate popped off.

What now?

Her strengths had always been in the arts and her ability to connect with people. Science was foreign to her, but she had raised Tom. He *lived* science, and after seventeen years of home experiments, she had learned a few things.

She studied the wires—red, green, and black. Her hands twitched between the three. Their doorbell at home used the same configuration; Tom had fixed it two years ago while she watched over his shoulder. She closed her eyes and summoned the image.

He'd chatted incessantly about the electricity.

What did he say?

He'd rambled about currents and proper grounding....

Finally, she heard his voice. "The red one is the hot wire. The green one connects to the motor and the black is a ground. It's important...."

She bit her lip. *What did he say next?*

"It's important the red and green wires don't touch. That would blow out the motor."

Channeling her inner Tom, she connected the red wire directly to the green one. A nasty shock zapped her finger and a puff of smoke swirled above the wires. She touched the control for the door and nothing happened. She shoved against the door, and it didn't budge.

I am a strong woman.

Her safety was only temporary. All Terry needed to do was shut off the electricity and pry the door open manually. Still, the process would take time, and time was all she wanted—time, and one last chance to confront Cooper.

Now I need a weapon.

She had searched the bathroom before, but this time she surveyed the room the way she imagined Tom might. Her eyes lingered on the stainless steel stool. The legs appeared sturdy—sturdy enough to be used as a club.

I am a strong woman!

She flipped the stool on its side.

How would Tom take this apart?

CHAPTER 65

Steven locked eyes with Vanessa. He had made her a promise, and his days of breaking promises had ended. *How am I going to find Doctor Beck?*

Tom caught his brother as he fell, and gently set him on the carpet. "We've got to go to the hospital! We need Doctor Beck."

Wickersham rolled on the ground at Steven's feet, still moaning from the aftereffects of his own taser.

Inspired, Steven grabbed him by the suit jacket, lifted, and yanked the diminutive doctor onto the table with a *thud*.

Wickersham screeched.

Steven leveled his gun at the man's head and spoke in a cool and calm voice, knowing that made it even more frightening. "Where is Doctor Beck?"

Wickersham's eyes twitched and he whimpered. "I don't know what you're... talking... about."

Steven aimed the nozzle at his forehead and held it steady. "I'll give you three seconds and then I'm pulling the trigger. *One.*"

Wickersham's eyes locked onto Vanessa.

"Two."

"Don't shoot! I'll tell you."

Steven pushed the barrel of the handgun hard against his plastic forehead. "Well."

"He's in the cellar with the interrogator. Don't shoot. We weren't going to kill him. We were going to let him go. You have to believe me." Wickersham squirmed and looked at Vanessa. "I'm sorry, Nessa. This wasn't my idea. He's not right for you."

Steven growled. "How do I find the cellar?"

"Take the back staircase. There's a key in my pocket."

Steven rummaged through Wickersham's suit pockets and pulled out an old bronze key. As he examined it, a bell chimed that startled everyone.

Steven removed the transmission inhibitor from his vest pocket. The device glowed red. "The inhibitor's been breached. All of the texts and messages they had sent will be released now. We have five minutes at most before others arrive. We'd better move fast."

He grabbed a dart pistol from the floor and promptly shot Wickersham, Sanders, George, and Cooper.

"I'll retrieve Doctor Beck from the cellar." He tossed a hand-sized disk to Tom. "That's a memory eraser. Pull the pin and leave it in the boardroom on your way out. It'll wipe their memories for the last few hours. Bring Jack and Cooper to the van. I'll meet you out front in five minutes. If I'm not out in time, leave."

Steven nodded at Vanessa, and they bolted from the room to save Darian, *if* they could save him.

Moses pulled the van in front of the industrial building, and let it idle.

They waited and stared at the lobby in silence. Time crept by.

"Five minutes since the inhibitor failed," Mary called out.

"He'll be here. We stay," Moses said.

"Five minutes thirty-seconds."

Moses shook his head and kicked Cooper's prone body on the floor of the van.

Aunt Jackie lay next to him. Tom couldn't leave her behind.

Tom held Jack's head in his lap. His eyes met Mary's. "I should have noticed the signs. He's been sensitive to noise and light. He's had these headaches. It was all there for me to see. I should have talked to Doctor Beck myself."

She squeezed his shoulder. "Stay positive, Tom. This isn't your fault. We'll take him to a doctor." She checked her watch and frowned. "Six minutes!"

Tom glanced at Gabriel, who shook his head. "If Moses says he'll be here, he'll be here."

Sirens wailed in the distance. The heat in the van became sweltering, and sweat rolled down Tom's face in rivers as his stomach soured. Time was running out. He had to get to the hospital.

Suddenly, Steven burst from the lobby with one arm around Darian's back, while Darian draped his arm over Steven's right shoulder, shuffling his feet and wearing loose-fitting gray clothes. Steven helped him into the back of the van, raced around to the front, and jumped into the passenger seat.

The tires screeched as they peeled away from the curb, but a Homeland Security SUV had already pulled onto the street behind them. The van sped away, but the SUV followed and pulled closer, sirens wailing.

"Nobody look back! Eyes front!" Steven flipped a switch.

Though looking forward, Tom caught the residue of a flash of blinding white light from the back of the van. It must have blinded the driver of the SUV, which crashed into a truck on the side of the road.

Moses turned right onto the West Side Highway before another Homeland Security vehicle could spot them. They were in the clear.

Darian slumped against the side of the van, his hair greasy with sweat. He winced as he moved, but his eyes locked on Jack. "What happened?"

"He fainted," Tom said.

"Tell me everything. I was worried this would happen."

"You're bleeding, Doctor Beck. Look at your shirt!" Mary pointed to a stain on the collar.

Darian grinned. "That's not my blood."

CHAPTER 66

Terry stomped back to his small room across the hall. Angry, blotchy red islands formed on his cheeks and chin where the tea had burned him. He splashed water on his face, but the red spots persisted.

He pounded the pedestal sink. "That bitch!" He always ended up hating the Maggies after a time, but he despised this Maggie more than any of the others.

"Look at these blisters!" He kicked the trashcan and sent if flying into his bedroom.

He opened the medicine cabinet, grabbed a bottle of potent pain suppressors, and swiped everything else onto the floor. With trembling fingers he popped open the bottle, removed five pills, and dropped two to the floor. He placed the remaining three on a plate and crushed them to powder with the flat side of a knife.

He had never taken more than two before, but the burns felt like a hot coil pressed against his flesh. He lined the powder into four long thin lines and snorted them, letting his bloodstream immediately absorb the narcotic.

Feeling instantly better, he wondered what he should do about Maggie.

She has to pay for this, but if I kill her, Cooper will fly into a rage.

Cooper killed all the previous Maggies, but Terry so wanted to kill this one. He paced his small room.

Maybe I could make it appear like a suicide.

"That won't work," he muttered to himself.

Cooper would still be angry. Terry was responsible to make sure the Maggies stayed unharmed until *Cooper* killed them. He suspected the last butler had failed at this part of his job and was never seen again. He would have to be smarter.

He continued pacing, each footstep angrier than the last. Visions of his hands around Maggie's throat so enraptured him he almost didn't hear the sound of an incoming text. Almost, but the ping was loud and had the distinctive ring tone he selected only for Cooper's messages.

He glanced at his phone. It displayed a one-word message—*Yorktown.*

He had no idea what Yorktown referred to, but he knew the codeword meant something had gone awry. He needed to dispose of the current Maggie, clean up, and leave the hospital immediately.

He stared at the message for a few moments, and had a hard time believing his good fortune. He shook his head and stared at the phone again. The message remained. He splashed more water on his face and took a deep breath. The message didn't change.

A smile bloomed across his face. *What a gift.* He felt like a child on Christmas Day.

"I can kill her. I can kill her," he sang to himself as he reached for his baton and practically skipped from his room.

He didn't bother to alert the armed guard that there might be trouble. This was all his.

CHAPTER 67

Steven clutched his phone a little too tightly. "We've had some difficulties at the meeting, Mr. Sheppard. The vice president is really the Cooper we need. His chief of staff is dead."

"That changes everything. What did you do with the vice president?"

"His mind has shattered, Mr. Sheppard. He's in the van, but he's gone. We've got a lead on Maggie's location. Tom and I need access to the Premium Wing of the Psychiatric Ward at the New York Hospital. Maggie is being held there. We don't have much time."

Moses sped the van up the West Side Highway, swerved around a slow moving coupe, and squealed the tires as he darted around a bus. The van lifted onto two tires but bounced back to all four a second later.

"Also, Jack's unconscious. He'll need to be admitted in the main hospital under Doctor Beck's care."

"I'll call you back in a few minutes."

Gabriel interrupted from the back of the van. "I want to join you guys. I could come in handy."

"I'm sure you would, Gabriel, but Homeland is looking for you," Steven said. "It's too risky. You need to stay in the van with Moses and keep an eye on Cooper. Mary and Doctor Beck will take Jack into the hospital and admit him."

Gabriel stomped Cooper in the side.

Steven shot him a sharp glare. "Don't kill him. We can deal with him later."

Moses swung the van off the West Side Highway at the 79th Street exit, and slowed the vehicle at the Homeland Security checkpoint.

Two armed agents patrolled the heavy metal barrier. Steven handed them his citizen's identification card, which gave him access to the more affluent areas of the city.

They nodded and the gate rose.

Sheppard called back. "I added Jack to the Sheppard insurance plan. He already has a private room. The hospital will admit him. That's the easier situation.... The news isn't as good about the Premium Wing. Access is only granted to patients and approved visitors.

"A Jessica Woodson is staying on the ward. My technology guy changed the information on your card. It shows that you're Michael Woodson's bodyguard. Michael is Jessica's brother and an approved visitor. I don't know anything else about Jessica. Unfortunately, we don't have time to change Tom's information. You'll have to say he's Jessica's brother and bluff your way in. That's the best we could do in so little time."

"Thank you, Mr. Sheppard. It will do."

Tom and Steven took the elevator to the Premium Wing.

The door swished open and Steven strode up to an armed security officer, who sat behind a half-circle mahogany desk in front of double doors leading to the ward. "Mister Woodson is here to visit his sister." He handed the guard his citizen card.

Tom stood a step behind him, looking uncomfortable in a lightweight gray gingham sport jacket, white shirt, and blue slacks—all clothes from the storage bin in the van. He tried to appear annoyed and tapped his foot.

The guard swiped Steven's ID. "Can I have Mr. Woodson's card, please?"

Steven leaned toward the guard. "I was supposed to bring the card, but I forgot." He noticed a tattoo on the guard's left forearm of two crossed rifles forming an *X*.

"Is there a problem, Steven?" Tom asked, his tone frigid. "I don't have all night. The benefit is in an hour."

Steven glanced back at him. "No problems, Mr. Woodson. The card reader is just a little slow."

Steven leaned closer to the guard and whispered, "If he finds out I forgot his card, he'll fire me. Last week, the car wasn't *properly* washed and he docked me a week's pay. I really can't afford to get canned. This is my first job since I left the Army. Give me a break."

The guard pointed to his tattoo. "I was a grunt myself. What division did you serve in?"

"The 36th Infantry Division out of Texas," he lied.

The guard smiled, glanced at Tom over Steven's shoulder and nodded. "He looks like a real ass. I hate the young ones. He's probably never worked a day in his life." He shifted his eyes across the empty hallway. "It's late, so no one's around. I'll let you in this once because you're a grunt, but don't forget again."

"Thanks."

The guard waved them in.

They entered the main hallway. Alternating white and black one-foot-square marble tiles covered the floor, soft yellow paint covered the walls, and hunter green doors with heavy glass windows led to private suites.

No other guests walked the hallway, but a handful of orderlies dressed in white roamed the corridor. A muffled scream escaped from behind one of the doors.

Tom's body tensed and with each step, his pace quickened.

"Stay in control," Steven whispered.

Tom slowed, but his left eye started to twitch.

Terry swept into the suite of rooms floating on a drug-induced euphoric cloud. Every nerve in his body burned. Finally, he felt complete. Finally, he could kill a Maggie.

"Where are you?"

He smiled and skipped toward the closed bathroom door.

"Come out and play, Maggie." He chuckled despite his best intentions. "I'm sorry I got so angry. I have a present for you. You can't hide from me."

The baton felt good and firm and dangerous as he slapped it against his palm.

"I guess I'll have to come in after you."

He felt light and airy, and a soft buzzing sound filled his head. He touched the control on the bathroom door but nothing happened, and the buzzing intensified. He stared at the control for a moment, uncertain what had happened, and pressed the pad again. Still nothing. The buzzing grew louder.

"What did you do to the door, you miserable *witch*?"

He threw his shoulder against the wood. It creaked but held, and the buzzing cascaded a waterfall. This time, he took a running start and leaped into the door shoulder first. It bent but didn't give way.

"I'm going to make you pay for this!"

Somewhere underneath the roar of the waterfall, he remembered that the door rolled into a pocket in the wall. He grabbed the side of the door and pulled, his fingernails digging into the wood as he tried to roll it, but it stayed planted. Niagara Falls crashed inside his head.

He stepped back. "I'm going to take my time with you!"

He breathed heavily and swayed with an uncontrollable urge to hit something—*anything*! He pummeled the door with a series of karate-style front kicks. He had no formal training but had spent many hours on the virtual simulator.

The wood cracked under the blows. He reared back and launched an eighth front kick, and the wood splintered, leaving the door shredded. He swung the baton at the gaping hole until it expanded enough for him to fit through. He smashed his hand against the sharp edges and blood dripped from his knuckles, but he didn't feel any pain. He only felt a carnal frenzy, wanting nothing but to kill Maggie, to strangle her and cry tears of joy.

He shouldered his way into the bathroom and.... It was empty. He stared at the air vent leading to the ceiling, which had been pried open.

"What the heck?" The vent was too small for anyone to fit into it.

He didn't notice Maggie slide up behind him.

She swung the leg of the stool like a Louisville Slugger, and the blow connected with a thud against his ribs. She could swear she heard bones broke, but Terry barely flinched as he yanked the metal leg from her hand. A sick smile spread across his lips, and she tried to turn and run, but he grabbed her hair and threw her through the jagged opening in the door.

She fell forward into the suite and tumbled onto her side.

A moment later he stood over her, straddling her with the baton in his hand. Blood dripped from his knuckles and his face flushed red. Sweat dripped from his forehead and an otherworldly glow lit his eyes.

"This is going to hurt," he said.

CHAPTER 68

Tom summoned all his willpower, fought against the panic, and slowed his pace. He scanned the hallway as he looked for signs of his mother.

Steven strode beside him, his gait smooth and unhurried and his demeanor calm and measured. He whispered, "Maggie will be held in a more secure part of the ward. Cooper would never risk holding her with the rest of the other premium patients."

Tom tried hard to rein in his imagination. His mother shouldn't be in a place like this. Horrible images flashed through his mind and made him shake. He glanced behind one of the green doors, and a young woman in a blue patient gown stared back at him, her mouth agape. Her hair had been shaved off, and her eyes blazed hot-black onyx behind her ash-white complexion. His heart clogged his throat.

His family had always been small, yet his mother filled it with enough love for one twice the size. When his father died, she could have retreated, turned away from the unfairness of his death, but she never did. She glued them together. Now, he had to save her. He was her last chance.

When they reached the turning point of the L-shaped ward, Tom noticed heavy steel double doors at the end of the hallway. A hulking security guard, pistol holstered at his side and electrified baton held in his hand, sat on a stool and blocked the path. A private elevator stood shiny and unused to the guard's right.

"Maggie will be behind those doors," Steven whispered. "We'll need to shove the guard's hand into that DNA reader to open the gates." A black plastic device resembling the outline of a hand was affixed to the wall next to the guard. "He'll have to be alive for us to use the reader. It measures pulse and DNA."

As they approached, the guard rose from his stool, twice as wide as Steven and towering a few inches over him. The giant tapped the baton sharply in his right hand. *Raymond Smith* was embroidered on his black shirt. He had a bent nose, a wispy thin mustache, and dead eyes.

Within six feet of the guard, Steven stopped. "Simmens sent me to relieve you. He wants me to work the rest of the night."

Raymond checked the time on his watch. "I still have another three hours. How come I've never seen you before?"

Steven shrugged. "I'm new. They stuck me with the midnight shift."

"Who's that?" He pointed the edge of the baton at Tom.

Steven smiled. "That's Doctor Polen. He's supposed to be some type of genius."

"He looks young to me."

Steven stepped forward and whispered, "You know these new eggheads. They race through school, but I doubt he's ever kissed a girl."

Raymond snorted. "I know the type. They're crawling all over here. I'll have to call in and check this out."

He reached for a cell phone in his pocket, and before he could react, Steven grabbed the baton, twisted it toward him, pressed the power button, and blasted him.

Steven held the thin stick steady as the guard fried. When Raymond slumped unconscious, Steven wedged his body against Raymond's weight and jammed his hand into the DNA/pulse reader.

Tom glanced over his shoulder. Halfway down the hall, two orderlies were laughing, oblivious to the quick alteration. The entire episode took no longer than ten seconds.

The steel door clicked open.

"Hold the door open for me, Tom." Steven dragged the heavy guard behind the steel doors and dropped him on the other side. "I'll wait out front. They'll know something is wrong if there's no guard. Be quick."

Adrenaline jolted Tom's body as he scanned the hallway and crept forward, uncertain what he would find. Butterflies fluttered in his throat. *Am I too late?*

The first door on the left led to a well-appointed office—empty. Tom's heart pounded. The next door on the right opened into an empty kitchen. His skin crawled, but he moved forward.

A photograph of a man's face and the name Terry written underneath it was fixed on the half-open door on the left. Tom swung the door fully open and saw a small, tidy bedroom—also empty. Still, the bedroom looked like someone had just left it, because the sheets on the bed had bunched up where someone had recently been sitting, and a trashcan had been tossed to the middle of the room.

Why would someone toss a trashcan?

Fear shook him, and he bolted down the hallway to the last door on the right.

CHAPTER 69

Maggie had been a good athlete when she was younger. She often told Jack he had inherited his tennis ability from her, as Paul had been a little clumsy.

When Terry stood over her, she did the only thing that came into her mind—she kicked upward, driving her foot into his crotch. If she had been on the soccer pitch, she would have curved the ball beyond the goalkeeper.

Terry looked totally stoned, but the blow registered. He doubled over and his eyes rolled into his head.

Maggie twisted away, scooted to her feet, and raced to the living area.

Terry recovered quickly and stalked after her, muttering to himself.

She darted behind a long oval cocktail table and kept it between them.

He waved at her with the baton. "There's nowhere for you to go. You'll need my DNA to get past the reader at the door."

Her heart galloped. "Cooper will be very angry with you if you hurt me. Leave me alone, and I won't tell him anything about this."

He flashed a sick, knowing grin. "Cooper's done with you. You're all mine and I'm going to enjoy myself."

He stomped to the left and swerved back to the right. Each time he moved, she matched him. The dance continued around the table for a few minutes, until he grabbed the edge and toppled it toward her. That forced her to the right, where he greeted her with a hard slap across the face that sent her sprawling to the floor.

Tears welled up in her eyes as he moved toward her.

I am a strong woman.

He kicked her while she was still on the ground, his foot pounding her broken ribs. Firecrackers exploded in her head.

He raised the baton, grinned, and....

The door to the suite crashed opened.

Tom stood in the doorway and glared at his mom's attacker twenty feet away. Only thick carpet separated the two. "Get away from my mother!"

He sprinted forward and tackled Terry before he could move. The two went down hard in a jumble of body parts. Tom twisted to gain the advantage, but Terry slashed the baton and jabbed him in the side, causing Tom to roll off him.

"I'm going to kill you both." Terry sneered, a crazy look in his eyes.

Tom lunged at him, but Terry moved quicker, dodging to his left, pushing Tom hard in the back and sending him tumbling face first.

Terry laughed. "You're pathetic. Just like your mom. I'm going to make you watch as I kill her."

Tom's vision clouded over, but he remembered his jujitsu training and Steven's warning to stay in control. He steadied his breathing and advanced, each step measured and menacing.

Terry's dilated eyes widened.

Tom threw a barrage of punches. After blocking the first three, his adversary's arms slowed, and Tom connected with a hard left hook to his solar plexus. Normally, such a blow would have crumpled any opponent, but Terry only stumbled back a step.

Tom growled and advanced. Terry tried a right front kick, but poor technique left him off balance, so Tom darted to the side and swept his attacker's other foot off the floor.

He fell hard.

Tom smiled.

The thug tried to get up, but Tom shot his foot out and kicked him in the side of the head. Bone broke. His nose bloodied and shredded, and he lay unmoving on the carpet.

Tom dashed to his mother's side.

She struggled to her feet and winced in pain, her breathing shallow.

"Are you okay?" He could hardly breathe. He had never seen her hurt before. He reached to help her, his concern so intense he forgot about everything else.

His mom got unsteadily to her feet.

Tom glanced down and saw a reflection off the cocktail table's shiny surface. He spun, but he was too late.

Terry swung the baton and connected hard with Tom's head, and darkness took him.

Terry cackled. "What a loser!"

His whole body shook with laughter. He felt strong and whole--triumphant. He *needed* this. He *needed* to kill them. He was *destined* to kill them.

He beamed a wide grin as he raised the baton to kill Maggie's son and embrace his destiny, his true self.

Clank!

Maggie had swung the shiny metal tray with all her might hitting Terry flush on the face.

He crashed to the floor, where new blood poured from his already broken nose and soaked his face.

She lifted the tray over her head again. "Leave...."

Clank!

"...my son...."

Clank!

"...alone!"

Clank!

Tom stirred and rubbed the side of his head.

She tossed the dented tray to the side, darted to him, and folded him into her arms.

"Where's Jack?"

He looked away, and her heart missed a beat.

CHAPTER 70

The next day, Darian walked stiffly, head hung low with a frown etched on his face. Random shooting pains still plagued him from his time with the interrogator, but he welcomed that pain. He deserved that pain. He wished it were worse. If he could dig a giant hole, bury hot coals in it and jump in, he would gladly do it.

He had spent the day with Jack, Maggie, and Tom. Jack lay unconscious and, based on the latest computer simulations, had only a day left to live. Despair and grief hovered over his hospital room in a dense fog.

It reminded Darian of how he'd felt when the Warden told him his mom had died—only more intense. He'd expected the worst for his mother, and knew her end would be bad—maybe not consciously, but the thought stuck in the back of his mind, ever present.

Maggie and Tom had received no such warnings about Jack. He was young and should have had a full life in front of him. His whole future was stolen away from them in a flash—a flash Darian had created.

He came clean to the family, explaining EBF-202 and his role in Jack's condition. He gave them all the facts and stood before them, waiting to be judged guilty, waiting for their wrath, waiting for them to scream at him and even to strike him. He deserved it, and would have welcomed it.

Yet after he finished explaining the situation, Maggie hugged him—the same awkward embrace she had given him four months earlier when Jack recovered from his coma. She forgave him and thanked him for the four extra months they had with Jack. She didn't believe he would have come out of the coma without his help.

Tom, on the other hand, wouldn't look at him.

Darian felt like the lowest creature on the planet—a dung beetle, perhaps. He needed a break from his vigil, so he somberly went to visit Lassie—the only test subject he hadn't managed to kill.

The kennel bustled with activity. The other researchers used a wide variety of dogs as test subjects, and it was feeding time. Lassie had her own room, being the last of his test subjects to survive. When he entered the small chamber, she playfully approached him, tail wagging, unaware of the pond scum he really was.

He pressed his back against the glass wall, slid down its length like slime, sat cross-legged on the tile floor, and stroked Lassie's thick fur. "I'm no good, Lassie."

She jumped into his lap, dropping her head on his thigh.

"I wish you could talk. You would tell me the secret. You know what I should do, don't you, girl?"

She lifted her head, stared at him, barked once, and plopped her head back down on his lap.

An autopsy now would be useless. The test results from her brain tissue would come back too late to save Jack.

He sat for a time, lost in his misery. An image of his mother drifted to his mind—young, healthy, beautiful. It was a child's fantasy. *Did she ever look like that?*

The mental picture morphed to what she had looked like the last time he saw her—her skin a sickly yellow, her face lined with wrinkles. A purple bruise marred her right cheek, and desperation flickered behind her eyes.

What did I really feel when she died?

He'd wept for the first time. Lord help him, he was relieved—relieved the bowl of ice cream came, and that he wouldn't have to worry about her any longer. Tidal waves of guilt and emotion had rolled through him as he mourned his mother for the first time.

He lost track of time as he sat with Lassie in his lap. He reached into his coat pocket and felt the syringe with EBF-202 inside. He carried the needle around with him everywhere he went now. After Jack died, he would inject himself with it. He had failed—not smart enough to discover the cure. Maybe with EBF-202's help, he could figure out the inhibitor before Wickersham found another patient.

He'd almost removed the needle from his pocket when the caregiver, Ed, entered the room carrying Lassie's bag of kibble over his broad shoulder. She jumped from his lap, wagged her tail excitedly, and barked at the familiar face.

"Easy, Lassie! You sure are excited today. Did Doctor Beck make you all riled up this morning?" Ed dropped the bag of dog food on the floor. "I'm surprised to see you during feeding time, Doc. Usually you're busy in the lab. Is everything okay?"

Darian managed a weak smile. "I've been better, Ed, but Lassie seems happy."

Ed opened the bag, dug out two large scoops of kibble, and dropped them in her metal bowl. She woofed twice more. "Usually she's quiet. She hasn't barked like this in months."

Darian glanced at Lassie, and then noticed the white bag of dry dog food. "When did we switch dog food? I thought we used a red bag."

Ed paused for a second. "It must have been three months ago. This food is cheaper."

"Three months!" Darian bounced to his feet. "How come it wasn't in her chart?"

"Gee, I don't know, Doc. We changed the food for all the dogs. They were supposed to send out a memo."

"Let me see that bag." He snatched it and scanned the ingredients. "Lassie is supposed to eat specialized organic food. It's important to regulate what she ingests as part of the drug trial. The beef used for this kibble comes from normal meat cows. These cows are given growth hormones."

An idea shot like an arrow through his mind. "Those growth hormones leak into the food. One of them must be inhibiting EBF-202!"

Lassie barked three times.

He raced from the kennel carrying the bag of kibble over his shoulder, spilling little dried bits of dog food as he ran.

Darian and Brenda studied the results from the mass spectrometer. The new dog food contained dozens of chemicals that had no reason to be there, and a half dozen different types of growth hormones popped up on the analysis, but Darian grimly ticked off the reason each one should have no effect on EBF-202.

"The key has to be in here somewhere," he said. He crossed his arms against his chest, sweat soaking his t-shirt.

Brenda pointed to the far end of the readings. "What about those proteins? They appear misfolded, like prions."

He highlighted the three proteins, and the screen shifted to a detailed molecular breakdown of the prions.

Prions were on Brenda's list of things that killed brain cells. "Certain prions cause Bovine Spongiform Encephalopathy."

Darian smiled. "That's mad cow disease. It causes brain degeneration."

"But none of these prions cause mad cow disease," Brenda said.

"True, but one of them must be inhibiting EBF-202 from working. The prions' tendency to degenerate brain cells must be counteracting the drug."

"Which one do we try?"

"All three!"

Darian switched on the music and AC/DC's *Back in Black* started playing.

CHAPTER 71

Three days later, Maggie watched as Tom hovered over his brother with arms crossed and eyebrows furrowed. Now that the worst was over, she'd tried to persuade him to go home and sleep, but he refused. He would not budge.

She smiled. Paul would be proud of his sons. They were different in many ways, but they had his heart. Paul had loved completely and unconditionally, and so did Jack and Tom.

When Doctor Beck explained the seriousness of Jack's condition, she'd wanted to roll up in a ball and block out the pain and the rest of the world. As a mother, she didn't have that luxury. Inside she felt unspeakable blinding pain, but outside she appeared a pillar of optimism. She had no choice. Jack and Tom needed her.

Now that Jack was recovering, she could breathe again. She allowed herself to think about the future and how lucky they had been. He would have a chance to grow old. Her family was almost whole. Almost.

Maggie took Aunt Jackie's death hard, blaming herself. She refused to talk about it with Tom. She should have trusted Aunt Jackie and told her Cooper's identity long ago. Maybe Aunt Jackie would have found a way to kill him.

Aunt Jackie was old enough to have been her mother, but Maggie never thought of her like that. She grinned. *What type of mother would*

Aunt Jackie have made? She could only imagine the first time she brought home a boyfriend. He would have run in terror, never to return.

Aunt Jackie had been her cantankerous older sister who never failed to be honest or thoughtful or caring in her own peculiar way. Aunt Jackie would have done anything for her. All Maggie had to do was ask.

Now she would have to go on without her, and she wasn't sure how to do that. Half of the plans behind operation Chastity Belt had originated with Aunt Jackie. She had volunteered to pay a visit to any partner who touched her. It was no idle threat. Maggie imagined Aunt Jackie decking Mr. Grabby Hands, and chuckled.

Tom turned to see what amused his mom, the question in his expression.

"I was just thinking about Aunt Jackie," she confessed.

Tom smiled. "She *was* one of a kind."

A soft knock came at the door. Rachel entered carrying a small bouquet of carnations and a serious expression on her face. "How's Jack doing?"

Maggie waved her in. "He's resting. Doctor Beck thinks he'll make a full recovery."

Rachel threw her arms around Maggie and squeezed her tightly. "That's great news!"

Rachel arranged the flowers into a small glass vase and made small talk with Maggie and Tom for a while. Chitchat wasn't high on the list of things she did well. She kept glancing at her watch and nervously looking out the window.

Maggie noticed a black limo in the parking lot and assumed Charles waited for her. "Why don't I walk you out? I'm sure you have a lot on your plate, and there's nothing you can do here."

"That would be great." Relief washed over her voice.

When they left Jack and Tom behind, Rachel touched Maggie's arm and leaned in close. "I have to ask you something. Do you want to see Cooper again? His mind has shattered, but you can still see him. You will be in full control. Perhaps seeing him one last time will help you gain closure."

Rachel's offer was more than the opportunity to see Cooper one last time. She had offered her a chance at retribution. She just couldn't say the words out loud.

Maggie paused for a moment. Cooper had terrorized her for twenty years. She would always have to live with the guilty knowledge she did nothing to prevent the other women from dying. The yoke choked her. She hated him as much as she had a capacity to hate.

Still, she wanted nothing to do with his death. He deserved to die for his sins, but she would not be an instrument in his passing. To protect her children, she would have gladly killed him, but he was no longer a threat to them and she wanted nothing more to do with him.

"It's enough for me to know he will never bother me or anyone else again." She glanced through the open doorway at her two sons.

I am a strong woman. Love makes me strong!

CHAPTER 72

Tom and Mary stood outside of Jack's hospital room. She smiled. "It looks like he will be fine."

Sitting up in his hospital bed, Jack held a small bowl of rice pudding in his hand. Maggie sat in a chair by the window while David, Jack's best friend and Mary's brother, hovered close to his side with a spoon in his hand, trying to grab a spoonful of pudding as Jack shifted the bowl to dodge his efforts.

Tom turned toward Mary, his face only inches away from hers. His head swam as if he had stuffed himself with mountains of cotton candy. He smelled cinnamon and roses and his heart skipped. Her emerald eyes shined brighter than usual. "I want to tell you something," he said, his voice serious.

"Yes?" She brushed her wavy red hair away from her face.

"There's something I've been meaning to tell you." He glanced into Jack's room. Jack flashed him a thumb's up sign. Tom had confessed to him what he intended last night. He thought it was about time.

Tom turned back toward Mary, his face reddening and his voice husky. "I love you."

"Oh, that. I knew that already."

"Really?" This wasn't going the way he had predicted or hoped. She smiled, but she didn't say anything in return.

Time slowed. He waited until he thought his head would burst. "Do you have anything you want to tell me?"

"No."

"Nothing?" He frowned and looked toward the floor.

She smiled, lifted his chin, and kissed him, her mouth and tongue melting into his. When they separated, he felt dizzy. "Was that clear enough?" She grabbed his hand and led him into Jack's room.

Jack winked at Tom and did his best to alleviate his brother's awkwardness. "So, did Aunt Jackie really say I was her favorite?"

Tom shrugged. "We always knew she was an odd bird."

Maggie chuckled. "I'm sure she loved you both in her way."

"Still, I was her favorite," Jack persisted.

"Can't we talk about something else?" Maggie said.

Tom draped his arm over Mary's shoulder. David shot him a disapproving scowl. Tom removed his arm, and Jack laughed and shook his head.

"Actually, there is something I want to discuss," Tom said. He locked eyes with his mom for a moment. "What other family secrets do I need to know?"

He lifted his hand and started ticking them off his fingers. "First, we had the Fourteenth Colony, then Cooper, and then Aunt Jackie's colorful past. I don't want any more surprises."

Darian strolled into the hospital room.

"Saved by the good doctor," Maggie said.

"How are you feeling, Jack?" Darian carried a thin tablet to record his notes.

"I have this irresistible urge to fetch a stick. Other than that, I'm doing fine."

"Good news on the medication front." Darian pointed to the IV bag hanging on a stand beside Jack's bed. It contained a saline solution with the three different prions he had found in the kibble. "We won't need to give you all those prions anymore. We've isolated the one that inhibited EBF-202. We'll be able to grind the prion into pill form once we determine the proper dosage."

"When can he leave?" Maggie asked.

Darian scanned his notes. "Let's keep him for a week to observe him." He glanced at Jack. "Do you have any sensitivity to light or noise?"

"Not anymore, Doc. I'm good to go."

Darian eyed Jack and checked the time projected on the wall. "I'll be back in a few hours. I have an appointment."

Darian scooted to the elevator, taking it to the top floor. When it reached the top he turned left, and moved swiftly, his flip-flops flopping against the soft rug and reached Wickersham's office in no time.

Vanessa and Clair were chatting in Wickersham's reception room. Clair looked up as he entered. "Doctor Beck, I didn't realize you had a meeting with Doctor Wickersham."

"I need to talk to the *Doctor* about the latest breakthrough. We are ahead of schedule."

"I'm sure he will want to hear about that right away." She lowered her voice. "He's been crowing about your new discovery for the last couple of days. I've never seen him this happy."

Vanessa squeezed Clair's arm. "We had better go. I don't want to be late for our lunch reservation." She pulled her toward the door.

"Do you know that Doctor Beck is single? I think you two might make a nice couple," Clair whispered.

She smiled, glanced over her shoulder, and winked at Darian. "We'll be back in an hour."

Darian marched into Wickersham's office. The memory erasing gas had worked better on Wickersham than Steven had thought. The gas prevented the brain from converting short-term memories into long-term memories. Perhaps Wickersham's frequent use of drugs or the combination of the gas with the electric jolt he gave himself with the taser enhanced its effectiveness, but he had lost two full days of memories.

Upon seeing Darian, Wickersham shut off his video game and beckoned for him to approach. "Doctor Beck, what a pleasure to see you. How are you making out on isolating the prion?"

Darian strolled toward Wickersham's huge oak desk. "I've isolated the prion. We should be able to make it in pill form for Jack in the next day or so."

"That's great news. I'm sure the tennis instructor's family is pleased. Congratulations! We should be able to make a public announcement about EBF-202 by the end of the week. I've already had my assistant start the first draft." Wickersham's voice bounced with enthusiasm. In truth, he had already bought plane tickets for the next Noble Prize presentation in Stockholm.

Darian stretched his arms as he approached Wickersham's desk.

"I think you owe me a debt of gratitude," Wickersham said.

"Why?"

"It was my decision to change the dog food. In my own way, I provided you with the breakthrough you needed."

Darian smiled. "Actually, that's why I decided to stop by. I want to thank you personally." He reached across the desk and unplugged the intercom system.

"What are you doing?" Wickersham reached for his pocket, but Darian grabbed his tailored wool suit jacket before he could retrieve the taser Darian knew he always carried with him.

"It's time you got exactly what you deserved."

CHAPTER 73

Rachel and The Professor stood next to Jack's hospital bed and watched him sleep peacefully. "Do you think he will be okay?" she asked, her brow creased with worry.

"Doctor Beck believes his condition has stabilized. His brain has reversed some of the latest development. I'm not an expert on these things, but the brain scans seem conclusive." He crossed his arms against his thin chest. "We should be past any immediate concerns."

"But you have reservations?" She eyed The Professor's body language.

He stroked his goatee as if it were an old stuffed toy that comforted him while he pondered her question. "We don't understand much about brain function. According to Doctor Beck, Jack's brain has been transformed, developed to an unnatural state. We don't know how that will change him."

He uncrossed his arms. "Psychics and healers have been reported throughout time. I've studied them for years. It's a hobby of mine. Most of the reports are easily dismissed, but others deserve consideration."

"So you think Jack might have become a psychic?"

"Almost certainly. If we believe what Tom and Mary tell us happened in the boardroom, psychic behavior is the most obvious answer. However, I'm worried he might have a more serious condition." He frowned, and worry lines rippled across his weathered face.

"What could be more serious?"

"The connection he had with Cooper was intense. Tom described him as shaking violently. He even smelled electricity flowing between them. Mary described the event the same way. When Jack separated from Cooper, he knew things only the subject knew, like where Maggie was being held, for instance."

He paused and faced her. "It's possible the subject's personality downloaded into Jack's brain in the same manner you might clone a computer."

"Downloaded?"

"Yes, it is possible Cooper lives inside Jack's mind. All his memories, thoughts, and impulses."

CHAPTER 74

The newscaster sounded grave. "The manhunt for the vice president and his Chief of Staff continues into its second week. Homeland Security believes domestic terrorists may have abducted him. So far, no operative leads have been discovered."

Charles Sheppard shut off the television with a click from a remote.

"It's a real shame the Vice President has gone missing. I understand Ethel Simmens is spending a fortune to find him," Jacob Benjamin said. "We certainly don't want him found or any other evidence traced back to us."

"No, we don't," Charles said. "I don't think we need to worry about that. The hospital's security tapes have been wiped clean, and no one seems very interested in finding his butler."

Jacob wandered toward the balcony. "I still have a hard time believing those terrible things Peter did." He shook his head. "How could he have fooled everyone for so long?"

"Believe it, Jacob. The Originalists have complete power. No one watched him too closely. He had all the money and power in the world to do whatever he pleased. I have no doubt he committed these horrible murders."

"What about Project Qing? Have you decided what to do with it?" Jacob stood slightly stooped, but his eyes were bright, piercing, and youthful.

"I've scuttled the research. Project Qing no longer exists, and as far as anyone else is concerned, there never was one."

"But Charles, imagine the good a drug like that could do. We could end warfare and bring peace to areas of the globe that have never known peace."

Charles stared at the New York City skyline for a long moment. "Project Qing would give unlimited power to whoever wielded it. Too much power, Jacob. Even with the best intentions, it would eventually end up enslaving humankind. We were created with free will. It's not for us to take that away."

Charles thought of his mother. She thought God had a higher purpose for him, that his biological parents had been sacrificed in a divine tragedy so the Sheppards would adopt him. He would fulfill that purpose.

Perhaps stopping Project Qing is my purpose.

Jacob walked back to the chess table. "It's a shame Steven has decided to work on his own. He's a very talented individual."

Charles smiled. "I don't think we've seen the last of him. For now, he's decided to track down the families of the other victims to give them closure."

Jacob slid his castle along the chessboard. "With the vice president out of the picture, the Originalists are going to need a new candidate for President."

"I don't like that gleam in your eye."

"Who better than the Secretary of Domestic Priorities, Charles? With you as President, we could accomplish much."

CHAPTER 75

The sun shone bright and hot and the air hung heavy and crisp. They stood in a clearing in a remote forest in upstate New York. The grass underfoot was long, green, and inviting. Oak and maple trees ringed the open space. A hawk circled high overhead, caught in the air currents.

Bound to an ash tree in the center of the clearing, Cooper's arms forming a "Y" shape with the rest of his body.

Gabriel, Moses, and Jack stood ten feet away from him with grim expressions on their faces. They had been waiting patiently all afternoon. Finally, Cooper's brilliant Mediterranean blue eyes focused with lucidity. The Professor had given them a potent experimental drug to bring him back from his shattered state. The drug was extremely dangerous and would only last a short time. Still, they only needed a short time.

Cooper's face slowly contorted from madness to sanity, like a sunrise over the horizon. When reality fully dawned on him, he pulled against his restraints in vain. Fear clouded his face. "What are you doing? I'm important, superior. I'm Peter Simmens!"

"We know who you are," Gabriel said. "You're Cooper, killer of women."

Cooper stopped struggling against the rope when he recognized Jack. "You're Maggie's boy."

"Yes, I am."

"Help me. Maggie is my special friend. Your mother *loves* me. She would want you to help me."

"My mother despises you! She always has. You're not fit to wash her feet."

Cooper scowled as hazy memories returned to him. He remembered taking Maggie and even going to the boardroom. After that, he only recalled fragments and jagged impressions. "She is nothing! I was born superior. I am superior."

Jack stared at Cooper, feeling numb.

Gabriel opened a thin file full of the gruesome photographs of the women Cooper had ravaged. He moved close to Cooper and lifted each photo to his face. He let the photo linger in front of his eyes until he replaced it with the next one. "Do you remember these women?"

"They were nothing—just prostitutes—nobodies."

Gabriel lifted a photograph of Izzy and shoved it against Cooper's face. "Her name was Isabella. She was an angel."

"You can't blame me for that one. I offered her a deal. She could have been the queen of the ghettos, but she refused." Cooper wrenched his body, swinging wildly, trying to free himself, but the bindings held. "Let me go! I can offer you a deal. I know you. You're Gabriel. I'll make you the king of the ghettos. I'll give you everything, a better deal than I offered Isabella. You'll be powerful beyond your imagination."

Gabriel glanced at Moses, who handed him a shiny new scalpel. Light sparkled off the surgical instrument's clean lines.

"No, no! I'll give you anything. I have money and power. You can be rich!" Cooper squirmed away from the scalpel.

Gabriel smiled. "There is only one thing I want."

He glanced at Moses and Jack, who both nodded in agreement.

Jack heard a familiar voice in his head. It sounded raspy and weathered like an old saddle. "Good job, sonny boy!" He touched Excalibur tucked firmly in his waistband and grinned.

THE END

Book Club Guide

1. Throughout the novel, Darian struggles with Wickersham's decision to use Jack as a test subject for EBF-202. Who has the more persuasive argument: Wickersham or Darian? Would your opinion change if it were certain Jack would have died without the drug?

2. One of the effects of EBF-202 is enhanced intelligence. Should we develop drugs to do this, or is that going too far?

3. Cooper believes exceptional people must start with exceptional genes. What would Charles Sheppard say to that argument? What role does nurture play in human development?

4. Who is to blame for Cooper's actions? Does Ethel, as his domineering parent, share some of his guilt? How much do you think she knows? How far should a parent go to protect a child who does bad things?

5. Maggie is constantly trying to convince herself that she is a strong woman. Is she? What examples show she is a strong woman? Did your opinion about her change throughout the book? Did she make the "right" decision not to tell the authorities about Cooper and protect her family?

6. Abuse, whether mental or physical, changes someone. Maggie felt responsible for Cooper's victims. Does she share some guilt? Would Maggie have tried to kill Cooper with the calligraphy pen if he didn't threaten her sons?

7. Romantic love is depicted from Tom's point of view and Vanessa's. How are the descriptions different? Is either one closer to a true version of "love?" What about Mary? How do you think she sees her relationship with Tom?

8. The country's economic climate is depicted as extreme. Who is to blame for poverty in our country? Should those in ghettos take the lion share of responsibility or, as Darian believes, do they just need opportunities and hope? What role does the government have in making sure poor people have opportunities?

9. This dystopian view of America features extreme political power and wealth concentration in a small percentage of "winners." Are we headed in that direction as a country? What measures could we take to prevent such an extreme version of the country from becoming a reality?

10. Aunt Jackie has a violent past. Can one act of love redeem her from a lifetime of questionable choices?

11. Jack, Gabriel, and Moses dispense their form of justice to Cooper in the end. Were they justified in doing so? Maggie obviously disagrees, but what would the other characters have done?

12. The novel takes place in 2041. How would it differ if it took place today?

ACKNOWLEDGEMENTS

Many people helped me to make this book a reality. Among them are my faithful beta readers who never fail to give me their time and wisdom. I would never have written this book without the encouragement, and even a little nagging, from those who read *Fourteenth Colony* and *needed* to know what happened next.

I would also like to thank all of the great people at Evolved Publishing, particularly my fabulous editors, Megan Harris and Lane Diamond. Not only did they greatly improve this book, they've made me a better writer. Mallory Rock deserves a shout-out also for making my random thoughts into art.

About The Author

Jeff Altabef lives in New York with his wife, two daughters, and Charlie the dog. He spends time volunteering at the Writing Center in the local community college. After years of being accused of "telling stories," he thought he would make it official. He writes in both the thriller and young adult genres. *Fourteenth Colony*, a political thriller, was his debut novel. *Shatter Point* is his second novel. As an avid Knicks fan, he is prone to long periods of melancholy during hoops season.

Jeff has a column on The Examiner focused on writing and a blog on The Patch designed to encourage writing for those that like telling stories.

You can find Jeff online at:

www.JeffAltabef.com - www.Twitter.com/JeffAltabef

or via email at JeffreyAltabef@gmail.com

WHAT'S NEXT?

WIND CATCHER
(Chosen - Book 1)
By Jeff Altabef & Erynn Altabef

Watch for this first book in the new *Chosen* series of young adult fantasies, coming March 23, 2015. For more information, please visit www.EvolvedPub.com

~~~~~

Juliet Wildfire Stone stands between two worlds. Her eccentric grandfather tells her stories about the Great Wind Spirit and Coyote, but he might as well be speaking another language. She's started to hear voices and see visions, but even they don't make any sense. All she wants to be is an average sixteen-year-old girl, but she has never been average—could never be average.

She is the Chosen and the Seeker Slayer, and our only hope.

Recently transferred to an exclusive school, Juliet is forced to choose between her new wealthy life and her Native American heritage. Unsure where she fits in, she stumbles upon a series of murders. Worried that her grandfather is involved, she discovers an ancient secret society, the Order of the Twisted Arrows—a society formed over two hundred years ago to keep her safe.

When the mysterious Seeker learns of Juliet's existence, he threatens everyone she loves in the world, willing to kill to have her.

Betrayed by the young man she loves, she must decide whether to run or to fulfill her destiny as the Chosen.
~~~~~

More from Evolved Publishing

CHILDREN'S PICTURE BOOKS

THE BIRD BRAIN BOOKS by Emlyn Chand:

Honey the Hero

Davey the Detective

Poppy the Proud

Izzy the Inventor

Larry the Lonely

Ricky the Runt

Tommy Steals the Show

Tommy Goes Trick-or-Treating

Courtney Saves Christmas

Vicky Finds a Valentine

Silent Words by Chantal Fournier

Thomas and the Tiger-Turtle by Jonathan Gould

I'd Rather Be Riding My Bike by Eric Pinder

Emlyn and the Gremlin by Steff F. Kneff

VALENTINA'S SPOOKY ADVENTURES
by Majanka Verstraete:

Valentina and the Haunted Mansion

Valentina and the Whackadoodle Witch

Valentina and the Masked Mummy

HISTORICAL FICTION

Circles by Ruby Standing Deer

Spirals by Ruby Standing Deer

Stones by Ruby Standing Deer

LITERARY FICTION

Torn Together by Emlyn Chand

Hannah's Voice by Robb Grindstaff

Carry Me Away by Robb Grindstaff

Turning Trixie by Robb Grindstaff

The Lone Wolf by E.D. Martin

The Daughter of the Sea and the Sky by David Litwack

Jellicle Girl by Stevie Mikayne

Weight of Earth by Stevie Mikayne

White Chalk by Pavarti K Tyler

LOWER GRADE (Chapter Books)

TALES FROM UPON A. TIME by Falcon Storm:

The Persnickety Princess
Natalie the Not-So-Nasty
The Perils of Petunia

WEIRDVILLE by Majanka Verstraete:

House of Horrors
Drowning in Fear
Fright Train
The Doll Maker

MIDDLE GRADE

NOAH ZARC by D. Robert Pease:
Cataclysm (Book 2)
Declaration (Book 3)
Mammoth Trouble (Book 1)
Omnibus (Special 3-in-1 Edition)

MEMOIR

And Then It Rained: Lessons for Life by Megan Morrison

MYSTERY

Hot Sinatra by Axel Howerton

NEW ADULT / CONTEMPORARY

Desert Flower by Angela Scott

Desert Rice by Angela Scott

ROMANCE / EROTICA

Walk Away with Me by Darby Davenport
THE TWISTED MOSAIC by Amelia James:
Her Twisted Pleasures (Book 1)
His Twisted Choice (Book 3)
Their Twisted Love (Book 2)
The Twisted Mosaic (Special Omnibus Edition)

Claire and J.T. by Amelia James

Secret Storm by Amelia James

Tell Me You Want Me by Amelia James

The Devil Made Me Do It by Amelia James

Home Is Where the Heat Is by Amelia James

Sugar and Salt (Sugar House Novella 1) by Pavarti K Tyler

Protecting Portia (Sugar House Novella 2) by Pavarti K Tyler

SCI-FI / FANTASY

Shadow Swarm by D. Robert Pease

Two Moons of Sera by Pavarti K. Tyler

Eulogy by D.T. Conklin

SHORT STORY ANTHOLOGIES

FROM THE EDITORS AT EVOLVED PUBLISHING:
Evolution: Vol. 1 (A Short Story Collection)
Evolution: Vol. 2 (A Short Story Collection)
Pathways (A Young Adult Anthology)

All Tolkien No Action: Swords, Sorcery & Sci-Fi by Eric Pinder

SUSPENSE / THRILLER

Forgive Me, Alex by Lane Diamond

The Devil's Bane by Lane Diamond

Whispers of the Dead by C.L. Roberts-Huth

Whispers of the Serpent by C.L. Roberts-Huth

YOUNG ADULT

Farsighted by Emlyn Chand

Open Heart by Emlyn Chand

THE DARLA DECKER DIARIES by Jessica McHugh:

Dalra Decker Hates to Wait (Book 1)

Dream Warriors: A Joey Cola Novel by D. Robert Pease

The Silver Sphere (Kin Chronicles 1) by Michael Dadich

The Sinister Kin (Kin Chronicles 2) by Michael Dadich

THE ZOMBIE WEST TRILOGY by Angela Scott:

Dead Plains (Book 3)

Survivor Roundup (Book 2)

Wanted: Dead or Undead (Book 1)

Zombie West (Special Omnibus Edition)

CPSIA information can be obtained at www.ICGtesting.com
Printed in the USA
BVOW04s2008100914

366012BV00004BA/43/P

9 781622 533121